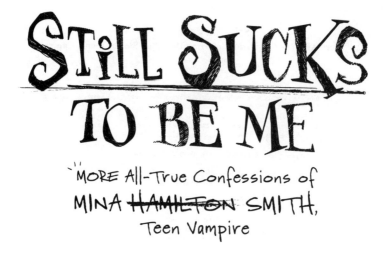

STiLL SUCKS
TO BE ME

"MORE All-True Confessions of
MINA ~~Hamilton~~ SMITH,
Teen Vampire

Kimberly Pauley

BOOKS FOR
YOUNG READERS

Still Sucks to Be Me
More All-True Confessions of Mina Hamilton Smith, Teen Vampire

©2010 by Kimberly Pauley

Published by Wizards of the Coast LLC.

Wizards of the Coast and its logo are trademarks of Wizards of the Coast LLC in the U.S.A.
and other countries.

Printed in the U.S.A.

Art by Emi Tanji
Cover photo by Allison Shinkle
Book designed by Emi Tanji and Kate Irwin

First Printing

9 8 7 6 5 4 3 2 1

ISBN: 978-0-7869-5503-9
620-25398000-001-EN

Library of Congress Cataloging-in-Publication Data

Pauley, Kimberly, 1973-
  Still sucks to be me : more all-true confessions of Mina Hamilton Smith,
teen vampire / by Kimberly Pauley.
    p. cm.
  "Mirrorstone."
  Summary: When newly-turned teen vampire Mina Hamilton, now Smith, moves with
her family far from their California home, her best friend Serena, and her vampire
boyfriend George, life is not at all what she expects.
  ISBN 978-0-7869-5503-9 (alk. paper)
  [1. Vampires--Fiction. 2. Moving, Household--Fiction. 3. Dating (Social
customs)--Fiction. 4. High schools--Fiction. 5. Schools--Fiction. 6. Family life--
Louisiana--Fiction. 7. Louisiana--Fiction.] I. Title.
  PZ7.P278385Sti 2010
  [Fic]--dc22
                                                        2009054384

U.S., CANADA,
ASIA, PACIFIC & LATIN AMERICA
Wizards of the Coast LLC
P.O. Box 707
Renton, WA 98057-0707
+1-800-324-6496

EUROPEAN HEADQUARTERS
Hasbro UK Ltd
Caswell Way
Newport, Gwent NP9 0YH
GREAT BRITAIN
Save this address for your records.

Visit our web site at www.wizards.com

For YOU

MYTH:	Vampires never die.
TRUTH:	Generally true. But they sure can fake it. RIP

1

I, Mina Hamilton, am officially dead. Officially, officially. You name it, I've got it: death certificate (which I'm not allowed to keep in a scrapbook, per the Vampire Relocation Agency rules), obituary in the paper (depressingly short, if I do say so myself, and ditto on the scrapbooking), and a funeral. A funeral which, incidentally, my family's personal VRA goon, Josh, would *not* let me attend.

What's the point of having a funeral if you can't go and see who cared enough to show up? I had an excellent disguise picked out and everything, but the Josh-erator put me under total house arrest.

Or should I say total *hotel* arrest. It's not like I—or for that matter, anyone in my family—can be seen in our house since we're all, you know, supposed to be *dead.*

But maybe I should back up for a minute here. In case you haven't been following my every move (and why would you be?), at the end of my junior year in high school, my parents dropped the v-bomb on me. Sure, I knew they were vampires (I mean, duh, I've lived with them my whole life) but the stupid Northwest Regional Vampire Council was making me choose if I wanted to be one too. That meant:

a) I had to attend vampire information sessions (aka pro-vampire propaganda classes) taught by this crazy vampire lady named Ms. Riley (aka Grandma Wolfington) so I could make an informed decision on my bloodsucking future,

b) which would have completely sucked except that I met George, my boyfriend and (who knows?) possible love of my undead life there, and

c) ultimately decided that, yeah, I'd rather be a vampire and stick with my family than get my brain washed and lose them forever. (Though I'd be lying if I said I were giving up my best friend Serena, because I'm not. She knows it all and I don't care what The Council says . . . okay, I do care, but *I'm* not telling them.)

So that brings me up to this week. One minute Mom's telling me it's time for us to die (and I'm like, "Huh? How much more undead can we get?") and the next, there's the Josh-erator at our front door saying The Council has decided that we can't live here anymore. But when you're a vampire, you can't just call up U-Haul and schedule a moving day like normal people. No, you get assigned a Vampire Relocation Agent who comes and hacks your whole life apart. He changed our last name, made up fake lives for us (Dad and Mom are supposed to be my brother and sister-in-law? Embarrassing!), and worst of all, he's shipping us off later tonight to some undisclosed location. And here I was hoping The Council and the VRA would be off our backs since we were all legal now and I was a bona fide, registered vampire.

I managed to get exactly one text out to Serena before the Josh-erator confiscated my cell phone:

Send text to (SERENA)

Me (3:44 pm): dnt frk out no matter wht nt dead del ths msg!! more 18r dnt txt bk!

Which was a good thing, since she'd have completely killed me if she found out I wasn't actually dead (like dead-dead, not just undead) after the funeral.

Not only did I miss my funeral, I also missed my own death. "Your presence is not necessary," was how the Josh-erator put it. Huh. That totally doesn't seem right to me, but the VRA and

3

The Council certainly know how to suck the fun right out of everything.

Josh did at least get me a copy of the article they ran in the newspaper about our so-called demise (after warning me at least five times that I'd have to destroy it after I read it). It was pretty nice, you know, as far as those things go:

Local Family Dies in Tragic Car Accident

Four people were killed in a road accident in San Mateo County early last evening. According to eyewitness reports, a large dog or other mammal darted in front of their car, causing the driver to veer sharply off the road and into the guardrail. The car, a silver-colored minivan, then reportedly continued over the guardrail to fall into the Pacific Ocean. The area, known as the Devil's Slide, has claimed many lives over the years.

Detective Lee of the San Mateo County Police Department commented, "This is one of the worst accidents I've seen in some time, and I've seen my share of tragedies. There's no way any of the family could have survived a fall of that height." The deceased include Bob and Marianne Hamilton and their seventeen-year-old daughter, Mina, as well as Mortimer Hamilton, the father's uncle . . .

It went on for a while about things like keeping your dog in check and the problem with the guardrails along the highway, and the controversy over whether or not the road should be rebuilt entirely, etc. etc. And there was a picture of the tail end of our minivan sticking up (barely) out of the ocean. I can't say I'll miss the thing; it was pretty much on its last legs anyway. Or last wheels. Whatever.

Those eyewitness accounts? All VRA plants. As well as the deputy they got the quote from and for all I know, the guy who wrote the newspaper article. If there's one thing you can say about the VRA, they're very thorough. And very, very present. As in around ALL the freakin' time. Maybe they do that on purpose so you don't have a chance to back out of the relocation or so you don't mess things up by popping up somewhere noticeable when you're supposed to be dead. Or maybe they just like to be annoying.

So here I am, stuck in a fleabag motel on the outskirts of my hometown. Mom and Dad are out conferring with the Josh-erator in some "undisclosed location" (i.e., probably some pancake house or something like that), which means I'm finally alone for the first time since this whole fiasco started. Uncle Mortie was supposed to stay and babysit me, but he disappeared right after the Josh-erator, muttering something about having to "take care of a few things'" (which probably means there's either a blonde or a hamburger in his future, or both if he's lucky). The Josh-erator may not trust me, but at least Uncle Mortie does.

Not that he should. Trust me, that is. Because the first order of business for the brand new Mina? One last big hurrah with my best friends. There's *no way* I'm leaving town without a party. And it's about time George found out that Serena knows about the whole vampire thing anyway. I hate keeping secrets from my boyfriend.

Since we're going to go out tonight, I need to figure out what to wear so no one will recognize me. But there's no way I can piece together a decent disguise with the stuff at this dump. I've only got my one VRA-allowed tiny little overnight bag of stuff with me that holds

a) my notebook from my vampire lessons, since I hopefully (but probably doubtfully) took notes on at least some of the stuff the Josh-erator keeps mentioning (and besides, it's not the kind of thing you want to leave behind for people to discover); and

b) my fav picture of me and Serena, and a prom picture with me and George and Nathan and Serena, all looking really happy (VRA contraband, but I hid them in my notebook); and

c) a couple of my favorite outfits (my Ella Moss dress, a pair of jeans, my fav shirt and a T-shirt I snitched from George that still smells like him); and

6

d) Mr. Lumps. Because there's no way I'm leaving my teddy bear behind. I don't care what the VRA says about it.

My only possible disguise option is to put on the shower cap that looks like it's been here since the nineties. Somehow I think that'd make me more noticeable than I am normally. I'd hope, anyway.

Time for plan B. I call Serena from the front desk of the hotel after I give the guy some story about how our room phone isn't working, just in case the VRA's checking up on our phone calls (I wouldn't put it past them). I tell her to bring some disguise-ready stuff and meet me at this cute little tea café place I saw around the corner from the hotel. It's not like anyone who knows me will be hanging out at some teahouse halfway across town eating crumpets or curds and whey or whatever it is you have with tea. We can get in disguise there. Or I can, at least. Serena doesn't really need one. Her normal look is a pretty good disguise.

MYTH:	Vampires can't cry.
TRUTH:	Tell that to the box of Kleenex I just went through.

2

I'm not, as a general rule, a very teary person. Okay, so I do cry at chick flicks and my dad has totally banned the Lifetime channel from our house, but it's not like I cry over cheesy commercials or anything like that. Yet I totally break down as soon as Serena pulls up in the Death Beetle in front of the tea place. This of course makes her turn on the sprinklers too.

I climb into the car and we cry on each other's shoulders for about five minutes until our backs are about to break from the awkward pose. Volkswagen Beetles, especially the old-school ones, are definitely not made for physical contact. Which, come to think of it, might be why Serena's dad gave her the car in the first place.

We finally get ourselves together and go into the café, which is when I notice Serena looks pale as anything and is wearing a black dress and some heavy (the part that's not totally tear-streaked) eyeliner. Oh no, I am not letting that slide!

"You're not going Goth on me again, are you?" I yell loud enough for two little old ladies next to us to look up in disgust.

"D'oh!" she says. "I'm in *mourning*. Haven't you heard? My best friend died in a tragic car accident!" Which causes us both to break into a fit of insane giggles and the two old ladies to get up and move to another table.

I guess I can't blame them, but I'm not about to explain what's really going on. Let 'em just think we're a couple of juvenile delinquents. That's what it always seems like the little old ladies think anyway.

"So what's your excuse for not calling me sooner? *Besides* going off a cliff."

"Hey, you're lucky I got that text out to you at all. This is literally the first time I've been alone since this whole thing started. I got *no* warning from Mom and Dad at all." Yeah. Ask me if I'm happy about *that*. I'll give you two guesses and one of them doesn't count.

"Where are they sending you?"

"All I know is that it's south of here." That's all I've been able to gather, even with my superhearing. What the heck good are übervampire powers if nobody says anything important remotely near you? Nada. That's what.

9

"Your mom and dad don't know either?"

"I guess not. They haven't said." They haven't said much, period. Which I am *beyond* over. But I don't want to get into *that* right now.

"So you think maybe LA? That's south."

"Maybe." Los Angeles seems like it would be the obvious choice. Big, lots of people, easy to disappear. I bet a ton of vampires live there. And I had glimpsed the initials LA on a piece of paper before the Josh-erator had whisked it out of sight.

"It's a drive, but it's doable. I could come see you on weekends once things get settled! I've got an aunt who lives there, so I've got a good excuse to go down. She's always asking if I can come and help watch her kids. She's got twins and my uncle travels a lot. Definitely before school starts I could get down there at least once. I could really use some time away from the family anyway."

"Maybe I could even meet you halfway or something, if I can talk my parents into a car." They totally owe me one for all this relocation nonsense. "I'm sure the VRA would kill me if I came all the way back here. I'm not even supposed to be out at all." I leave out the part where the Josh-erator was threatening me with "dire things" if I left the hotel room. No need to make her worry, and what the VRA doesn't know won't hurt them.

"So what have you been doing since you 'died'?"

"Ha!" I say. Shoot, I could spend an entire half hour on the packing trauma alone, but I do my best to condense things down to the main points:

a) The Council sucks and is all up in our business (as per usual); and

b) The VRA is a bunch of nosy busybodies who have confiscated everything I own, including all communication devices (so I won't be tempted to make contact with anyone who isn't supposed to know anything) and all memorabilia (like yearbooks and photos, since they'd be identifying factors or some such nonsense); and

c) If I hear the Josh-erator go, "Okay, pop quiz!" one more time, I may whittle a stake out of my toothbrush and do him in myself; and

d) I am so ticked that the VRA didn't let me attend my own funeral. How wrong is that?

"It was nice," Serena says. "For a funeral, anyway."

"Did a lot of people come?" I hope so. It would kinda suck if no one cared enough to show up. Not that I had a lot of friends other than Serena. But still. I mean, I did die an untimely death at a young age. Isn't that supposed to count for something?

"Yeah, pretty much the whole school showed. Even Bethany

was there. And Ms. Reed and Ms. Tweeter were totally bawling their eyes out the whole time! I'm kind of ticked, actually. I squeezed an onion to get some juice just in case I couldn't work up enough tears, but with all the waterworks they had going, nobody noticed me one way or another."

"Wow." Geez, I hope Ms. Reed didn't still think I was pregnant because I checked out that teen pregnancy book by accident. I probably gave the poor woman nightmares. Talk about a dedicated librarian.

"By the way, what was up with your weirdo vampire friend?" asks Serena. Off the top of my head, I'm not even sure which vampire friend she must mean. Maybe Linda? I haven't seen her since she turned, so maybe the former poster girl for the Chess Club went all crazy ninja or something. Or maybe Lorelai wore her cheerleading outfit. I wouldn't put it past her.

"Who? What happened? Somebody scare the locals?"

"Some freaky Goth chick with a serious attitude problem. She was all skulking around. Now tell me the truth: I didn't look that stupid when I was Goth, did I? Please tell me I didn't. I had style, right?"

"A Goth chick?" Whoa. I've never hung out with any Goth chicks other than Serena. That could only have been Raven, crazy vampire wannabe from my vampire training classes who had it

12

in for me over some stupid guy. Maybe Grandma Wolfington let Raven turn after all even though they kicked her out of class? Otherwise, she should have no idea who I am anymore, since they should have done the whole brain-wiping thing on her. Either way, I can't imagine why she would have shown up at my funeral, unless she actually thought I'd died for real somehow and wanted to gloat. "Did she say anything to you?"

"Yeah. It was kind of weird. She asked me if I was a friend of yours—actually, she said 'the deceased'—and I said you were my best friend, but she should've been able to tell without asking. I had some great fake tears going. You should have seen me. I swear I should be an actress."

"That was it?"

"No, that's when it got bizarro. She got right in my face and said, 'Wouldn't want to be you.' I thought maybe she meant, you know, about you being dead and everything, but it was really strange how she said it. Then she poked her finger at me and said that she was my worst nightmare. She was like stupid creepy, if you know what I mean."

That definitely had to be Raven. She was always poking her finger at me too. What did she mean by all that? Is she trying to get back at me through Serena or something? It's not like it's my fault she got kicked out of class. Not exactly. Mostly.

"Are you sure she was a vampire? She say anything else?"

"I dunno. How can you tell? She just looked like she wanted to bite me or something. But she didn't say anything else. Some girl in a cheerleading outfit came over and the Goth chick disappeared, like, poof! I forget what the cheerleader's name was, but she seemed pretty nice. For a cheerleader. I can't believe she wore her little cheer suit to your funeral though."

"That's just because you don't know Lorelai. She was in my intro class too. Good people. I heard she got accepted to some pre-college cheerleading camp thing. Besides, she knows I'm not really dead." Dead-dead anyway. I'm just, you know, undead. I doubt if she even owns anything black. Wait, I take that back. I bet she's got at least one perfect little black dress in her closet somewhere. Or a bunch of them in multiple hem lengths so she'll be prepared for any situation.

Which reminds me. Clothes. I point at the overstuffed purple backpack she brought in with her. "So, what did you bring for disguises? Tell me it's not Goth stuff."

Serena plops the bag on the table and nearly knocks a flowery little china teacup filled with sugar cubes off the table. She starts pulling out a bunch of hats and sunglasses. "No Goth. I just mostly brought stuff for your head since I figured that's what you'd need to hide the most."

14

I grab a bright yellow tennis visor with a flower pasted on it and try it on. Very PTA mom. I think I'll skip the black cowboy hat with the sheriff's star and the bright yellow construction helmet though. Where does she get this stuff?

"How's this look?" I add some big heart-shaped sunglasses, and she gives me a thumbs-up and a big grin.

"What do you need it for, anyway?"

I lean forward and whisper, "Okay, here's the plan. You, me, and George. We hit the town and take in all of our favorite places. We go to Chili Pepper's and get a couple of slices of pizza. Run by the Coffee Café for an espresso. And, of course, a Fat Elvis milkshake from Dingle's. George gets off work at four and we can pick him up then."

Serena sits back and puts the bag back on the floor by her feet. "You told George about me? About how I know about the whole v"—she glances at the little old ladies who are staring at us and she lowers her voice—"the you know. Things. And stuff."

"No, not yet, but there's no time like now. As long as we avoid any creepy-looking guys in suits, we should be good. The VRA guys are pretty easy to spot, if you know what you're looking for." I lean down to check out what else is in the bag. These glasses are really a little too big for me. I can feel them slipping

15

off my nose. Score! I pull out a pair of glittery cats-eye-shaped sunglasses. No one would ever think to look for me in these. I trade glasses and strike a pose for Serena. "Whaddaya think? Totally très not me, right?"

Serena doesn't look like she's feeling it. She shakes her head.

"It doesn't have to look *good*," I say. "It just needs to look not me."

"Not the glasses. Min, I just don't think it's a good idea."

"What? The disguises?" They are kind of silly, I guess. Maybe I should go for something less noticeable.

"All of it. Didn't you tell me the other day that those guys can, like, totally wipe your mind? And that your parents got fined again just because you turned without filling out some form? And how much trouble everyone could get in, including me, if they knew that I knew?"

"Yeah, but—" How can I leave town without a last hurrah? I thought she'd be all over this.

"We probably shouldn't even be *here*. Showing up at Dingle's and Chili Pepper's and all that? That's just insane. We could get in huge trouble."

"When have you ever been worried about getting in trouble?" I mean, come on, Serena's usually the one who gets me in trouble with her crazy ideas.

16

Serena starts packing up all of the hats and glasses left on the table. "Since it could get me brainwashed and my best friend and her family relocated to Siberia. Or who knows what."

"Well, why did you even come and meet me here at all?"

"I wanted to see you again and say good-bye, but I didn't know what you were thinking. I probably shouldn't have come. You shouldn't be out in public. This was a bad idea."

She leaves some money on the table for our hibiscus tea, which we barely touched (smelled really good but tasted like uck), and stands up. "Come on, we should go."

I follow her out, but now I have no idea what to do. My last hours at home and my best friend doesn't even want to spend them with me. This isn't remotely how I pictured things going.

MYTH: Vampires have to be invited in.

TRUTH: That'd be the polite thing, but it isn't strictly necessary.

WELCOME

3

Serena drops me off around the corner from George's place once she does a drive-by and sees that his car is there. It was all I could do to talk her into driving me here instead of frog-marching me back to the hotel.

I lean in the Death Beetle's window. "You really won't come in with me?" I have to try one more time.

"Min, you know that's not a good idea. It'll only make things more complicated and dangerous. You know I love you. I just want you to be safe." She gives me a sad smile. "Now get inside before someone sees you!" She waves one last time and drives off.

I know it's not the last time I'll ever see her, but this just feels so final and awful. I don't like it at all.

I keep my head down and walk to George's place, then I stare at the door for a few minutes before going in, which is silly since

18

I'm sure he's realized I'm here already. I can hear him in there watching TV (that whole superhearing thing can be pretty handy), and with his creaky front steps, I know he heard me coming. He's probably wondering what I'm doing standing on his front porch.

Okay, maybe Lorelai with all her dating advice is right. I *do* tend to overthink things sometimes.

I open the door and run right into George's arms. *Yeesh.* He's getting really good at that whole silent stalking thing. Not that I think he's actually gone stalking anyone or anything for real. But he totally could. I didn't hear him get up from the couch at all. I guess his silent stalking is better than my superhearing.

"Hey, Mina," he says as he hugs me. "I was wondering if you were going to come in. You do know that whole thing about being invited in is a crock, right?" He gives me one of his crooked half smiles. It registers just a 3.5 on the George amusement scale.

"I know, I know," I say and just let myself melt into his arms.

"How'd you escape the dreaded clutches of the VRA?"

"You didn't think I'd skip town without seeing you one more time, did you?" I neglect to mention how I got here but he doesn't notice anyway since I distract him with a flurry of kisses. Works every time.

I guess I should look on the bright side. I was hoping to get some time alone with George today to talk about the big stuff.

19

Like where our relationship is going now that I'm being forced to relocate. Gah. The VRA sucks. This really isn't a conversation I'm ready to have yet. We've only been dating a couple of months. I mean, it's all been good, but still. I feel like I'm barely used to *having* a boyfriend. And while a long-distance boyfriend is better than no boyfriend, what I'd really like is a move-along-with-me boyfriend.

We go sit on his lumpy couch and I take a deep breath and look him in the eyes. Ever since he turned, his eyes have been like that crazy mood ring my uncle Mortie fobbed off on me one Christmas. Except prettier. And only in vampire-like shades of blue and green.

They are a dark and stormy gray-blue today, which doesn't bode well for me asking him about future plans. But it *is* now or never.

"So . . ." Yow, I suck at this. I really have no idea how to say this. "I'm thinking we're probably going to LA. Do you think you'll be able to visit me soon? Or, you know, I've always heard it's a great place to live." I can hardly stand to look him in the eye as I say it, but I manage to keep my eyes on his. "What do you think?"

"Um," says George. "I don't think—" He clears his throat and looks away.

Yowch. I sit back on the couch a bit. That definitely doesn't sound like a yes.

George takes my silence as an opening, I guess, since he keeps going. "I probably should have brought this up when I first started thinking about it, but I knew you wouldn't be happy, so I've been putting it off." He takes my hand in his and gives it a little squeeze. *So* not good. He's not going to use this whole relocation drama as an excuse to dump me, is he?

"I'm leaving." He holds up his hand as my mouth drops open purely of its own accord.

"What? The VRA's moving you too? Where? Do you know where?" And does he know somehow that it's not where I'm going? Did they tell him? Is the VRA trying to split us up or something? Why are they out to ruin my life?

"Hold on. The VRA isn't relocating me." He pulls me back down on the couch. I hadn't even realized that I'd stood up. "I'm going to go visit my parents. I know how you feel about them after what they did to me, abandoning me all those years. *I know.* But I just keep coming back to the fact that they *are* my parents. The only ones I've got. I feel like I've got to take a chance and get to know them. I want to . . . I don't know . . . know where I came from. You know what I mean? You understand, don't you?"

Oh. Wow. Didn't see that one coming at all. His eyes cycle an even deeper shade of blue, like the ocean just past the breakers during a storm. But no, I don't understand. Why would he want anything to do with them at all, after they abandoned him to the foster care system when they decided to become vampires?

"I—" I don't know what to say.

He leans over and squishes me in a big, huge bear hug. It's a good thing I've got supervampire strength too. Otherwise he probably would have broken my ribs. "I promise I'll do my best to stay in touch. I don't want to lose what we've got. I just feel like I've had this hole in my life for all these years. I've got to try and fill it."

Exactly what does he mean by that? He never said anything about a hole before. Does what we have together not help fill that hole? And what does he mean by he'll "promise to do his best to stay in touch"? Is it just me, or does that sound like the kiss of death? And I do not remotely mean that in a vampiric sort of way.

"Um—"

"Please, Mina? Don't be mad," he says into my hair.

"I'm not mad," I say really quickly before he can confess to anything else. He squeezes me even harder and lets out a huge sigh of relief. "I'm just surprised is all," I squeak out.

"I know. I'm sorry. I should have told you before—"

"I don't suppose your parents are in LA, huh?"

"No, they're in Brazil."

"Brazil?" That's another country entirely! That's like . . . well, I don't even know exactly how far away that is, but it's a long, long way.

"Yes, they've been working down there off and on since they turned."

Oh, so that's where they were all those years that George was in foster care. Gallivanting around the beaches in Brazil. That's just pathetic. Why does he want to go spend any time with *them*? Instead of me? I don't get it at all.

George takes my silence as acceptance this time and gives me another bone-crushing hug. "I knew you'd understand. I really can't wait to see them! Your relocation really came at the perfect time! You'll be so busy moving that you won't miss me at all! Things couldn't have worked out better!"

Well, I don't know about that. I can think of a lot of ways things could have worked out better. I'm thinking they couldn't have worked out any worse.

1. I finally get a boyfriend and a ~~life until~~ death
   (ugh. whatever) and now he tells me we're going to be
   separated. For some undetermined but way too long
   period of time. By, like, an entire ocean. Or whatever
   is between the United States and Brazil.
   Brazzzil.

2. I totally suck at geography.

3. I also have to leave behind my best friend and all
   my stuff and fake my death to move somewhere.
   (Probably LA, which could be kind of cool, but not
   really, considering all the other sucky stuff around the
   whole moving thing.)

4. My parents apparently still think I'm a little kid who
   only needs to know stuff on a need-to-know basis.
   Well, you know what? I need to know. Why don't they
   get that?

5. And did I mention that said boyfriend said he'd "do his best" to keep in touch? Do his best? Is that like "I'll do my best to get my homework in on time" best or "you're one of the most important things in my life" best?

6. AND my last hurrah with my best friends turned into one big downer after another. I already miss them and I feel like they don't even care I'm gone. My vampire superstrength can't fix this trainwreck. What good is being a vampire when it won't help with the important stuff?

MYTH: Vampires are always in control.

TRUTH: Apparently, this doesn't remotely apply to me.

4

George drops me off at the roach hotel (okay, so maybe it isn't exactly infested, but it sure looks like it could be) and I have my only piece of luck of the day. Uncle Mortie is sitting on the bed and watching TV, but Mom and Dad and the Josh-erator are nowhere to be seen.

"Getting in a little face time with the old boyfriend before we go, eh?" Uncle Mortie wiggles his hairy eyebrows at me.

"Yeah," I say and sit down next to him. I'm too depressed to think of a snappy comeback, which Uncle Mortie notices right away.

"Trouble in paradise?"

"George is going to Brazil to go visit his deadbeat parents for who knows how long. Not to mention I'm leaving behind everything I know to move who knows where." And a weirdo Goth girl is making bizarro threats to Serena for who knows why, but I keep that part to myself. That's a secret even Uncle Mortie might tell my parents, though I bet he wouldn't tell The Council.

"Ah," he says. "Brazil. Great beaches. Did I ever tell you about the double-jointed trapeze artist I met who was from Brazil? She was—"

"*Uncle Mortie. So* not helping."

He puts an arm around my shoulders. He smells kind of like bacon and barbecued meat. He must have gone to get a burger like I thought. Of course, Uncle Mortie usually smells like some kind of food, so maybe not.

"George is a good guy. I like him. And you like him, right? Maybe even *luurrrrvveee* him?"

"Uncle Mortie!"

"What?" he says innocently. "Isn't that what you girls say nowadays? I swear I heard that in a movie."

"Maybe if I was a member of the single-digit IQ club. But yeah, I like him." I like him a lot. And maybe I do *love* him, but there's no *luurrrrvveee* involved.

"Just give him some time and space to do his thing. 'To boldly go where no man has—' "

"Uncle Mortie, enough with the 'Star Trek,' okay?" I kind of head butt his chin. He's such a goober.

"Okay," he says. "Pep talks aren't really my thing anyway. Besides, we need to get ready to go to the airport. I'm supposed to be your chauffeur. Bob and Mari are going to meet us there with the goon." He gets up and heads for the dirty bathroom.

"The airport? We're not driving?" LA is a little bit of a drive, but not killer.

"Drive?" Uncle Mortie emerges from the bathroom holding three dingy towels and the only washcloth that didn't have a hole in it, all of which he promptly stuffs into his suitcase. "No way am I spending that much time in a car with your dad. I'd probably want to strangle him after three days. After four, all bets would be off. Five, and I couldn't promise you that you'd be alive either."

Um, days? More than *five* days? You'd have to be driving at a snail's pace to take that long to get to Los Angeles. A snail in a full body cast. Not that Dad's any kind of speed demon, but still. Even he could make it in a day. "Where *are* we going? I thought we were going to LA?"

Uncle Mortie reaches to unplug the phone and stuffs that in his bag too. "LA? Why would you think we were going to—Ah." He sits back down. "Kiddo, we're not going to Los Angeles."

"Where are we going?"

"I'm not supposed to say," says Uncle Mortie. He picks up

the Gideon Bible and looks at it for a minute and then puts it back down.

"We're leaving *today*. Why all the hush-hush anyway? I did the whole turning thing. Aren't I part of the family? Why are you all keeping everything from me?" I have this insane urge to throw a tantrum like when I was three, but I hold off. For now. But I do shut the dresser door before he can take the channel guide.

Uncle Mortie pulls his hand back and blows on his fingers like the drawer got him. Like it was even close. "I didn't say I *wasn't* going to say. I said I'm not *supposed* to say. The VRA apparently thinks you might be a flight risk since you're still young. A fledgling, so to speak. But that's a bunch of hogwash."

I *knew* Uncle Mortie would come through for me. "So where exactly is it they're sending us to anyway? Siberia?"

"I'm going to New Orleans."

I do a double take, but Uncle Mortie has a completely straight face and I don't think even he would joke about something this big. Oh. My. God. New Orleans? As in New Orleans, Louisiana? That's, like, just as bad as Siberia practically. I mean, it's more than halfway across the country from California. Serena is going to freak. I plop down on the hard bed and nearly bounce my bag off onto the floor.

"Wait, what do you mean, 'I'm going to New Orleans'? We're not?"

"I've got some big plans in the city. Your dad has a new job . . . outside the city. But we've wasted enough time. We're going to be late if we don't get out of here."

He hustles me out the door and cranks up the music as soon as we get in his rental car. (The VRA confiscated his big yellow boat of a car, which is the only good thing they've done, as far as I'm concerned.) We make it to the airport in record time. The way Uncle Mortie drives, it's a good thing we're practically indestructible.

Apparently, the VRA has some serious connections at the San Francisco airport. The Josh-erator and my parents are waiting for us in some posh area called The Strix Lounge where the only other people waiting are vampires. Probably other VRA victims. They've got a pinched peevish look about them.

I decide to go for the full-frontal attack on the Josh-erator. I've obviously been playing way too nice so far. I walk right up to him sitting in a plump leather chair with his ever-present briefcase at his feet. "You're sending us to *Louisiana*? What kind of crazy is that?"

"Now, now," he says in the annoyingly warm and friendly tone of voice he seems to use every time I ask a question he doesn't want to answer (namely, every single one). "I'm sure you're going to love your new home, Mina! Why don't you just have a seat? I just have a few final things to go over and an information packet to give you and then you'll be on your way!"

"Mortie—" says Dad, but Uncle Mortie just shrugs and swipes a handful of peanuts from a table. He's got my back.

"I've had enough information packets to last me a lifetime," I say. Even a vampire's lifetime. "What about LA or San Diego or, I don't know, *anywhere* other than Louisiana?"

The Josh-erator gives Dad a your-daughter-is-beyond-annoying look and then just ignores me, handing out the stupid packets one at a time, starting with Mom. I let mine drop to the ground. Sadly, it's all stapled together, so it just kind of falls in one lump.

"You'll be contacted by a local Council representative once you reach your final destination. If you have any questions, you know where to reach me. I'll be sending on your personal effects—those I can, of course—as soon as possible."

He gives me another one of his thousand-watt smiles (which do not compare in any way, shape, or form to George's). "It's been a pleasure working with all of you. As always, please be sure to destroy any paper documents once you have committed them to

31

memory." And with that he hightails it out of there faster than you can say "vampire chicken."

"Mom," I say. "Seriously, this completely sucks. What am I supposed to do in Louisiana?"

"The same thing we're all going to do." She picks up my packet and hands it to me. "Make the best of it."

WHY IT STILL SUCKS TO BE ME, CONTINUED

1. I have to give up my entire life and all my stuff (well, okay, almost all of my stuff) while my boyfriend is traipsing around Brazil, rubbing suntan lotion on bronze Brazilian goddesses.

2. And I am not moving somewhere cool like Los Angeles.

3. No, I'm moving to Louisiana.

4. Louisiana.

MYTH:	Vampires can fly.
TRUTH:	Yeah, in airplanes.

5

I have to say that flying is a totally different experience as a vampire than as a regular person. Basically, you're sitting in this flimsy seat that you could crush with your bare hands, listening to all these creaks and pops and other scary noises that the people around you can't hear. And the worst part? You can also hear every conversation going on in the whole plane, including

- a) the pilot and copilot arguing about some reality TV show and apparently not paying any attention whatsoever to the plane,
- b) a couple of flight attendants debating which guy in First Class is cuter, and
- c) some disgruntled passenger in the back of the plane complaining about the lack of free snacks.

It's really kind of nerve-racking. I mean, if the plane goes down due to a couple of bonehead pilots who can't agree on whether or

34

not the blonde with long legs or the brunette with the big butt should win the grand prize or not on some stupid TV show, I'll probably die a flaming death along with everyone else. I don't think even a vampire can survive a drop of 30,000 feet. Pretty sure, anyway. It definitely wasn't in the brochure.

The rest of the fam seems completely okay with all of this, but I guess they've had longer to get used to it. Dad's reading some boring history book (surprise), Mom's watching the in-flight movie (nothing good), and Uncle Mortie is rocking out on his old-school CD player. And thanks to the Josh-erator School of Light Packing, I don't even have a book to take my mind off of things. All I've got is my vampire lessons notebook and the information packet. I'm not desperate enough to read my old notes, so I break out the packet.

Dear Mina Smith, formerly Mina Hamilton:

I snort. "Uncle Mortie, I still can't believe they're changing our last name to Smith. Isn't that like the most common last name in the entire country?"

He takes off his headphones and wiggles his eyebrows at me. "And why do you think that is?"

Oh. *Hmmmm.* That makes me wonder about my old sixth-grade math teacher, Mrs. Smith. I always thought there was something different about her.

Attached please find a biographical profile of your new identity. We strongly advise you to study this document carefully and commit it to memory before destroying it. You are also strongly cautioned against keeping any memorabilia from your old life that might serve to identify you in any way. This includes yearbooks, driver's licenses, birth certificates, and any other identifying documents. New documentation will be provided to you by your agent as necessary.

Great. The Josh-erator was lying about me getting most of my stuff back. I bet he didn't even let Mom keep my baby pictures since she's supposed to be my sister-in-law now, and Dad is supposed to be my brother. I should have packed up some of my stuff and hidden it or given it to Serena for her to keep for me. Now I bet I'll never get any of it back. The good stuff anyway. The stuff I actually care about.

I'll have to see if Serena can sneak into my house and steal some of it for me. They won't be expecting that and she can always just pretend if she gets caught that she wanted to have something to remember me by.

The Vampire Relocation Agency (VRA) welcomes this opportunity to assist you in your upcoming relocation. Your personal agent is Josh Douglas. Please feel free to call upon him at any time during the process with any questions, comments, or concerns.

A follow-up survey will be forwarded to your new address. We appreciate your taking the time to let us know how we are doing.

You can bet I'll be filling out their little survey.

Sincerely,

Lucas Porter
Regional Coordinator

Mina Smith Biographical Profile

Name: Mina Smith

Brief Family Bio: Mina Smith was born in Seattle, Washington. She is the second child of Adam and Briggita Smith née Mueller.

Her older brother is Robert "Bob" Smith, who is her elder by eleven years. Adam and Briggita died in a tragic snowmobiling accident in Boulder, Colorado, five years ago when Mina was twelve. She was subsequently taken in by her brother, Bob, and his wife, Mari, and the family moved to Santa Barbara, California.

I think we've *driven* through Santa Barbara before. Hopefully no one asks me anything about it. Though I guess people in Louisiana probably wouldn't know if I messed up anyway.

Bob and Mari have no children of their own and have happily raised Mina. Mina and Bob's uncle, Mortimer, is their only living relative. He lives in New Orleans, Louisiana. Mari worked as an office assistant at an elementary school until she was downsized. Soon after Bob was laid off from his nontenured teaching position at Santa Barbara Community College. So Bob and Mari decided to move the family to Louisiana to be closer to Mortimer.

Mina was a solid A/B student at a midsize school in Santa Barbara. She participated in her school's French club, school newspaper, Drama Club, and track and field. She was voted Most Likely to Win an Oscar in her junior yearbook.

Birthday: June 1st

Chronological/Apparent Age: 17/17

It goes on for a while with a bunch of other inane factlets about my life. Or rather, my fake life. At least they didn't change my birthday. Or my grades. Most everything else is a bit of a mystery. I didn't really participate all that much in clubs and I am definitely no drama queen. Well, okay, Uncle Mortie might say I am, but

39

never like in an actual drama class. I transferred out of that in ninth grade. Whoever made this stuff up really should have paid a little more attention, but maybe they were going for opposites. I dunno.

New Location: Cartville, Louisiana
New School/Career: Cartville High School, senior

"Hey, Uncle Mortie, where exactly is Cartville, anyway? Is it a suburb of New Orleans or something?"

"Probably. Isn't the Big Easy the only city in Louisiana? Hey, I'll be right back. Going to see if I can snitch some nuts from the stewardesses. I think the redhead was giving me the eye."

I seriously doubt that, but Uncle Mortie's nothing if not optimistic. About redheads, anyway.

So I try pumping Mom for some more details. I poke her on the shoulder. "Mo—sorry, Mari." She turns away from the in-flight movie and lifts up her headphones.

"What do you know about Cartville?" I ask. "Anything you can tell me now that Josh isn't around?"

"I'm sure it will be really nice," says Mom. Which I guess answers my question—she has no idea either. She's already got her headphones back on and is staring at the movie.

I poke her again. "Do you think it will be close to New Orleans? Maybe we can tour around once we get there?" I imagine eating some of those yummy Frenchish doughnut things called beignets I saw on some Food Network show about New Orleans, preferably with George once he comes to visit. Or walking through the French Quarter with him and checking out the street musicians. I've heard New Orleans is a good music town.

"Come on," I say. "At least give me something to look forward to."

She shrugs. "I can't wait to meet our new neighbors."

"Our neighbors?" I laugh. "Did you not pay any attention to the neighbors we just left behind?" Mrs. Finch was like the devil in old-lady skin. And that weird guy a couple of doors down with the yard full of ugly yard art and slowly rotting newspapers? He was just scary. Why would I want to hang out with neighbors? I want to hang out with my friends. Who live in *California*. Well, except for George. But you know what I mean.

Mom whips off her headphones again. "Mina, why can't you look at this as an opportunity? Don't you think it will be nice to start fresh? It may not seem like it right now, but the VRA has our best interest at heart. They're trying to help us."

"Yeah, whatever." She gives me the *shush* face, so I go back to reading. I could live without the VRA's help, that's for sure.

MYTH: Vampires are cold to the touch.

TRUTH: We prefer to be called "cool."

6

"Mari! Mina! Look alive!"

I unplug my headphones and try to come back into focus. In my pre-vampire days, I'd totally have been asleep. Now, I just feel completely zoned. We've been on the road for at least three hours since landing at the New Orleans airport (where Uncle Mortie ditched us to go pursue whatever his new venture is in the city), driving through increasingly blah-looking country. No coastline, no ocean, and lots of farms. And cows. Lots of cows.

So much for Cartville being a suburb of New Orleans. I gave up that hope after the first half hour.

I look out the window and see . . . well, not much. Dad is driving slowly down the road. I can see a gas station, a couple of shops (half of which look abandoned and the other half look like they've been there since Uncle Mortie was a kid), a hardware store, and not much else. Dad stops at a blinking red stop light. It's just sitting there flashing on and off.

"Welcome to Main Street, Cartville, USA! Small-town living at its best!" says Dad.

"Um . . ." I am at a total loss for words. This isn't a *small* town. It's . . . tiny. Tinier than . . . like so tiny there's not even a word for it tiny. Even Mom is kind of quiet, which I bet means Cartville is also way smaller than she thought it was going to be too.

"Are you sure this is it?" I say. "Maybe this is just like the slum part or something?" Not that it looks particularly slummy. It just looks . . . small. Definitely no beignets or espresso. Is there even a library?

"Of course this is it!" Dad says. "We just passed the city-limits sign! Now, let's see. I just need to turn right on Cypress Street . . . and hey, Mina, look! There's the high school! Looks like you'll be able to walk to school from our new house! Isn't this great?"

"Dad, I think I could walk to school from pretty much any place in this entire town." Going to a new school is *not* something I am remotely excited about. Being able to walk to it? Not a bonus. But I guess walking is better than taking the bus since I don't have a car. Though I'd kinda been planning on begging for one. You know, riding the guilt train for all it's worth. Looks like I have no excuse now. Do they even need buses here?

43

"Okay!" says Dad in his grin-and-bear-it-everything-is-under-control voice. "Here we are! 512 St. Ann Avenue! Our new home sweet home!" He parks the car and bounds out the door with Mom close behind. I get out of the car, but with a lot less bounce. Home sweet home? They have got to be out of their minds.

Our old house wasn't exactly stellar. It probably could have fit inside the first floor of one of the McMansions that the A-list kids like Nathan and Bethany lived in (and totally took for granted). And it needed painting and probably could have used some better landscaping (which Mrs. Finch was always hinting about).

The new house? It would fit in the first floor of our old house. And as far as atmosphere, let's just say it pretty much looks like a box. With a roof. And it's purple. Not like a normal Victorian-style pale lavender either, but purple purple. Like Barney purple. Like Barney ate a bunch of blueberries and then barfed them up.

Not to mention the leftover plastic goose dressed in a purple (of course) raincoat sitting in the front yard. With three little baby plastic geese wearing matching purple bonnets.

"Please tell me we're just renting." I kick at one of the baby geese and knock it over.

"Mina, don't be so negative." Mom picks it up and looks at it a minute, then sets it next to the mommy goose again.

Ha. The only thing I can be positive about is that the situation keeps getting suckier and suckier every time I turn around. Maybe they want to go all Dullville and be neighborly or whatever, but they didn't have to drag me down with them. Then she dishes the real scoop on our not-so-luxurious digs. "We can't afford to buy a new house until the VRA is able to release our funds to us. But I'm sure if we just do a little clean up, this place will be just fine."

I shrug and grab my one dinky little bag from the back of the car. I think it would take a lot more than some bleach and elbow grease to make this place presentable. At least I won't be spending our first night in the new house unpacking . . . since I have basically nothing to unpack. But I'm not at all surprised that the VRA has us by the throats, so to speak.

Dad is already inside and exploring, which takes him a grand total of about five minutes. There are two bedrooms, a kitchen (with lavender tile and pee yellow cabinets with happy little daisy-shaped knobs), a single bathroom (yet more lavender plus a truly hideous floral shower curtain), and a kind of combined living room/dining room with olive green shag carpet (at least it wasn't purple). Not exactly palatial. The bedrooms are about the same size and both of them have queen-size beds (which I suppose is more for show than anything else, since we don't sleep). I lay claim to the one with two windows by putting my bag in it. They can at least give me that.

"Dibs," I yell out. "I call the one with the desk." It's got a missing drawer, but I guess that's better than nothing. I set my suitcase down on the red bedspread (another thankfully not-purple thing) and look around. "But you can have the lamp." I think I'm a little too old for a lamp with a headless pony on it. Besides, that's the stuff nightmares are made of. Other than that, there's not much in the room, just a dresser (painted white, with chipped gilt edges), and a closet (no door, just a beaded curtain).

We meet back in the kitchen and stand there looking at each other. D'oh. "What're we supposed to do now?" I look back and forth between Mom and Dad. Seriously. What do you do when you don't have any of your stuff?

"Well," says Mom. "I guess maybe we could go shopping? How about some Pop-Tarts? We can get your favorite."

It's right on the tip of my tongue to say, "Yeah, where? Is there another town nearby?" when we all hear footsteps coming up the walk. Maybe I'm just nervous from all the little pep talks we've been getting from the VRA, but I can't help but wonder who it could be. No one should even know that we're here. Or is it maybe a VRA goon coming to check up on us already? What, were they following us?

46

I think Mom and Dad must be a little paranoid too, because Dad says quietly, "I'll get it. You two just stay here." I guess you can never be too careful when you're a child of the night or whatever.

He waits until the person, whoever it is, knocks. Then he plasters a friendly smile on his face and opens the flimsy white paneled door. "Hello," he says. "Can I—"

"Well, hello there! So nice to meet you! I'm Eugenie Broussard, your new neighbor. And you're . . . ?"

"Um, Bob. Bob Smith. We just—" Dad sounds a little nonplussed, but I can't blame him. The lady sounds like a force of nature. I could've heard her across the house even if I didn't have superhearing.

"Oh, it's a 'we' then. I see. So you're not a single gentleman? Well, where's the rest? I'd love to meet all of y'all. Is it just a missus or do you have a whole passel of kids back in there? The old Blanchard place ain't that big, so I don't suppose you do, but you never can tell, can you?"

Mom hides a snicker behind her hand and whispers to me, "We'd better go save your dad." I'm all for offering him up for humiliation, but my curiosity gets the best of me.

We come up behind Dad, and Mom puts her hand on his shoulder. He looks like a fish out of water, with his mouth just kind

47

of slowly opening and closing. "Hi there," says Mom. "I'm Mari Smith, Bob's wife. And this is Mina, Bob's little sister."

Oh yeah. Can't forget that. Not sure I like the "little" part there though. After all, I'm almost as tall as Dad is.

Mom pokes me in the side with her elbow. Right, manners. "Hi. Nice to meet you," I say.

Eugenie is a big-boned lady with lots of curly blonde hair piled up on top of her head and a smile about as wide as her entire face. She's wearing kind of a fancy and very colorful floral dress for just kicking around town, but maybe they dress up here. Or maybe she was hoping for a single gentleman.

"Nice to meet you, Mari and Mina! What interesting names! Where are y'all from? Don't sound much like y'all are from 'round here."

"We're from California. We—" starts Mom.

"Oh, California! Can't say as I've ever been out that way, but always wanted to go. All them beaches and movie stars! You ever meet yourself any of those movie stars or those super-skinny models, Mina? Young girl like you, I imagine you've had your eye on a few, ain't that right?"

"Oh yeah, I was hanging out with some models just the other day. We pretended to eat some ice cream together." *Snort.* Mom gives me a look. Oh, come on! Like California is just full of famous people.

"Really!" says Eugenie like she believes me. "You don't say! And Mari! You've got yourself some beautiful red hair there. Always did love red hair." Eugenie somehow reaches around Dad and gets an arm around Mom's shoulder and starts walking inside like they've been best buddies for years. "Now, I tell you what: When you need a touch-up, you just let me know. I own the beauty shop. It's called Eugenie's, after my name, you know, and I give the best haircuts in town, if I do say so myself. Course, there ain't another salon until Hainesville, but y'all don't want to go there anyway." She sniffs and looks from me to Mom and back again. "Owner's just a little young thing and what she don't know about hair! I like to had a heart attack when I saw what she done to Mabel Mouton last June before her daughter Jessie's wedding. Mabel comes to me now, I tell you what."

Mom looks at me kind of helplessly but all I can do is raise my eyebrows at her. I don't know what she expects me to do about this lady. I've never met anyone like this in my entire life. And hair is so not my thing.

"Um, Eugenie, I'll definitely keep that in mind," Mom finally chokes out.

"You do that, dearie. And you too, Mina. I 'spect I could tame those curls for you, though girls these days, I tell you, it's a wonder they've got any hair left at all the way they treat it. Why, just the other day—"

49

Mom jumps in before Eugenie can work up a full head of steam. "Eugenie, I'd love to offer you something to drink, but I'm afraid we haven't had time to go grocery shopping yet. We were actually just headed out the door. Perhaps you could recommend a place for us?"

"Well, of course I can! There's J & E Grocery just over on Main Street, you more'n likely passed it on y'all's way in. And there's a Dollar General over on Duson Avenue. But if you're lookin' for something a mite bigger, there's a Piggly Wiggly over in Jennings. It'll take you a good twenty or thirty minutes to get over that way, though."

A Piggly Wiggly? What kind of a store is that? Don't they have any normal stores here? It's a good thing we don't actually have to eat. But I guess we have to buy food to keep up appearances, especially if Eugenie's going to be popping by on a regular basis. And somehow, I think she just might.

Mom is trying to steer Eugenie toward the door when our new neighbor turns her eye on me again. "You gonna be starting up at Cartville High, Mina? You look the right age. Senior?" I nod, but I'm not sure if she even notices. "I'll be seein' you there then. My son Grady's a senior too, and I volunteer over at the front office in the mornings. Great school and great kids! I bet everybody'll just eat you up, bein' a California girl and knowin' models and all!"

"Oh," says Dad, totally ignoring the model thing. "Maybe you could tell Mina a bit about the school?"

"Why, certainly! Go Cougars! There's eighty-nine seniors this year. Would've been ninety, but Bobby Duschamp dropped out to work on an oil rig at the end of last year. Even so, it's the biggest senior class since I went to school there!" She laughs a big, hearty laugh and pokes Dad in the chest. "I bet you can't guess when that was!"

Dad is saved from answering by my jaw dropping to the floor. "Eighty-nine? Seriously?"

"Yep! Four hundred and thirty-two total in the school. Been gettin' bigger and bigger every year! Why, the whole town's grown to 1,255 people."

"Are you kidding me? That's less people than went to my old high school, McA—"

"Mina!" says Mom. What? Oh, yeah. What was the name of my high school supposed to have been? Not McAdam. Um, crap. I just shut my mouth with a snap, but it doesn't matter anyway since Eugenie just goes on like I didn't say anything.

"I guess I should say 1,258 people now! But enough about Cartville. Why don't y'all tell me a bit about yourselves?" She plops herself down on the couch (faded, lumpy, and purple) and pats the cushion next to her like she owns the place. "I'm all ears!" Ha, I don't doubt that!

51

Dad catches the sound of a car stopping outside the same time I do. *Another* visitor? Already? What, is Cartville like Louisiana's Grand Central or something? Can there be more than one Eugenie in a single tiny town?

Mom answers the door this time while Dad is stuck sitting next to Eugenie, who has now started in on his hair. (Apparently, she thinks he could use some highlights. Oh my God.) It's another blonde lady who looks to be around Mom's age with a huge, toothy smile. She does kind of remind me of Eugenie, but much smaller and more sophisticated (at least as far as her clothes go).

"Why, Ivetta!" says Eugenie, jumping up in midsentence. "Whatever are you doing out this way?" Is it just me, or does she look a little suspicious? Who is Ivetta, anyway? And what's up with the names? Seriously, maybe that's what you do in a small town—sit around and think up unusual names for your kids.

"Eugenie! And here I thought I'd be the first to greet the Smiths. I suppose I should have known you'd get here before me!" Ivetta smiles wide at Mom. She and Eugenie could probably get walk-ons in a toothpaste commercial. "Eugenie's a regular welcoming committee unto herself around here."

Eugenie sniffs a little at that, though I don't know why she'd find that insulting. I guess the truth hurts. She stands up and smoothes some invisible wrinkles out of her dress. Or maybe there actually are wrinkles. Hard to tell with all the flower power going on.

"Well, I should be gettin' on anyway. So nice to meet all y'all. Interestin' to see you again, Ivetta."

Ivetta waits until Eugenie's down the walk before saying anything. "Don't worry about Eugenie. She's a huge gossip, but she means well. She's just not real fond of me since I stopped getting my hair cut at her salon. She was payin' a little too much attention to my lack of aging."

Mom looks her up and down. "You must be . . . ?"

"Oh, sorry. Forgot the introductions, didn't I? Ivetta Pierce, regional continuing education coordinator extraordinaire! There aren't any Council agents stationed up this way, so I kind of act as an all-around greeter and educator. So nice to meet you all! We've heard so much about you! Hadn't had anyone *really* new move to the area in quite some time. Years, really! Very exciting!"

Lovely. I guess that means I'm the only vampire teen in town. My social life is gonna rock. Not.

"Except, of course, for Dr. Jonas, but you knew that!" I did? Who the heck is he? I don't think I've ever heard of him. But Dad is doing his bashful grin. Ivetta goes over to him and gives him a huge whack on the back, which almost knocks him over. She's got a lot of oomph for a little lady. "That was quite a coup for you!

53

I heard there was big competition for his internship. Y'all should be very, very proud."

Um, wait. "What internship?"

"Why, honey, your daddy—oops, excuse me—your *brother* landed himself one of the most coveted jobs in the vampire world! They probably taught you about Dr. Jonas in your intro classes. He's a legend! We're very proud to have him here in our little corner of the world. He's been pretty hush-hush about what he's researching. Though I've heard some things." She gives a quick wink-wink like I'm supposed to have any clue what she means.

"Wait, we moved *here* because Dad got a job with some legendary vampire dude? Not because the VRA decided to drop us in the middle of nowhere?" Ivetta's smile slips a bit. "No offense, Ivetta." At least not to her. Mom and Dad can take offense if they want to. I know I'm offended. Did they not think I would figure out that it's their fault we're here?

"None taken, sweetie. This area is a little blip of nothin', but it's a nice one." She starts fumbling around in her purse and backing toward the door. "But it sounds like y'all have a bit of talkin' to do. How about I just drop off some information for you and be on my way? Lookin' forward to talkin' to y'all again!" She drops some brochures (surprise) in Mom's hands and then takes off, letting the door slap shut behind her. I don't let Dad out of my sight.

"When were you planning to tell me that it's your fault that we're stuck here? In this hole-in-the-wall?"

Mom sits next to Dad and puts her arm around his shoulder. "Mina, this is a once-in-a-lifetime chance for your dad. Even a vampire's life. You should be happy for him. Dr. Jonas only takes on a new intern every hundred or so years. You know how much your dad loves history. This is his chance to learn from the best."

I'm still staring at my traitor dad. "You could have told me. Or given me some input at least."

He finally clears his throat. "The VRA thought—"

"Forget it," I say and bang out the door after Ivetta. It lets out a loud creak, but I don't care. Let it break. They can't blame this fiasco on the VRA anymore. This is all their fault. Dad's anyway, and Mom's by association.

WHY IT STILL SUCKS TO BE ME, CONTINUED.
(Yet again.)

1. Cartville. Do I need to say more?

2. Sure, my parents are so excited about how my dad
   gets to fulfill his lifelong dream of studying history
   or whatever (what is up with that, anyway?) with some
   famous creaky old vampire, but what about my dreams?
   Not that I know exactly what they are, but they sure
   didn't include getting stuck in the middle of nowhere
   with no friends and no boyfriend.

3. But the absolute worst thing is that it's so totally
   unfair that here I am, some all-powerful (ha),
   all-knowing (yeah, right), in-control (totally not)
   vampire and my parents still get to dictate everything
   I do.

MYTH:	Vampires are antisocial creatures.
TRUTH:	Not usually, but enough is enough already, people.

7

I've been running through the countryside (I don't technically need to exercise, since the muscles are there no matter what I do, but at least it makes me feel like I'm doing *something*) or camped out in my room for the last three days while Mom and Dad play the Happy Neighbor game. They get all excited and crazy friendly every time someone comes over. Like puppies. It's absolutely disgusting. Mom has already joined some cooking club (bet she won't be breaking out the old blood pudding recipe for *them*) and Dad has been talking about fishing and hunting *while* wearing a John Deere baseball cap. I think they're taking this whole fitting in thing a little too seriously.

Cartville is like a black hole. It's like being totally cut off from civilization. I haven't been able to call Serena because there are no cell phone stores here, and I can't call her on the landline while my parents are home. I haven't been able to send an e-mail to tell George to rescue me because the "new" laptop Ivetta dropped off is basically a giant solitaire-playing paperweight until we get Internet access.

I'm on my fifty-third solitaire game of the day when I hear the now-familiar sound of Eugenie's pumps clicking up the sidewalk (at least she's not evil like our old next door neighbor), but this time I can hear that she's not by herself.

Great. More company.

"Mom, do I have to do this? Now? It's Friday night. I was supposed to go out with the guys. Lonnie's having a party." Ah. Must be Eugenie's son, Grady. I've heard her telling Mom all about him.

Eugenie clucks at him. "You be a good boy and be neighborly. Mari said Mina's having a hard time adjusting to things around here. She don't know anybody her own age and it'd be nice if she met a few of you young folks before school starts. I know you'll just love her to death. Mari says she has a really nice personality." Gah. Thanks a lot, Mom. Not. It's no wonder he's dragging his feet up the walk. That's a death sentence if I ever heard one.

"But, Mom—"

"No ifs, ands, or buts," she says firmly. "Get going. Here's the keys to the truck. Just make sure you put gas back in it if you spend all night going up and down the Loop. I'm going across the

58

street to visit with Mabel for a while." I hear her footsteps go back down the path and across the street. Then a few more slow steps up the walk from Grady.

Lucky for him, I'm planning on helping him out.

I wait at the door and answer on the first knock. Might as well get this over with.

"Hey! Whoa—I . . . uh . . ." Guess I surprised him with the preemptive door opening. Grady is pretty cute, in a healthy-jock-farm-boy kind of way. Not like the whole Wesley farm boy thing in *The Princess Bride* or anything, but attractive. He's got wavy light brown hair with some natural sun streaks in it, some pretty beefy biceps under his slightly too tight T-shirt and a totally confused expression on his face.

"Hey, you must be Grady, right?" Might as well get right to it so we can both get on with the rest of our lives. "Look, I'm sure you've got better things to do tonight than show me around town." I grit my teeth and smile at him as best I can. "And honestly, I've seen pretty much all of it already. So I'm good to go. I mean, stay. Stay at home." Smooth, Mina, real smooth. Showing off my nice personality all right.

He blushes, clears his throat a couple of times and then runs a hand through his hair, which causes his bicep to actually ripple. Does he have to practice that? Is that natural? Where're my friends when I need them? Lorelai would totally love him, George would be cracking on his obvious überness and I bet Serena would freak him out.

"Oh, no, I told my—I mean, it's no trouble at all," Grady says. "I didn't have anything else planned. I'd love to show you around and introduce you to everybody."

Um, okay. That's a total lie. Didn't he just tell Eugenie a totally different story?

"Don't worry about your mom." I wink at him before I think better of it. Crap. Don't want to give him the wrong idea. "I'll tell her you took me around and showed me a good time and all that. You can go hang out with your guy friends or your girlfriend or whatever." I start to ease the door shut.

He blushes a little darker but puts his hand on the door over the top of mine. "Oh, I don't have a girlfriend. Really, I'd love to take you out. There's a party over at Lonnie Pratt's tonight."

Um . . . *what*?

I'm trying to think of some other polite way to tell him "no, thanks" when Mom takes it out of my hands. "Mina would love to go!" she calls out from the kitchen. She comes out to stand behind me in the doorway and I give her a glare over my shoulder.

Grady quickly takes his hand off mine and leans against the rickety door frame. Mom gives me a push in the back and I almost trip out the door. "Thanks so much for offering to show Mina around. I think it will be great for her to get a chance to meet some other kids her age instead of hanging around here with me and her brother."

Oh, so that's the story. I bet they want a little alone time together. It is a small house and with me having hearing just as good as theirs and the whole no-sleeping thing . . . yeah, I bet they're just dying to get rid of me for awhile. Well, if that's the case, I'd rather not be here. I mean, I *know* where I came from and everything, but that doesn't mean I want to *really* know-know, you know?

"Fine," I say. "Mo—uh, Mari. I'll just be gone a couple of hours. I'm sure I don't want to take up too much of Grady's time."

He smiles real big and friendly at me. Now I can see that he really is related to Eugenie. "You can take up as much of my time as you'd like," he says and takes my hand as I go down the stairs.

Seriously, this whole Southern hospitality thing is hard to get used to.

WHY IT KINDA SUCKS TO BE A VAMPIRE

1. The whole superhearing thing. Sure, it might sound great (ha, ha, very punny), but what it really means is that you hear everything. Even stuff you'd rather not hear. Like your parents doing you know what. And people all around you all talking at the same time. The next door neighbors arguing. The dog down the street chasing a cat. The list goes on and on. It's really distracting. And sometimes gross (see note about parents).

2. And the whole supersniffer thing? Just as bad. You'd be surprised how many people smell. I mean, I'm sure they don't smell to other people, but when you can smell someone baking a chocolate cake three houses down, you can also pick up on the BO of the guy next to you, even if he does wear deodorant. (Or, as usually seems to be the case, wa-a-y too much cologne. And could someone please ban Old Spice? What is up with that? Even my dad is cooler than that.)

3. Having to wear sunglasses whenever it's sunny.
It wasn't so bad in California where, like, everybody
wears them. But here? I'm going to stick out like
a sore thumb. Not that I'm sure other people don't
wear them too, but none as dark as the ones I need
to wear. I bet they're going to think we're acting like
stuck-up movie stars or something just because we're
from California.

4. Accidentally doing the extend-a-fang thing when you
don't mean to and biting your lip or tongue. (Hey, it
takes practice to get it right.) Just because you're
a vampire doesn't mean you can't hurt yourself.
And man, let me tell you, fang through the lip
seriously hurts.

5. The drinking blood thing. I'm getting used to it, but
it still is kind of gross. Mom says it's all in my head,
but I don't know. Why couldn't it have been chocolate?
I could totally get behind that.

MYTH:	Vampires are suave party animals.
TRUTH:	Suave? who actually says that?

8

We get to Lonnie's and I start to get out of the truck under my own power. This obviously goes against all Southern protocol because Grady comes running around the truck. I guess it's kind of nice, but at the same time it's kind of annoying. I mean, what, does he think I'm some delicate flower who can't handle getting out of a big old truck by herself? Cheese.

He holds open the door of his truck for me and takes my hand to help me out, which feels kind of ridiculous since technically I could pick up the entire truck with one hand. But not like he knows that. I guess it's more of the whole Southern charm thing. George opens doors for me, but he doesn't try to help me in or out or anything. He knows me better than that. I just hope he's not busy opening up a cabana door for some bikini babe right now.

Grady leads me to the door of the house like I couldn't find it on my own. I can already hear unidentifiable country music turned up way too loud (actually, as far as I'm concerned, any country music that is actually audible is way too loud) and a crowd of people. "Now, Mina," he says, leaning close to my ear, "if anyone in there gets fresh with you or gets a little too close, you just let me know and I'll take care of it."

"I think I can take care of myself," I say. Then the door flies open and nearly hits me in the face. A couple of guys come pouring out.

"Grady!" yells one and pounds my knight in denim jeans on the back a couple of times hard enough that Grady has to let go of my hand. "I haven't seen you practically all summer! How you been, man? How's Baby? Lookin' good this year?" He's a big, beefy guy with close-cropped blond hair and hands that look large enough to palm a pumpkin.

"Good, Lonnie. And Baby's great. Fat as ever. How 'bout you?" Man, I hope Baby isn't what he calls his girlfriend. How rude.

That's when Lonnie notices me. "And who do we have here?" He whistles and gives me a huge smile. "You're definitely not from around here!"

I guess it must be pretty obvious, since everyone keeps telling me that. Maybe I should just get a T-shirt that says, "That's right, I'm not from around here" on it. It'd save time.

"This is Mina," Grady says, and plops his arm around my shoulders. "She just moved to town from California."

I step forward to shake Lonnie's hand. "Nice to meet you," I say. "Hope you don't mind that I'm crashing your party."

"Not at all," he laughs. His hand completely engulfs mine. This dude is HUGE. "You can crash at my house any time you want. Any time at all." He throws an arm around both me and Grady at the same time and pulls us into the house. I feel a little bit like Goldilocks being hugged by Papa Bear. I'd be surprised if Lonnie's not on the football team. Shoot, he could be the entire defensive line all by himself.

"Grab yourself somethin' to drink. You know where everything is, Grady." Then Lonnie leans his head over to whisper in Grady's ear. "Kacie's not here yet, but you better watch out, man. I heard she's coming." I pretend I can't hear anything, since I technically shouldn't be able to. But I can't help but wonder who Kacie is. Unless she's Baby?

The house is completely packed with kids. Some are drinking beer, which smells even grosser to me now than it did before. (A bonus for my parents, I guess, since there's no way I'll ever drink the stuff. Not that I did before, but now . . . ew. Let's just say that when you get right down to it, dog piss actually does smell better than beer.) The music is blaring some whiny country song about somebody doing somebody wrong or something like that.

I haven't been to a lot of parties and only one that you could call an A-list party, but this is definitely nothing like that one at all. No fancy designer clothes, no catering, no expensive cars parked out front. (In fact, hardly any cars at all. Does everyone around here drive a pickup truck?)

It's actually kind of nice. I'm totally not grooving to the lame music, but at least I don't feel completely out of place either.

Grady waves his free hand and yells to me over the music, "If you wanted to meet people, this is the place for it! Lonnie throws the best parties. This is pretty much everybody, right here!"

"You know it!" Lonnie yells back and releases us from his bear hug to go hug a new girl who came in right behind us.

Grady parades me around the room and introduces me to a bunch of people, most of whose names I forget as soon as they say them. Too bad supermemory isn't one of the things you get when you turn. Now *that* would be handy. He finally parks me on a couch and tells me to save him a seat and he'll get us some drinks. I tell him soda and he nods, though he looks a little surprised. I guess people from California are supposed to be serious partiers or something.

I'm kind of having fun just sitting there and watching the people ebb and flow around me. Everyone who walks by the couch actually stops to at least nod or say hello to me. They really are friendly here, though a bit, um, excitable. I can hear a group of guys in the backyard holding some kind of drinking-wrestling contest. From here, they all sound like they're losing. Or winning, I guess, depending on your viewpoint.

Grady finally comes back over and sits down on the couch as close to me as he can get. Granted, he had to squeeze in between me and some girl who I already forgot the name of, but who apparently really likes my hair and would give Eugenie a run for her money on the nonstop chattering front.

She's not the only one. Grady certainly does talk a lot for a guy. I learn that he

a) was on student council last year and expects to win student body president this year,

b) wants to go to Tulane University after high school to study Veterinary Science, and

c) apparently likes to flex his biceps a lot. I get more than one glimpse of them as he keeps messing with his perfectly tousled hair.

I finally interrupt him. "I'm gonna get another drink. Do you want anything?" Everything goes kind of quiet. Not like completely dead silent since there's still some jangly country tune going on and the guys outside are still battling it out, but there's a definite lull in the conversations going on directly around us. The girl on the other side of Grady kind of clears her throat and shifts as far over as she can get, like he's got the plague all of a sudden.

What, is it totally against the rules for the girl to get up and get a drink for a guy?

"Uh-oh," I hear Grady say under his breath.

I look up to see a kind of pretty (if you like sharp angles and no curves), petite blonde girl dressed in skintight jeans that leave absolutely nothing to the imagination (and I mean *nothing*) and a teeny-tiny sparkly pink T-shirt (I swear, it could have been Barbie's) giving me the evil eye from the doorway. I'm guessing she might be Kacie, whoever that is, since I see Lonnie standing behind her frantically waving at Grady. The girl comes sashaying over to stop right in front of us.

"Who's your new little friend, Grady?" she asks in this really annoyingly sweet voice, ignoring me completely. I can already tell she's going to be my new favorite person. Not.

I stand up and stick out my hand like I'm too stupid to notice that she obviously hates me already. "Hi! I'm Mina. I just moved to Cartville and Grady's mom was nice enough to ask him to show me around and introduce me to people. Are you Grady's girlfriend? It's nice to meet you!"

69

There. That'll hopefully do it. The last thing I need is some chick hating on me for no good reason. But I can see by the look on her face that I've somehow managed to say exactly the wrong thing.

"No," she practically spits at me. "I'm *not* Grady's girlfriend."

O-o-o-kay. I'm not really sure what to say to that. Sorry? Guys suck? Good for you? So I just stand there with a stupid smile on my face, counting to ten in my head until Grady hauls himself off the couch and clears his throat.

"Hey, Kacie. How's it goin'?"

Is that all he's got? Oh man. I gotta get out of here.

"So . . . ," I say. "Um, Grady, thanks for showing me around, but I did tell my mo—my sister-in-law—that I wouldn't be too long, so I think I'm going to head out."

I sidestep around Kacie, who's standing there glaring back and forth at me and Grady with her hands on her bony hips. Lovely. The last thing I need is a catfight at my first party in town.

Grady grabs my hand and tries to stop me.

"Oh, no, it's a really long walk back to town. I'll drive you."

Dude. This guy is clueless. Cute, but clueless. If Kacie had lasers for eyes, he'd be a smoking pile of goo on the floor by now.

70

"No, really, I'm good. It's a nice night for a walk. And maybe you should, you know . . . stay here." I start backing up, hoping he'll finally take the hint and drop my hand.

He looks like he's going to argue when a hand mysteriously appears between us. A strong, capable hand attached to a tall, thin, pale guy with piercing blue eyes, a shock of dark auburn hair, and full red lips. He takes my hand like he's going to shake it or maybe even kiss it, making Grady drop it in the process.

Where did he come from? It's like he appeared out of nowhere to step in front of Kacie.

"Perhaps I can be of assistance. I was on my way out anyway." The guy whisks me out of there before anyone has a chance to say a word. We're already outside and in his car, something fast-looking and red, before I hear Grady go, "Hey—"

I don't need to check the stranger's nonexistent pulse to get the real picture. Looks like I'm not the only bloodsucking teen in town after all.

MYTH: Vampires have an innate sense of direction.

TRUTH: Maybe. But I seem to have an uncanny knack for getting lost.

9

"So," says Cameron, the mystery vampire guy, "you must be one of the new VRA victims that we've been hearing about." He's got a slight French accent, but more regular French than the Cajun-French spoken around here. It kind of adds to his whole air of coolness.

"That would be me. And my mom and dad, but now they're supposed to be my brother and sister-in-law. What're you doing here in the middle of nowhere? I didn't think there'd be any other vampires my age in a place this small." Especially supernova hot ones. Not that I noticed.

"You'd be surprised how many vampires there are in Louisiana. We've been here since the beginning."

Oh. Hey. I wonder just how old this guy *really* is. Maybe he just looks like he's my age. Can I ask? Is it impolite? Is asking a vampire his actual age like asking a woman if she's pregnant when she's not? Maybe I should ease into it.

"So how long have you been here? Do you like it?" I can't imagine he does, but who knows.

"I like it well enough, I suppose. I travel a lot, but I always come back to Louisiana. So I guess you could say that I've been here all my life. And death, for that matter. I'm part of the Carter Clan."

Am I supposed to know what that means? Is this another one of those things I should have paid more attention to in vampire class? Gah, G.W. was right. I hate that.

"There are a lot of us around here still, though there aren't many of us actually in Cartville itself anymore. And I get the feeling John and Wayne will probably be rolling into town any day now."

"Um . . ." Okay, I guess I am going to have to ask since I haven't understood anything he's said yet. "I'm really new to this whole vampire thing. Who are John and Wayne? Are they part of this Carter Clan whatchacallit too?"

He arches an eyebrow at me, but keeps driving. "You've never heard of John and Wayne Carter?"

I've heard of John Wayne, does that count? Seriously, how many ways can I admit to being stupid?

"Nope. I only just turned like a couple of months ago."

"Ah," he says, shifting gears. The trees and cows outside are just a blur. "I'm surprised they didn't mention the Carters in your vampire prep classes. You took those, right?" He raises an eyebrow at me. "Or were you an unauthorized turning?"

Does he know G.W. or something? I am so going to ask George and Lorelai if they know who the Carters are. When I can. Oh, wait. "I missed the first class. I think that was the history one."

"Well, John and Wayne Carter are vampires, obviously, who came to the States back in the late 1600s from England. They founded Cartville, but they also lived in New Orleans for a time until they got caught, back in the early 1900s."

"Caught?"

"Yeah, one of their humans escaped."

One of their humans? Is he kidding me, I hope? "What, are they like Black Talons or something?" I laugh a little nervously. Surely this überhot vampire guy can't possibly be part of that whole human-hating scene, right?

Cameron downshifts and swerves a little as we take a corner a bit too fast. "Why do you say that? The Black Talons were outlawed by The Councils, as I'm sure you know. They must have mentioned that in your classes."

"Oh, right. It was just a joke." I try to muster up a funny ha-ha laugh, but it falls kind of flat. There, now I've done it. Gone and insulted the only vampire (maybe) teen around. "Anyway, you were saying?" I stop myself from playing with the seat belt buckle.

"John and Wayne were caught red-handed with a bunch of humans in their house in New Orleans. They were tried and 'executed' "—he takes his hands off the wheel long enough to make little quote marks in the air—"and they've been traveling the world ever since. There are Carter Clan members everywhere."

Oh. So I guess John and Wayne just go around indiscriminately turning people wherever they go? Isn't that kind of against the whole Council don't-do-anything-without-telling-us-first thing?

"So I guess John or Wayne turned you?" I hope that's not too personal a question to ask. I'm not really up on the whole vampire etiquette thing. They didn't cover that in class.

"Wayne did. I just came back to town last year. I've been gone for awhile." He abruptly turns off the headlights on his car and makes a sharp left. I look around and have no clue where we are. We're surrounded by trees and that's pretty much it. I should have been paying attention. Oh, man, what if he *is* like a Black Talon or something? Do they hurt other vampires or just humans?

Dad always told me to never go anywhere with strangers. What was I thinking?

75

Okay, I know what I was thinking. I was thinking, "Gee, stay here with the about-to-go-postal Southern belle or leave with the sexy vampire dude?" It had seemed like a no brainer at the time.

"Um, so where are we going exactly?" And please don't say: *You insulted my bloodline. We're going to some secluded cabin so I can kill you, muwhahaha!*

"Didn't I tell you? I thought I'd show you the local blood bar, Ernie's. There's really only one, but I know you and your family haven't been by yet because I'd have heard about it if you had been. I thought you'd like to meet some of the other vampires around here."

Well, that's a lot better than the alternative. "Hopefully they'll be friendlier than Kacie." We both grimace at the same time. "Hey, is there a local vampire-friendly butcher anywhere too? Mom was looking."

He raises his eyebrows at me again. "Oh, so your family are pig swiggers? Ernie can hook you up there too, if you want."

"Excuse me?" I'm not sure whether to feel stupid or insulted. Or both.

"You *are* new," he says. "A 'pig swigger' means you primarily drink animal blood rather than human blood."

"Oh. Well, my mom and I do. Dad, too, mostly." No one ever called us pig swiggers before though. You'd think there'd be a more polite way to say it. Maybe it's just a Southern thing. I can't see some California vampire running around calling people "pig swiggers."

He keeps driving with the lights off (not that we really need them anyway) until we come to a clearing where about ten or so cars and trucks are parked. I still can't see anything but trees though. No buildings or anything. Or vampires.

Creepy. Where is everybody?

He parks his car and waves at me to follow him. I guess the Southern hospitality thing only applies to the non-vampire folk. I follow him, even though I can hear my dad yelling at me in my head. But what else could I do now that I'm here? It's not like I have a clue where we are, other than in the woods. And as far as I can tell, half this state is woods—or fields—once you get out of New Orleans.

"So . . ." I say. "Do the vampires around here know some secret vampire invisibility trick or something?"

Cameron laughs and walks over to a particularly tall tree with feathery-looking branches. "Just look for the cryptomeria," he says.

I jump back and look down at my feet. "The what?" I take a big step to stand right next to him. "Gross! Is this some kind of a graveyard or something? Am I walking on dead people?"

"Cryptomeria, not crypt." He gestures at the feathery tree. "That's what kind of tree this is. They're often used around here to mark underground locations. The entrance to Ernie's is under this one."

Oh. Yeesh. He must think I'm a complete loon after my little two-step performance. But who names a tree after a grave? And who would *know* that the tree was named that? It just looks kind of like a Christmas tree to me.

He pulls on an ancient-looking iron ring set into the ground and a trapdoor opens up. I guess they're real into secrecy here. I'd have totally missed that if I were just walking by. Not that I would have been walking by, since we're in the middle of FREAKING NOWHERE.

I head down a narrow flight of stairs and he closes the trapdoor after us, then squeezes past me to lead the way. It smells musty and earthy and makes me think of being buried alive. (Which is totally not appealing to me. I don't care how undead I am.) I can still see, but only barely. Even vampires have to have some light.

The ground slopes down and we keep walking for about five minutes. Then Cameron abruptly stops and I run into his back, which is very solid and very masculine and smells very not musty. Kind of like really good cologne, but better since there's nothing fake about it. I catch myself taking a deep whiff and then stop.

What am I doing? I have a boyfriend and he smells perfectly wonderful too.

"Sorry," I mumble, and step back a few steps.

He opens a door, reaches back for my hand, and pulls me into a candlelit room full of vampires . . . who all immediately stop talking to turn and stare at me like I'm some kind of alien demon spawn.

MYTH:	Vampires are organized into clans.
TRUTH:	Only clandestinely. Ha, ha.

SMITH

10

There's an ancient-looking wooden bar in the middle of the room with a pudgy bald bloodtender (Ernie, I'm guessing) behind it. Other than that, there are a few plain wooden tables scattered around and an old-school jukebox in a corner playing something guitary (thankfully not country music). Most of the vampires are gathered around the bar, but a few are back in the corners. The only light is from a bunch of candles scattered around the room. All in all, the vibe is very fourteenth century. Except for the jukebox, which is more circa the fifties, I guess, since it has actual records in it.

Everyone stares at me and Cameron for a long minute and then just goes back to whatever they'd been doing before we came in. Ernie grunts and gives us a brief nod.

I guess I'm not such big news after all.

Cameron leads me to the bar and squeezes us in to stand between two grizzly looking guys. Definitely a lot different than the only other blood bar I've ever been in, where everyone was dressed in all kinds of crazy clothes from a bunch of different eras. Everybody here pretty much just looks normal. Like country normal, but normal.

Well, as normal as a bunch of vampires ever look, I guess. Given the whole mostly buff, no-aging, pale-skinnedness of us all. I wonder how vampire farmers explain away the whole lack of a farmer's tan thing?

Cameron nods at Ernie. "I'll take an O negative," he says, "and a Special K for Mina here."

"Special K?" What, they serve cereal at the bar?

"Pig's blood is all type K. Ernie keeps a couple of sows out at his place."

"Oh." Ugh. He didn't need to do that. I really prefer not to think about exactly where the blood I'm drinking comes from.

Ernie grunts at us again and slaps some glasses down on the bar. A young-looking guy in the back of the room grumbles something about "damn Cullenist" loud enough for me to hear (well, me and everybody else, since we've all got superhearing). What's he talking about? What did I—oh wait, yeah, those vampire books with the sparkly vampires. Great, now I've been branded like I'm some kind of a vegetarian vampire freak.

Cameron juts his chin at the guy on our right, the smelly one in overalls who probably hasn't shaved in this century. "Mina, this is Lowell. He's a Carter as well. And supposed to be my uncle, now that I'm back in town. I'm staying with him at his place. Lowell practically lives in the back room here at Ernie's though, so I'm usually on my own."

I stick out my hand to Lowell, but he just barely nods at me.

Cameron grimaces at him and tries again. So much for friendly. "Lowell teaches out at the high school, but I doubt if you'll have him for a class."

"Oh? What do you teach?" I can be polite, even if he's not going to be.

"Shop," he says.

Um, yeah, don't think I'll be taking that one. And honestly, the thought of this guy with power tools is a little disturbing.

"Anyway," says Cameron, obviously giving up on Lowell, "on your left is Roy." This one looks younger than Lowell and isn't as smelly, but his fashion sense is about on the same level. Plaid really doesn't look good on anyone.

Roy stands up to face me, weaving a little. "So, what year are you?" Roy asks, looking directly at my chest. Gross.

I try to cross my arms in the cramped quarters and mostly just succeed in elbowing both Cameron and Lowell in the chest. "Um . . . senior?" Why in the world does this old guy want to know what year I am in school?

He snorts at me. "No, I meant your turning year."

Oh. Is this the equivalent of the whole "what's your sign?" conversation or "what's your screen name?" for vampires? Cheese. "I just turned this year."

"Fresh blood. We need some of that around here. Especially the young, pretty kind." He reaches between me and Cameron to poke Lowell in the shoulder, who just grunts in return, not even bothering to take his nose (and beard) out of his glass. What is it with these people and grunting? And they call *me* a pig swigger.

"So, how about you?" I ask, trying to change the subject and keep his eyes focused upward.

"Nineteen fifty-four. Lowell here is an 1862."

"Yep," drawls Lowell. "I was part of the Civil War influx."

I nod like I know what that means. I refuse to admit to not knowing something else for the rest of the night. I foresee some research in my future. I could ask Dad (I'm sure *he'd* know), but I'm still not talking to him.

Roy gives me another toothy smile and leans into me. *Blech.*

Does he realize he's old enough to be my dad? Actually, more like my grandfather. Maybe even great-grandfather, depending on how old he was when he was turned. He doesn't look like any kind of spring chicken, let me tell you.

That makes me wonder again. "Cameron, what was your year?" I'm guessing it's okay to ask, since Roy did. Cameron doesn't look as old (or hairy) as Roy, but I guess he technically could be even older. Though not creepier. *That* I think I'd be able to tell. After meeting these guys, I'm not so worried about Cameron's intentions anymore. Though he could have picked better people to introduce me to.

"Oh, Cameron's not one for sharing," drawls Lowell, standing up to put an arm around both Cameron's shoulders and mine. He pulls us close. Close enough I can tell he's been drinking something in addition to the A negative. A *lot* of something.

"Lowell, cut it out." Cameron squirms out of Lowell's grubby hold. But Lowell just pulls me closer.

"Hey," growls Roy. "I saw the fresh meat first." He leans forward like he's going to try and kiss me or something. I go to step back but Lowell's still got my shoulder in a death grip, so I put my hands up to block Roy (there's NO way he's getting anywhere near my lips) but find myself suddenly pulled away. Roy and Lowell bump heads and both step back cursing.

"Why don't I get you home," says Cameron, his hands still warm on my shoulders. I don't know how he moved that fast. I'm not even sure what he did. I just know I'm grateful. "It's a little *too* friendly around here tonight."

THINGS I SHOULD FIGURE OUT

1. Just exactly how old is Cameron anyway? He never really answered my question. Not that I care anyway. I'm just curious.

2. How important are the Carters to the history of vampires? I should look up the Carter stuff. And clans. They just sound so Genghis Khan.

3. And what was that about the Civil War influx? I bet Dad knows all about that one. It sounds like some kind of History Channel thing. That is, if vampires had their own History Channel. Which we don't, I don't think. Though who knows, there are like five billion cable channels. If they can have a Pakistani cricket channel, maybe we've got one too.

4. Wait. Could Cameron be from the Civil War time too? He looks like he's my age, but he could actually be like a hundred and fifty or something. Which is kind of freaky, if you think about it. 'Cause if he looked like he was hundred and fifty, you know, that would be completely different.

5. Not that I'm interested. I have a boyfriend. Who's practically on the other side of the world, probably sunning himself on a beach right now. Well, I guess not sunning given the vampire thing. Oh. What if he's got some Brazilian babe slathering him with sunscreen?

MYTH: Vampires can communicate telepathically.

TRUTH: I wish. Then I'd know what George was up to.

11

As soon as there is enough daylight that there might be stores open (ha, if I can find any), I tell Mom it's time to go electronics shopping. Or else.

I go for the power punch of parental guilt and tell her I need a cell phone because, if I was going to go out without a car of my own, I might need to call home for a ride. She totally buys it. What parent with a teenage daughter wouldn't? But the real reason is I'm going to go totally insane if I don't get a cell phone soon. I don't think I've ever gone this long without talking to Serena before, especially not with so much stuff to tell her. Not that I'm supposed to be calling her or anything, since she's supposed to think I'm dead. And I'm going to have to go, like, miles away from the house to make sure Mom and Dad don't hear me talking to her, but I'm going to talk to her tonight somehow if it kills me. Not that it could. You know what I mean.

Dad is stuck hanging around the house since the cable guy is supposed to come today and set up our Internet connection and TV hookup. Dad had finally figured out that it was actually possible to get connected to the real world from here. You just had to talk to Eugenie, who talked to her brother Amos, who talked to some guy he knew, who set it up with the cable company to get someone to come out to our place. Or something all convoluted like that.

Mom and I drive all the way to Jennings, the town with the Piggly Wiggly. (It turns out that it's a pretty normal grocery store and carries Pop-Tarts, so I'm good.) We hit the electronics store first and pick up a cell phone for each of us. Since the VRA still has all our funds tied up and Dad hasn't started up with Dr. Jonas yet (what the big rush was with getting us here, I certainly don't know), we wind up with last year's models, but I talk Mom into getting the texting package anyway. I think she is feeling the guilt. And she should. Who's ever heard of having to drive to another town to go shopping?

Then she hits me with this: "Why don't we get your back-to-school shopping done while we're here? There's a SaveMart."

Okay, so I'm not exactly a style maven and I definitely wouldn't

89

know enough to make it through even one episode of just about any show on the Style Network. But geez. I at least tried to have *some* semblance of fashion before. I mean, I wasn't like haunting the cool boutiques or anything, but I at least did my shopping at an actual *mall*.

I guess Mom can tell I'm less than thrilled, since she puts an arm around my shoulders. "I know this is a big adjustment, Mina. We'll just buy a couple of basics now, and after the VRA releases our funds we'll go shopping in New Orleans, okay? I'm sure they've got at least some of the stores you're used to. And at least you'll be out of the stuff they left us in the house. I wouldn't mind a new shirt or two myself."

I snort. That's an understatement. Ivetta (who apparently is the do-it-all contact here) has less than no fashion sense, at least when it comes to finding stuff for other people. She'd given us an assortment of not-so-matching clothes to go along with our not-so-matching furniture. The best outfit I'd been able to scrape together was a pair of ratty jeans and a T-shirt with some cartoon character that I'd never even heard of on it (some bug-eyed cat). Mom has been knocking around in a frilly purple and pink sundress that was so-o-o-o not her. If anything, it looked very Eugenie. And Dad? Well, come to think of it, he doesn't actually look much different. He still just looks like Dad.

So we spend a couple of hours trying to piece together some decent outfits out of the racks at the SaveMart. As I score a surprisingly nice red shirt off of the sale rack, Mom gives a little telltale throat clearing. Uh-oh.

"Mina . . .," she starts off and then clears her throat again. That's definitely a bad sign. It can't be the shirt—the neckline is high enough to even be Dad approved.

"Yeah?"

"I was just thinking . . . you know, since we're in a brand new place with . . . well, essentially brand new lives . . . now is the perfect time, don't you think, for all of us to turn over new leaves?"

What kind of new-age mumbo jumbo is she talking about? How much more new can things get? I keep flipping through the sale rack.

"I just mean . . ." She sighs. Wow, this is so unlike Mom. She's usually the take-charge gal. "Your dad is trying something new and expanding his horizons. And I'm not sure yet what I'm going to do next, but it definitely won't be teaching. I'd like to try something new myself. And you . . . well, I think you've got the perfect chance here to really shine. Make new friends. Maybe . . . maybe try to keep a *positive* attitude when you meet people."

"Exactly what are you trying to say? I'm *positive* I don't know what you mean."

"Just that you might try being a bit more open-minded about people. Just . . . you know, be nice. Nicer. I don't mean to say you aren't nice already."

No? Well, it sure sounds like that's what she's saying to me. Geez, from my own mother!

She sighs again. "This isn't coming out right. I'm sorry. What I mean to say is that I know things are rough on you, especially with losing Serena and then George moving to Brazil."

"*Visiting* Brazil."

"Okay, *visiting* Brazil. I'm just saying that I'd like you to take this as an opportunity and not as a setback. There are lots of people out there who would love to be able to reinvent themselves and we've got the chance. We can be anything, do anything."

"Oh? I'd like to be in California again. I don't see that happening."

"I know, sweetie. That's just what I mean. We all need to accept the reality of things and move forward. I just think you should *try*, okay?"

"Like what, exactly?"

"Well, what did you think of that Grady fellow? Eugenie says he's a nice young man."

Of course she does. She's his *mom*. He could be an axe murderer and she'd probably say he was just misunderstood. Not that he is, but you know what I mean. "He was okay. Kind of full of himself. Why?"

"No reason." She flips through a rack of jeans like her life depends on it and clears her throat again. Just what is she trying to say?

"I thought he was quite handsome," she says.

"Yeah, for an overly muscular pretty boy who probably carries a mirror around so he can check his biceps out from every angle. So?"

She sighs for like the three millionth time and stops messing with the jeans. "I just think you ought to keep your options open."

My options? What options? I'm living here because I have no options. "I think you're going to have to spell it out for me, Mom."

"Okay, okay. I think George is a wonderful boy, but he is half a world away. And you're so young. There's no reason to tie yourself down, especially when you have literally lifetimes in front of you."

"You think I should dump *George* for *Grady?*" Holy cheese, what has she been smoking? That's like dumping Prince Charming for the troll under the bridge. Not that Grady is remotely troll-like. But you get the point.

"No, no, honey. I'm just saying that you should keep your options open. Keep an open mind."

Yeah, whatever. George is an awesome boyfriend. Besides,

a) It's not like I've got a lot of experience in the whole boy department. She should be happy I even *have* a boyfriend at all. Even if he's in Brazil and hasn't bothered to write to me for over a week. He's still my boyfriend. (I think.)

b) Grady is cute, but seems about as interesting as a hole in the wall, not to mention he's got a bunch of baggage (i.e., around 110 pounds of baggage in a sparkly pink T-shirt).

c) And hello! Grady is a non-vampire. Mom turned just so she could stay with Dad. Why would she even suggest I take a look at a regular guy? Sounds like heartbreak city to me. Of course, I haven't told her about Cameron, who *is* a vampire. And is really cute in a non-big-bicep kind of way.

d) But hello again. Awesome boyfriend. Don't need a new one.

I guess Mom can tell I'm not really buying it. "And I'm not saying that you'll ever be able to replace Serena, but who knows who you might meet tomorrow once school starts? You never know."

No one could ever replace Serena and I don't need anyone to. Of course, she doesn't know that. But to even suggest it . . . cheese.

94

"How are you liking Eugenie as your new BFF?"

She grimaces a little. Got her there. "I get your point. But she's growing on me because I'm keeping an open mind. And that's all I'm asking you to do too. Okay?"

"Okay," I say grudgingly. I can try to be nice. But no one, and I mean no one here or anywhere else, will ever replace Serena. Or George.

I start texting as soon as we get in the car to go back to Cartville.

Send text to(SERENA)

Me (4:53 pm): HT, UT?

Me (4:54 pm): Hey S

Me (4:55 pm): my nw phn

Me (4:59 pm): UT?

Me (5:02 pm): u ok?

Me (5:10 pm): TXT ME!

It's not like Serena to not have her cell phone with her. Maybe she just doesn't recognize the number? But she should be expecting something from me by now. I've got so much to tell her and I want to make sure Raven isn't bothering her. I wonder if I could sic Linda on Raven? She's training in the Vampire Corps, the über-crazy enforcers of the vampire world, now—or something crazy like that. Though she did hang out with Raven some in class. I never could figure out why.

Send text to(GEORGE)

Me (5:15 pm): G!

Me (5:15 pm): H&K

Me (5:16 pm): XOXOXO

Me (5:17 pm): gt nw phn

Me (5:18 pm): WUWH :(

Me (5:20 pm): UT?

Me (5:22 pm): Brzl ok?

Me (5:23 pm): G??

So much for finally getting a cell phone again. Where is everyone?

MYTH:	Vampires don't show age.
TRUTH:	Usually. Unless they're really, really, really old

OLD!

12

Dad is in a complete tizzy when we get back. I think at first it's because we're all connected to the world again, but then I notice he's gone all happy homemaker on us. He has set out like five different pitchers and carafes full of blood (which was pretty much our entire supply at the present, since we still hadn't figured out a local "pig swigger" contact. Okay, other than Ernie, but I hadn't exactly told them about dropping by a blood bar with a sexy vampire stranger I'd just met, so-o-o . . .) and little trays of sandwiches and things like that. There's even a dish with little bitty pickles, with toothpicks to stab them with.

"What's up with the Rachael Ray, Dad?" That is, if Rachael Ray had gone all vampire, which I would seriously pay money to see. Big bucks. I can't even imagine how big her fangs would be.

"Dr. Jonas is coming over! He'll be here any minute. Hurry, get changed! Do you have a dress? Can you comb your hair?"

Wow. This dude must be seriously big time. I've never seen Dad so excited. Or freaked out. He even buttoned his shirt wrong, but Mom reels him in and fixes it. I don't think he notices. He's practically hyperventilating.

The doorbell rings while I'm changing into one of my new outfits (not a dress, since I didn't buy one, and besides, I'm not that excited to meet some ancient historian dude) and I hear Dad squeak out a high-pitched "He's here!" before Mom shushes him and gets the door. By the time I get out there, they've already made their introductions and are sitting kind of awkwardly in the living room, staring at each other. Well, Dad at least. He's staring at Dr. Jonas like he's covered in gold or something.

Which he isn't. Though he does have this look about him like he should be covered in dust. He doesn't actually look *that* old, just a little bit of peppery gray in his hair and kind of a craggy face. He was probably turned when he was in his forties or maybe even fifties, like Uncle Mortie, but there's something about him that just screams ancient. Maybe the smell. He smells old. Like mothballs and whatever that smell is they get in old-people homes. Cottage cheese? Dust bunnies? Metamucil? I bet even non-vampires can tell he's an antique.

I wonder what year he is?

Dad jumps up like a puppet on a string. "Dr. Jonas, this is my daughter, Mina."

Dr. Musty gets up too, but a lot slower. I go over and shake his hand. "Nice to meet you," I say and smile my best you-employ-my-Dad smile though it kind of pains me to be nice to him when he's also the reason we're stuck in Cartville.

"The pleasure is all mine," he says in a wispy, paper-thin voice. Wow, dude even *sounds* ancient. Does he really dig up prehistoric vampire secrets, or does he just remember stuff?

Dad offers the good doctor a selection of cow, pig, or sheep blood and I'm relieved when he just takes a glass with a thanks and sits there sipping it, rather than ragging on us for being pig swiggers. That's really been kind of bugging me. I don't see how you can call somebody any kind of swigger or anything related to a pig and have it be completely harmless.

"So," says Dr. Musty, "how have you been enjoying Cartville so far?"

"Well, it could be worse," I say. "I guess you could have been researching Siberian bloodsuckers." They all turn to look at me. What? It's true.

Dad laughs nervously and then goes on and on about how "quaint" Cartville is. Maybe I don't have the right definition of quaint. Mom tactfully says something about how nice the people are.

"Yes, most of the people here are very welcoming, until you start digging into things they don't want dug up," Dr. Jonas says in his wispy voice. "I'm speaking, of course, of the Carters. This has been one of the more difficult research challenges of my career."

"Some of them seem kind of nice," I blurt out, forgetting (once again) about that whole not interrupting your elders thing. And this dude is definitely my elder, probably by like a thousand years.

"Oh, and to whom are you referring?" Dr. Jonas looks down his nose at me. Maybe he's old school, with the whole "be seen and not heard" thing.

I shift a little in my seat. This probably isn't the best way to tell Mom and Dad about the whole after-the-party blood bar visit. "Um, Cameron? And a couple of others. Lowell, I think? But Cameron seemed really nice. Not so much Lowell." And hot. Cameron, that is. But NOT dwelling on that.

"Oh? And where did you meet them, perchance?"

I don't think I like his tone or his line of questioning. Geez, he's worse than Mom and Dad, who are also now looking at me quizzically like I was out doing something wrong. What's their problem? Didn't Mom tell me to get out there and meet people?

I lean forward to grab a pickle from the coffee table. "I met Cameron at a party that Grady Broussard took me to."

"And Lowell was there?" He sounds incredulous, in a whispery sort of way.

I can't help but laugh. Lowell would look like some kind of trolling geezer at a high-school kid's party. Which I guess he kind of was. "No, Cameron took me to Ernie's after the party."

"Ah," he says, and leans back in his chair, satisfied at last. Man, I bet this is how he interrogates his research victims.

"You went to a party with Grady but left with another boy?" Mom sounds scandalized. Dad just glances apologetically at Dr. Musty, like he can't believe his daughter would do such a thing. Cheese.

"It wasn't like that. This girl Kacie was all mad at me for being there with Grady and I didn't want a scene—"

"Oh, yes," says the sage Dr. Musty. "Kacie Kinsley. She's been after Grady Broussard for quite some time. They did go out a few times, but nothing serious. At least, not on Grady's part."

Why in the world does he even know that? We all stare at him.

He shrugs delicately and takes a tiny bite of a little tuna fish sandwich. "It's a small town," he says. "I think you'll find that you'll soon know everyone's business."

Huh. Sounds like a crazy place to send a bunch of vampires to hide out in, if you ask me.

"And who is Ernie?" Dad asks.

"I was going to tell you about that," I say, resisting the urge to glare at Dr. Musty. "Ernie's is the local blood bar. Cameron said it's about the only place to go around here for blood. It's in the woods just a couple of miles outside of town."

"You went to a blood bar without telling us?" Mom looks even more scandalized now. For heaven's sake, it's not like I'm a little kid anymore.

"I didn't know that's where we were going until we got there. Besides, you've been looking for a blood supplier. I thought you'd be happy." They could at least say thank you, couldn't they?

Dad stands up like he's going to pass around the tray of cookies he's holding on his lap, but stops in front of me instead to give me the evil eye. "So, you just went somewhere where you didn't even know you were going, with some boy you didn't even know, without telling anyone about it?"

Okay, when you put it that way, it does sound a little bad. And I did have a little moment there where I thought Cameron might go all hack and slash on me, but everything turned out okay, didn't it?

I shove the pickle in my mouth and take a couple of the cookies.

"I'm *fine*," I mumble as I chew. "Nothing happened. And in case you've forgotten, I do have that whole vampire superstrength thing and whatnot going for me now." Not to mention I could totally kick butt before any of that too. "And I told you, Cameron is really nice. Right, Dr. Jonas?" I leave out the part where he saved me from being groped by Roy and Lowell. I could have taken care of myself anyway.

He stares at me. "It remains to be seen. He's new to the area and I haven't been successful in interviewing him."

"Funny, he said he came *back* last year. It definitely sounded like he'd been here before." I pop a chocolate chip cookie in my mouth and then wish I hadn't. Dad must have baked them.

Dr. Musty leans forward like a bloodhound on the scent of something big and hairy. "Oh? And what else did you learn there at Ernie's? Did he say anything about the Carters to you? Ask you any interesting questions? Perhaps mention any affiliations he might have?"

Affiliations? Like what? Key Club? Geez, this guy is weird. And nosy. I hope Dad doesn't go all weird from working with him.

"No-o-o . . . just that Lowell was a Carter too." And that stuff about how John and Wayne used to keep humans, but I leave that out. Probably he knows that already anyway and if

103

my parents don't, they don't need to know it right now. Weirdo Carters. "Hey, how come they haven't had to change their names?" That's totally not fair, now that I think about it.

"They have used many identities over the years, but they do tend to stick to their chosen names. The Carter brothers and their Clan are not known for their rule-following abilities."

"Well, it doesn't seem to be hurting them anyway. The VRA should get a grip and let the rest of us keep our names too."

Mom gives me a warning look.

Dad glances nervously at Dr. Musty and leans forward in just the same way. He half whispers, "You are certain the Carters didn't mention any affiliations?"

"Yes, I'm sure!" I look at Dad and suddenly feel sorry for him. He is so obviously trying to impress this guy. He's even started talking like him. I decide to throw him a bone. "Oh, yeah. There was one thing. Cameron said John and Wayne are probably on their way back to town."

"*Very* interesting." Dr. Musty turns to Dad. "At least your daughter's bad judgment brought some new information to light. The brothers coming to town will, I daresay, make our jobs that much more difficult in the coming months. But forewarned is forearmed." He sighs. "And I had a feeling I was so close to making the connection."

My bad judgment? Who the heck does he think he is? Oh yeah, the reason I'm stuck in this town. Well, I guess I can add "nosy" and "pompous" to the list of stuff I don't like about him, and I've known him for only half an hour.

MYTH:	Vampires don't sweat.
TRUTH:	Good thing, what with all the running I've been doing.

13

Praise the Internet gods!

After Dr. Musty leaves, I go out on my nightly run (i.e., excuse to get out of the house). When I come back, Dad has finally gotten the Internet set up.

I spend the rest of the night online and sending e-mails to everyone I can think of: Serena (five times), George (eight times), Lorelai (twice), Linda (what the heck, once), and Uncle Mortie (I was really getting desperate).

I got back exactly one reply, from Linda, who was in the middle of some top-secret training program (or so she said, though how secret is it if she could tell me that much?) and didn't have time to do more than say "Hey!" and "Isn't being a vampire COOL?" I will never get that girl. I wonder if she got her bee and butterfly tattoos before turning? I know she was thinking about it, and you can't get them after since you heal too fast for them to take. I e-mail her back again to ask if she's seen Raven at all.

The next few hours I spend going through my meager supply of clothes (thanks, Josh-erator, O Killer of Fashion) for my first day of school in the morning. This is my first time picking out my outfit without Serena, which makes it that much more depressing. Especially since the last time I had any contact with her at all was really kind of a bust.

It's pretty easy to pick out my most stylish outfit, since I don't have a lot of choices: a pair of decent jeans that I'd snuck in my bag when the Josh-erator wasn't looking, and that one slightly retro red shirt I'd found at the store. All I can say is that the VRA better do whatever it is they need to do and either send us some more fundage or my stuff. They *said* we could get it back. Not that I trust them.

Though it's probably just as well that I don't have my whole wardrobe since I probably would have wound up changing outfits a million times without Serena to be my mirror. Why couldn't they have put off relocating until after my senior year? I was just really starting to get comfortable in my old school. Now I have to start all over again.

I really wish Serena were here.

I go back to the computer to send her one more message and

see that I've finally gotten a reply from her. About time! I was seriously about to start calling the police with an anonymous tip or something. The date stamp says 9:00 a.m., which is about 7:00 a.m. for her in California. Which worries me, since it's way early for her (school doesn't start out there for another week or two). It means either (a) something is dreadfully wrong, or (b) she stayed out so late with Nathan that she was still up.

Turns out that it's (a).

> hey girlllll!
>
> about time u wrote!!! ur up L8 . . . no rest 4 the wicked, rght?? Got ur txt yesterday, srry didn't snd back. trouble at home with the rentals. Mom & Dad are into it big time.
>
> they argue ALL THE TIME now!!! it SUXXXXXXX!!!!! h8 it! Wish u were here. Nate is gr8, but not the same. :-/
>
> went school shpping all by myself yesterday. ver ver sad. Saw a dress tht u would luv!
>
> U should stop stressing ovr tht stpd goth chick. don't waste the email space. i haven't seen her. tld u she was jst being weird.
>
> I miss u! Write bk soon, k? Gotta go, the horror is banging on the door.
>
> luv ya,
>
> serena

Oh man, that sucks. I'm glad Raven's not bugging her, but this is worse. Serena's mom is this really nasty woman who spends all her time and energy on Serena's little beauty queen sister. I bet that's what she and Serena's dad were fighting about. He's the only one in the family who's decent to Serena at all. Now I feel like an idiot for sending her those five e-mails full of nothing but me complaining about how crappy Cartville is and how I can't get in touch with George. Having your parents at each other's throats is way worse. Gah.

hey S—

that suxxxxx rocks. I'm so sorry!! I wish i could do somethin. if u think of ANYTHING u need at all, let me know and i'll do whatever i can. Anythin 4 U!

i hope they work things out. =(Tell Nate to take u out & spoil u rotten. U deserve it.

Sending you lotsa hugs. XOXOXOXO

miss u!

Min

I feel so useless. Serena's going through this really nasty situation and I'm stuck halfway across the country where I can't do anything about it. Not that there's a whole lot I could do, but I could at least get her out of the house. I miss our monthly Girl's

109

Night In. I bet she does too. My mom is more like a mom to her than hers is. And way nicer. And prettier. Not that that makes a difference. Just saying.

I send one more e-mail to George and then spend some more time online. Which is totally the wrong thing to do when you're trying NOT to think about how your boyfriend apparently can't find the time to e-mail you or call you or even send you a teeny-tiny little text.

Because what do I do? I google Brazil, where apparently the girls all run around in these skimpy little bathing suits. And I do mean skimpy. Have you heard of the Brazilian? It's a type of bikini waxing thing where they essentially take off all your hair. Down there. Seriously. Like really ALL of it. Places where you didn't even think you *had* hair.

Yet another thing I didn't want to learn from the Internet. Even as a vampire with a pain threshold of who knows what, I don't want to think about that.

Though it's slightly less painful than thinking about George cavorting around on some Brazilian beach with a bunch of Brazilian-waxed bikini babes.

(MORE)

^ REASONS WHY IT SUCKS TO BE A VAMPIRE

1. Since you don't sleep, you've got a lot of hours
   of the day to fill. This maybe doesn't suck if you
   have lots of money and live in New York City,
   where there's always something to do. But if you live
   in a sleepy little tiny town like Cartville, it bites the
   big one.

2. Seriously. I think I've run through the entire county
   by now and there's nothing going on at night except
   for bored cows staring at me and stuff growing.

3. Especially with the only alternative being spending time
   online. There's only so much surfing you can do.
   I mean, really, did I need to spend two hours watching
   videos of cats playing piano and people falling down?
   I'm going to live forever, and I still feel like I wasted
   hours of my life.

4. And all these souped-up superpowers are absolutely
   useless when it comes to helping out your friends
   and making them feel better. Unless I had teleportation
   powers. That would be useful. Impossible, but useful.

MYTH:	Vampires don't care what mere mortals think of them.
TRUTH:	Hey, I may be a bloodsucker, but I'm still a teenager. I can't help it.

14

I'm watching yet another stupid cat video when I hear dad singing off-key in the shower, which mean's he's deliriously happy to be getting ready for work AND I'm nearly late for my first day of school. Agh! Curse you, Lolcats!

I run the couple of blocks to school with my mostly empty backpack (schedule from the Josh-erator, two pencils, one pen, and some college-rule paper) and in through the main door. Maybe I should have gone in early like Mom said or at least figured out where the office was ahead of time.

The school feels really small after going to McAdam for the last three years, but big enough that I can't find the office. It's not like a one-room schoolhouse or anything, but it's way smaller than my old school. And very blah looking. The whole thing is made of concrete block, like a prison or something, and all the walls are institutional gray. Every door looks like every other door, which also doesn't help.

And the cafeteria smells weird. Like wet dog and Cheetos. I can smell it everywhere I go as I run through the rapidly emptying halls. Chalk one up for being a vampire. NOT.

I'm really glad I don't *have* to eat, especially considering it's just the first day of the year. I don't know how I'm going to stand the smell after it's had some time to build up. Gah. I can just imagine Taco Salad Thursday. I need to ask Mom if there's some way you can block the whole supersniffer thing. I mean, she worked in a middle school back home in California, and I'm sure it smells just as bad as here. Maybe worse.

I finally ask a janitor guy where the office is (four more doors down, duh). And there's Eugenie, filing papers. I'd forgotten she said she volunteered at the school too. It's almost good to see a familiar face.

"Hey there, Mina, sweetie. You runnin' a little behind? Spend a little extra time on your hair? Or"—she squints her eyes at my head—"maybe not."

Hey, my hair isn't that bad today. I hope. I didn't actually check it before I ran out of the house. "Um, yeah. Hey, Eugenie. I guess I need to check in."

She clucks her tongue at me and pulls a compact mirror and

113

a bottle of Aqua Net out of her purse. "Why don't you let me see what they gave you while you check out those curls. Don't wanna make a bad impression your first day!"

"Um, right. Well, here's what I got." I hand her the letter the Josh-erator gave me and take the mirror. Yikes. I run my finger through my wild hair a few times and give it a light touch of hairspray, but there's not really much I can do without a brush. Or a flamethrower. I set the mirror and the hairspray on the counter.

Eugenie glances at the letter and then flips through a file drawer and pulls out a folder with my name on it. It's so weird to see "Mina Smith" instead of "Mina Hamilton." I don't know if I'll ever get used to that. And what'll it be like a couple of hundred years from now? Who knows what my name will even be? Hopefully something better than "Smith."

"You know what, honey? I'm gonna stick you in AP English." Eugenie scratches something out and then scribbles on both my copy and whatever she's got in her files. She gives me a wink when she's done. "Your GPA is good enough and you had Honors English at your last school. I'm not sure why you weren't in there to begin with. You really ought to be thinking about your transcript for college, you know. At least you were already signed up for Calculus with Mrs. McNeal. She's an excellent teacher."

Like I even had anything at all to do with my schedule. But I don't tell her that. "Um, okay." I doubt if it makes much of a difference anyway. And as bored as I've been, a little extra homework actually sounds kind of good.

"If you have any questions, you just come on by anytime. I told Mari I'd take care of you. Now then, let me call your student mentor to come pick you up and show you where everything is."

"That's really not necessary," I start to say, but she just shushes me and picks up a phone.

"Mrs. Hebert? Could you please send Henny to the front office?" She smiles at me again and says, "You're just gonna love Henny, I know it. I'd've gotten Grady to show you around, but Henny just begged and begged. She's dying to meet you!"

Again, I have to ask: where do these people find their names?

Henny gets there in no time and bursts in through the door at full speed. She's quite a bit shorter than me (shorter, in fact, than Serena, and that's saying something) and has some crazy fuzzy brown hair and a round face. And she's smiling. Of course.

"Mornin', Eugenie! And you must be Mina! From California, right?"

"Right, um, Henny." She nods happily. She reminds me a little bit of Linda, except without the weird vibe. Okay, and maybe not the Chess Club vibe either. She's more like a little mini pep rally on short legs.

"Let me take you to your locker first. It's right by mine." And with that she takes off out the door like a little jackrabbit.

"Don't forget your schedule and your locker combination!" Eugenie hands me some papers and then gives me a little wave and another big smile.

Henny is already halfway down the hall and she's still talking. I guess she didn't even notice I wasn't right behind her. ". . . it here, I'm sure. Though I bet it's nothing like what you're used to in California. I've never been there, but I've heard it's real nice. I did go to Florida once to go to Disneyland. Or is it Disney World? I forget which one's which. Did you go to the original one out there in California? Is it any different? I guess all Mickeys and Plutos look the same. But enough about that. I heard you went to Lonnie Pratt's big back-to-school party with Grady Broussard." She whistles and gives me a wink as I catch up to her. "Grady's quite a catch, but you might want to watch out for the other fish, if you know what I mean. Though I also heard you left with Cameron Carter . . . is that true?" She actually stops talking long enough for me to answer her.

"Yes, but it wasn't—"

"Interesting," she says. "Very interesting. Cameron just started here at the end of last year. He was the last new person we got before you, but I guess he's related to a bunch of the Carters

116

around here somehow, so it's not like he's really a stranger, ya know? He's pretty hot too, in a really distant kind of way, but some girls like that kind of thing. But he's always ignored all us local girls. I heard he doesn't date. Never heard of him leaving a party with anyone before. I don't know why he even goes to them, always sits himself down in a corner and stays there all night. Where'd he take you?"

Boy, a little nosy, isn't she? And it's not like I can tell her about Ernie's. I shrug and almost lose my backpack. "He took me home. It was no big deal. I just needed a ride."

"But I thought you went to the party with Grady?"

Okay, I guess this must just be a small-town thing, like Dr. Musty said. Either that, or else everyone I've talked to is just incredibly nosy. Or I have "sucker" written all over my face (probably right underneath where it says "not from around here").

"Well, kind of. It wasn't like a date or anything like that. And there was this girl Kacie—"

Henny holds up her hand. "Say no more. I get it. Hey, here are our lockers."

I fumble with the papers Eugenie gave me, trying to find the one with the locker combination on it, and manage to drop all of them. They scatter around my feet and I stoop to pick them up. When I stand up again, there's Henny with my locker door already open.

"Here you go!" she says cheerfully. "I had that locker fresh-man year. They never change the combos here. My mom's old locker down the hall still has the same combination as when she had it."

Well, *that's* safe. Why do they even bother having locks at all?

Henny is in only two of my classes (physics and the weird health class they stuck me in called Food & Nutrition . . . which so-o-o doesn't apply to me, but how am I supposed to explain that?) but she meets me at the door after every single class to walk me to the next one. I don't think I could get away from her if I tried. And she's not the only one either. Everyone, and I do mean *everyone*, seems to want to talk to me or just stare at me. It's kind of creepy. Not that I necessarily liked being Invisible Girl at McAdam, but being Girl Under a Microscope is kind of worse. And Grady has managed to meet me after three of my classes even though he's only in one of them (Calculus, so apparently there's a brain in that cute head of his). By lunchtime I'm totally ready to leave. Or at least give my hair a really good brushing.

I'm seriously thinking about ducking out a side door when Grady throws his arm around my shoulders and steers me to the cafeteria.

When we walk in, I swear that the whole place goes quiet for a beat and then the conversation picks up again. And they are *all* talking about me, even the teachers. It's crazy. With my superhearing, I can hear just about every word (and it's totally giving me a headache). Here's just a sampling:

"Have you seen the new girl's eyes?" (Oh, c'mon! I mean, they are really ultrablue now, but I don't look like a total freak or anything. I don't think. I hope.)

"I am totally getting that shirt she has on. Do you think it's from one of those famous stores on Rodeo Drive? It must be." (Ha, little does she know. Try SaveMart, sweetie. Not that I would ever admit that.)

"Is she talkin' to Grady? Do you think she's talkin' to Grady?" (Um, hello, he's standing right next to me, so yes, I'm talking to him. Wouldn't it be rude not to? I so do not get the South.)

"Little snotty, if you ask me." That's from Lowell, but one glance in his direction shows that there's only one other teacher sitting remotely close to him and the man's leaning the other way. Maybe Lowell always smells bad.

Not that I had superhearing back at my old school, so I can't technically confirm this, but I can tell you right now that never, at any point in my high-school career to date, have this many people ever talked about me. At once. Or maybe ever, other than at my

119

funeral. I doubt if this many people even noticed me the whole time I attended McAdam. Seriously. It's really nuts.

It's also about to drive me totally insane. It's been bad enough all day in classrooms (though having to concentrate on listening to the teacher actually helped, go figure), but in here it's just like a wave of chatter. Actually, more like wave after wave after wave and I'm starting to drown.

It does seem to help block out all the noise when you try to listen to just one person. So I focus on listening to Grady as he splits off from me to go through the hot-lunch line. I take the cold line since it's shorter and will hopefully help me get out of here sooner.

"So, who's the hot new girl with the whacked-out eyes?" I hear some guy ask Grady. Ohmigod. Is he really talking about me? Hot? Me?

"Hands off," says Grady. "I saw her first."

Excuse me? What kind of Neanderthal does he think he is? No, wait. What kind of girl does he think *I* am? Is that what all his oozing Southern charm has been about? So much for that. I guess guys are all the same everywhere. Well, not all guys. George isn't like that.

Though, okay, I have to admit that I am a little bit flattered that the guy called me the hot new girl. But also offended about the whole caveman mentality thing they've got going on. I swear, if all girls could hear as well as vampires, most guys would not be getting any dates.

"What about Kacie? She's gonna show up any minute."

"What about her?"

The other guy laughs. "Your funeral, man."

Great. I obviously need to let Grady know that

a) I have a boyfriend,

b) I'm *so* not interested (I don't care how much of a cute-farm-boy thing he's got going on, we have less than nothing in common), and

c) he needs to deal with his Kacie problem, whatever it is. I'm not going to tackle that one for him.

I grab a tray and just pick up a yogurt. I don't really feel like eating anything at all and I really want to get out of here, but that would look funny and if there's one thing G.W. drilled into me, it's that you have to keep up appearances. Unfortunately, my lunch selection sets off a new storm of gossip and I hear at least three girls behind me in line put back the stuff on their trays and just grab a yogurt instead. What is up with these people? Is this what it feels like to be king of the A-List like Nathan? Except, you know, as a girl?

It's really kind of irritating. Who knew? I wonder if Nathan ever gets annoyed? I bet he does. But I also bet he hides it better than

I ever could. Good thing it's just the whole "new girl" status. I bet it will all rub off in a few days.

I debate grabbing some more food, but then I figure it's their own fault if they can't think for themselves. Maybe tomorrow I'll get like one of everything and eat all of it. That would really mess with their heads.

Henny finishes paying and leads me over to what can only be the popular kids table. And who should the queen bee be except the one and only Kacie? She's right smack in the middle of the table, right in the middle of the lunchroom—staring daggers at me and Grady, who's wrapped up his caveman routine (apparently, he thinks he's the king of the school, since he cut in line and has already paid) and is making his way to the table.

So I squeeze in right next to Kacie and everybody obliges by scooting down with only a little bit of whispering and one "whoa." That gives Grady a pause, but he sits across from me after a minute or two. Henny happily jams herself in right next to me. I can't tell, but maybe she's not normally at the A-list table. Grady definitely is (people moved out of his way without him even asking) and Kacie looks like she owns the place.

Not that this is at all like the A-List Land that I'm used to. That is, used to watching from across the McAdam cafeteria.

These kids don't seem quite as, I don't know, polished? Not

like shoe polished, but like schmoozing polished. Like Nathan. I think he could charm anybody, anywhere, any time, of any age. So far, everyone here seems more normal. But there's still the whole clique thing going on. There are no Goths that I can see, but there's definitely a group of artsy kids over to the right and a group of nerdy kids in the far corner. I guess some things are universal.

Kacie didn't say anything to me as I sat down, so I give her a huge smile, which I'm sure bugs the heck out of her. The best defense is a confusing offense. That's my motto. I don't actually have anything against her, other than her attitude. Not that I want to be her new best friend either. But I would like to just have a decent last year of high school. As decent as possible in this Podunk place. And, you know, I appreciate where she's coming from. I liked Nathan for years and nothing ever came of it. For me, anyway. It kinda worked out for Serena. But anyway. Who knows how long Kacie has liked Grady? They're both obviously the leaders of the pack at this school and that's usually a match made in heaven.

"So," I say, "Kacie, right? I think we met briefly at Lonnie's party?"

She just glares at me some more, doesn't even bother to nod or anything. Nice.

"Well, it was nice to meet you."

Still nothing. Even Henny has abandoned me to talk to some girl sitting on the other side of her. Grady keeps making eyes at me, like he's begging me to stop. Well, no one has ever called me a quitter.

"My name's Mina, in case you didn't catch it."

"What kind of a name is *Mina*?" She practically snarls it at me. Okay, so "Mina" is a little weird, but get a grip.

"German," I say through slightly gritted teeth. "It means 'love.'" I am not going to let her know she's starting to get to me. "How about Kacie? Is that short for something? It's an interesting name. I've never heard it before."

She just stares at me. Man, this girl has a chip on her shoulder the size of . . . I don't know . . . Grady, I guess.

"I really miss my best friend Serena and my *boyfriend* George," I blurt out. Okay, random. But I didn't know what else to say. If she missed the boyfriend part, then she's deaf. Even Grady appears to have heard it, since his foot mysteriously moves away from mine under the table.

"What about Cameron Carter? He seems nice to you?"

I'm not really sure from her tone what she's getting at, though I can tell from her pulse (which has practically doubled since I sat down) and her sweat (which is so not Eau du Pleasant) that she's still highly pissed at me. Maybe it isn't just Grady she's mad about. Maybe she's just got lots of issues. Maybe she just wants all the hot guys to herself. Greedy girl.

"I don't really know Cameron all that well, since I just met him at Lonnie's party and all he did was drive me home, but he seemed nice enough." Is that diplomatic enough, I hope?

"I don't know where you come from, but around here a *nice* girl doesn't leave a party with a different boy than the one she came with."

Whoa. Okay, that's it. I've had more than enough of playing the nice girl. Mom can't say I didn't try. The old me wouldn't have made it through even half of that conversation. I stand up. Everyone at the table who was paying attention to our little exchange (which was, apparently, every single last one of them) sucks in their breath in one collective whoosh.

"Not that it's remotely any of your business, but the only reason I left the party with Cameron was because your panties were so far up your butt over Grady just sitting next to me that I could tell what color they were as soon as you opened your mouth. And it's probably not *nice* to say that, but it's the truth."

In a figurative sense, anyway. I'm talking some green panties. As in jealousy green. But I think she gets my drift from the slack-jawed reaction I get from that one. Or maybe she's just stupid. From the stunned looks all around us, other people are definitely

125

getting it. Or maybe she's just not used to anyone calling her or her underwear out.

"And furthermore, I don't know where *you're* from, but where I come from, when people are *trying* to be nice to you, you at least *act* like you're nice back."

This is where I'd *really* like to invite her outside, but there are quite a few reasons not to do that, like

a) being as I've got superstrength and what not, I could totally accidentally kill her, not that she isn't annoying and already a pain in my rear, but that doesn't mean I actually want her dead (and it'd be a total waste of blood);

b) Mom would totally kill me (I did say I'd try to be nice); and

c) so would Dad. Not to mention the Southeast Regional Vampire Council.

So instead I just turn to Henny and tell her thanks for showing me around all day and that I'll see her tomorrow. And I just leave.

I can feel the whole room staring at my back as I walk out. The cafeteria falls completely silent—except for Lowell chuckling to himself over in the teachers' corner and Grady whispering to Kacie to shut up. Kacie finally manages to snap her mouth shut.

Oh, wouldn't I have loved to shut it for her.

WHY SCHOOL SUCKS

1. School always sucks. It just does. I don't care what Uncle Mortie says about the good old days. I think he just doesn't remember. After all, he is, like, ancient. Not like vampire ancient or anything, but normal old-guy ancient.

2. But being the new kid at school sucks even more than normal suckage. Because everyone is staring at you. ALL the time.

3. And being the new kid who also happens to be a senior is even worse, since all the rest of the seniors have been there for three years together and they're already all gossiped out, so of course you're the new target.

4. And being the new kid who also happens to be a vampire with superhearing so you can hear every little thing everyone is saying about you? Major suckage. Though I did appreciate some of the comments about my butt. No one ever told me I had a great butt before. Not that someone actually told me today, I just overheard them. So I guess technically someone could have thought I had a nice butt before, but I seriously doubt it. Ha. Vampire buns of steel. That's what I'm talking about.

MYTH:	Vampires are loners by nature.
TRUTH:	Then why can't I ever get rid of my parents when I need some privacy?

GET OUT

15

I try texting Serena on the way home, but I don't get a response. Gah. Try George and get the same thing. What good is a cell phone if I can never reach anyone on it? I send Serena one more text saying I'm going to call her in ten minutes and she'd better be there. Or else. Or else my brain might explode, but hey.

Mom must have had an inkling that my first day at Cartville High probably wasn't going to be my best day ever. She's taking a batch of chocolate chip cookies out of the oven as I open the door and doesn't even mention that I'm home way early. The smell is absolutely heavenly. I thought cookies smelled good before, but now, it's just amazing. It almost makes up for the lingering smell of the cafeteria. Almost.

She takes one look at my face and wisely doesn't say a word, just hands me a cookie and takes one herself. We sit at the chipped

128

Formica kitchen table (seriously, this place is so decrepit it's starting to depress me) and chew.

I'm on my third cookie when she says brightly, "I've got some good news!"

"We're moving back home?"

She just hands me another cookie. "No, I signed us up for a class."

Okay, so she thinks, somehow, that *more* school is going to make me feel better? "What, how to speak Southern?"

"No," she says in the same bright, cheery voice that she's been using way too much lately. "It's a shape-shifting class. Kind of like continuing education for vampires. Remember all those brochures that Ivetta left? Well, the shape-shifting one sounds like fun, don't you think? Your father and I never took any classes before, since we were kind of on the down low—isn't that what you kids call it? Anyway, I thought it would be fun. You know, like a girl bonding thing."

"I—"

"It will be great! Just the two of us . . . your Dad is too busy, you know, and it's supposed to have some really practical applications. I think it would be good for you. Show you some of the good things about being a vampire, you know? Maybe we could meet some other local vampires. Hang out a little. And I've never tried shape-shifting before." Mom takes a bite of a cookie and stares at the ceiling. "Well, I did once, but it didn't work out exactly . . . but anyway, what do you think?"

She sounds so excited and for-real bubbly that I don't have the heart to tell her I'd rather eat live flies than take another Council-sponsored class. And I get the feeling that if I don't agree, this is going to turn into one of those all-nighter talks about what's good for me and how I need to adjust to my "new" life. Not to mention, I'd have no hope of sneaking out to talk to Serena. I check the clock on the microwave—five more minutes until I'm supposed to call. Time to suck it up.

"Sounds great."

Even though I don't sound all that enthusiastic (hey, Serena's the actress, not me), Mom gets even more excited.

"Wonderful! I can't wait. Honey, this will be such fun!"

She's all smiles, no fangs. I manage to smile back at her. At least one of us is happy. Well, make that two of us. Dad comes through the front door just then practically bouncing up and down.

"Hey! How are my two favorite girls? What do you say we blow this pop stand and go out tonight? I heard about another blood bar a few towns over. I can't wait to tell you about my day today! Dr. Jonas is just amazing!" He stands there beaming at us like a heavy-duty flashlight. I have the urge to tell him to take a breath, but I don't. He and Mom just stand there grinning at each other like crazy people.

Sometimes they really depress me. I mean, I love my parents. I do. Even when I'm mad at them, I still love them. Bloodsucking vampire freakishness aside, they're pretty cool as parents go. I know they do their best, most of the time. Or, at least, they try to. They didn't abandon me like George's parents did to him and they don't argue all the time and call each other names like Serena's parents. They just drag me halfway across the country.

I'd really like to be happy for my dad since he obviously thinks Dr. Musty is the best thing since, I dunno, refrigeration or sliced bread or music videos. But so far, all I've been served up on my plate is a big oozing pile of suckiness with a side of suck it up.

"Uh, I'm going to skip out tonight. It's been kind of a long day." Besides, I need to get them out of the house and beyond hearing range, so I can give Serena a call.

"Oh, I completely forgot to ask! Mina, how did your first day of school go?" Dad pulls up a chair and puts on his best concerned-dad face. See, that's what I mean. They do try. But sometimes they just don't get it.

I glance at the microwave clock again. Three more minutes. I talk fast. "Well, the cafeteria smells like a garbage dump, everyone was preoccupied with my butt, and some girl hates me already."

"I'm sure she doesn't really hate you," he says, totally disregarding the butt comment. Which I expected. "Maybe you just need to get to know her better. Maybe she's just jealous. After all, you are my beautiful girl." He reaches over and fluffs my hair. Oh, cheese.

"I know what you mean about the cafeteria," says Mom. "That used to get me at work. You get used to it after awhile. Mostly." Great. I was hoping there would be some kind of Jedi mind trick to dealing with it. What did vampires back in the Dark Ages used to do when they didn't even have, like, toothpaste and good soap? I suppose I could ask Dr. Musty. I bet he'd know.

"Well, you guys better get going!" I start shuffling them toward the door.

"Are you sure you don't want to go with us? I heard this place is pretty nice. Dr. Jonas told me about it. They even have karaoke!"

Double cheese. Vampire karaoke? That makes me want to go even less. Besides, talking to Serena will cheer me up way more than Dad belting out an off-key version of *Love Shack* or *Bohemian Rhapsody*.

"No, I'm fine. You and Mom could probably use some alone time."

They head off without too much more fuss. I think the idea sounded good to them too, once they thought about it. That's a great trick, actually. Parents have needs too. If you can cater to those and to your own at the same time, total win-win. Plus you get brownie points.

I wait until they're far enough away that they can't hear me and I pull out my cell and dial Serena. Four rings and she finally picks up.

"Hello?"

"Serena! It's me!"

"Hey, M—Willy! Nice to hear from you! Hold on a second, let me get up to my room." I hear her fiddling around for a couple of minutes and some babble in the background that must be the holy terror (i.e., her little sister). "It's safe now. How are you? I miss you!"

"Willy?" I've been called lots of things before, but that's a first.

"Well, I couldn't call you Mina in front of my mom. It was the first thing I thought of. We were watching a movie with that goofy actor guy. Besides, Willy is kind of cute."

"Yeah, yeah, funny," I say. "I've missed you, you goober." I really have. I've got so much stuff to tell her that I almost don't even know where to start. It just starts coming out all at once. "Serena, you won't believe what happened to me at lunch—"

"Hang on just a sec." I can hear her yelling at someone on the other end of the phone. "Can't you just leave Alexis alone for one second, you guys! She's not your interpreter, Mom. Tell him yourself!" Serena gets back on the line. "Sorry about that."

"Is everything okay?" I say. "What was that all about?"

"Things with my parents are getting really bad. They won't even talk to each other directly anymore. I absolutely refuse to be their go-between, so they're using Alexis. I guess the good thing about that is they have to watch their language."

"Oh man." Grown-ups can be worse than little kids sometimes.

"Yeah. I saw Dad looking up apartments for rent online. I think this really might be it."

"I'm so sorry." What else can I say? It really seems like there should be something better to say, but heck if I know what it is. Gah, I hate stuff like this.

"It's okay. At this point, I think it might be for the best."

"Still sucks."

"Yeah." She's quiet for a minute and I debate about whether or not to tell her about my almost throwdown with Kacie. I really want to get her take on what to do about her, but suddenly it feels kind of wrong. I don't want to worry her with my problems. She's got big enough problems of her own.

"So what were you saying about lunch?" she asks.

"Oh, nothing. We, uh, had pizza today." I lie down on the lumpy couch and prop my feet up. There's no comfortable place to talk in this stupid house. "I miss you, but at least the kids here seem pretty nice."

"Don't tell your parents. You should still try to guilt them into buying you a car so you can come visit me! How far a drive is it from Louisiana anyway?"

"Uncle Mortie said days, but he's not exactly good with facts and figures. Do you think the Death Beetle could make it halfway? Maybe we could still meet up somehow." I wonder if there's anywhere cool halfway between here and California?

"Of course the Death Beetle could make it! Speaking of which, guess what? Somebody is taking the whole Death Beetle thing too seriously or something. They've started leaving offerings! You think it could be Bethany? I think she's still mad at me about getting Nathan."

"Offerings?"

"Yeah, this really gross dead bird's foot all spray painted black a couple of days ago. And then some bloody feathers this morning. But I guess I could have hit a bird and just not noticed. Oh, ugh. Do you think I hit a bird?"

A dead bird's foot? Spray painted black? Um. I sit up again. This could be bad. "I know you keep telling me no, but are you sure you haven't seen that weird Goth girl around?" Raven technically shouldn't know a vampire from a hole in the ground anymore, but maybe the goons missed something when they wiped her brain. Maybe they missed a few things.

"I'm positive! And why would she be leaving me dead bird stuff? You think she's some kind of devil worshiper or something too? Geez, Mina. Just because she's Goth doesn't mean she wants to sacrifice goats."

Not a devil worshiper. Well, probably not. But that sounds an awful lot like a Black Talon kind of thing. I mean, who would spray paint a dead bird's foot? "Just keep an eye out, okay? If she does show up, you call me. I mean it." I can't imagine the goons really did miss anything, but maybe Raven has, like, ghost memories or something. I've heard that was possible, especially if you felt particularly strongly about something. And she hated me pretty bad.

"Okay, okay. I've got bigger things to worry about, you know."

She doesn't have to remind me. Her whole life sounds like crap right now and all I can do is offer up pathetic "I'm sorries."

"Well, how about Nathan? How're you guys doing?" That's gotta be a good topic. Nathan rocks. I settle back down on the couch so the Nathan Appreciation Hour can begin.

"Oh, he's okay." Uh-oh. That's it? From her tone, it sounds like all may not be well in Nathan-Serena Love Land.

"Just okay?"

"He's perfect, actually."

"And this is bad because . . . ?"

She sighs. "Really, Mina, he's just *too* perfect. I mean, I talk to him about the stuff with my parents and he tries to be comforting and everything, but he's never had anything bad happen in his life. His parents are just as perfect as he is. He gets everything he wants. Everybody loves him. He just doesn't get it."

Oh. Yeah, I could see that about Nathan. It's good to be king. Not like it's his fault. He just got lucky in the whole birth lottery. "I'm sure he's trying."

"I don't mean to sound down on him. He's the perfect boyfriend. Really. I couldn't ask for anything better. He's been taking me out every chance he gets and getting me out of the house so I can get away from all the fighting. And he keeps sending flowers and these really sweet cards. I just . . . I don't know. I miss you, I guess."

"I miss you too." Why oh why did Dr. Musty have to pick now to need an assistant? I should be there with Serena. Maybe I can find a way back somehow. Even if I could just visit for just a little while, it would be better than nothing. I wonder if I could talk my parents into a plane ticket? Who could I say I was visiting? Lorelai? Linda? No, that wouldn't work. I don't think they'd buy it. Not to mention the Josh-erator would have a cow. But there's got to be something I can do.

137

We talk for another hour and I'm even more depressed after we're done talking. Not that it wasn't great to hear Serena's voice, but

a) hearing her reminded me how much I miss her, and

b) how much it stinks to be basically friendless in a new place where I don't have anyone to talk to at all, and

c) I didn't even get to vent about the whole Kacie thing (which, okay, by comparison is trivial, but still, you know, normally Serena would've come up with something off the wall to say about it that would make me feel much better), but mostly

d) it really sucks that I can't be there for her when she really needs me.

MYTH:	Vampires don't show up in photographs.
TRUTH:	How silly. The truth is that we're not supposed to leave photographic evidence just lying around. I mean, think about it.

16

The teachers at Cartville are all okay, but none of them are anywhere near as interesting as Ms. Tweeter was with her crazy costumes and props. The most interesting thing any of them wear is plaid.

After six weeks, school is getting so monotonous that I'm actually totally excited when they call my name over the loudspeaker for senior photo makeups. I go to the library and find Cameron there, as well as a few other seniors who must have missed getting their picture taken at the end of summer. They immediately shut up and start staring at me when I walk in. Gah! So annoying. Even worse, the guys all stand up straighter and give me the eye and the girls copy the way I lean against the wall. Which totally makes me want to do something crazy, like stand on my head but then who knows what'd happen. Maybe they'd all do it. So instead

I pretend to look at the Open Your Mind to Banned Books poster on the wall.

Cameron walks over to me and I ignore the little flurry of excitement that causes from the peanut gallery. Though he is looking exceptionally fine in a blue button-down long-sleeve shirt that brings out the color in his eyes.

"Don't worry," he says. "They treated me the same way when I first got into town. They do get over it after a few months. Mostly."

Not so comforting, since I can tell the girls are eyeing him the way the guys are eyeing me: like a lapsed vegetarian sizing up a double cheeseburger. I guess I should say something instead of just standing here and staring at him like the rest of the girls.

"So . . ." Ack, I can't think of anything to say! "Uh, how are you?" Nice conversation starter, Mina. D'oh!

But Cameron doesn't seem to notice my lame question. He smiles. "I'm doing pretty good. Really busy. We've all been getting ready for John and Wayne to get home. They should be here any time now."

"I guess it's been awhile since they've been around?" I don't really care, though I guess Dad and Dr. Musty would probably like to know. Not that I think I'm going to tell them. Let them dig it up on their own.

"I think they were last here in the sixties. Not that much has changed around here since then."

Hey. Does that mean that Cameron is older than my mom? Like her real age? Didn't he say that Wayne or John turned him here in Cartville? Or did he say? Now I can't remember. Is he even older than that? Did they turn him in the sixties or before then? This is making my head hurt, especially when looking right at him and he *so* doesn't look a day over eighteen. And he's looking at me with those pale icy blue eyes and slightly raised eyebrows.

I decide to change the subject. "Um, I guess you missed getting your senior picture taken over summer, huh?" Yeah, I'm brilliant. Just brilliant.

He looks at me like I'm an idiot. Which I am. "Yes," he says, kind of gently, "I don't—we don't—want our picture taken."

"Oh, right!" Duh, I'm a HUGE idiot. G.W. drilled that into our heads about a billion times. Never leave photographic evidence because it will always come back to haunt you. It's kinda hard to explain away a picture of yourself a hundred or two hundred years later. Not that I imagine someone's first thought would be "hey, I bet you're a vampire," but it's better to be safe than sorry. Part of the VRA's annoyingly thorough service is to scrub as many photos of you as possible from everywhere they can. I laugh like

I meant it as a joke, but I doubt if he buys it. *Sigh.* "So what should we do? Leave?"

He scoots closer to me and lowers his voice so it comes out as this husky kind of whisper that, I admit, gives me goose bumps. The other girls give me the serious eye too. "That would be too suspicious. Just follow my lead."

Huh. I wonder what he's planning? I hope it doesn't mess up anyone else's photo. If I were them, I'd hate to have my senior photo messed up. Though after looking through Mom and Dad's yearbooks before the VRA destroyed them, maybe it would ultimately be a good thing. But before I can ask what he's planning, the photography teacher (Mr. Benoit, who also happens to be the yearbook supervisor) gets there and *tsk tsks* at the half of us who must not have gotten the memo (I didn't) and didn't wear fancier than normal clothes. Cameron, of course, did. I'm starting to get the feeling that he's one of those vampires who actually *is* in control.

Cameron keeps fading back in line and I follow him until we're last, trading places back and forth with this one skinny girl who keeps picking at a gigantic pimple on her chin. Finally I lean over and tell her it popped already and would she just get on with it? She looks kind of offended, but goes ahead and poses with her hand glued to her chin.

It's finally our turn. It's just me, Cameron, and the kooky photography teacher.

"Good lord, what is this mess you're wearing?" Mr. Benoit tugs at the hem of my crazy cat T-shirt with his nose turned up like it smells.

"Sorry. I didn't know we were supposed to dress up." I glance back at Cameron. I hope I'm doing the right thing. Cameron said to follow his lead, but he hasn't done anything other than stand in line so far.

"Oh no, this won't do, not at all," Mr. Benoit says. He rummages around in his camera bag and comes back with this bizarrely floral piece of fabric that he drapes around my neck and upper torso. Then he tells me to stand in front of the backdrop.

He fusses with the fabric until I'm sure that I look like some kind of flowery burrito. "Artful, we want artful!"

It's a good thing this picture isn't going to turn out. I'm sure it would be the kind of picture that would haunt me the rest of my life, just not how G.W. would have envisioned.

Behind Mr. Benoit, I can see Cameron getting closer and closer. I watch as he silently comes up right behind the guy. Oh no. He's not going to bite him, is he? That's so, I don't know, twelfth century. And totally NOT Council sanctioned, I'm sure. Do I try and stop him? Pull Mr. Benoit to safety? Get in the way? Warn the dude he's about to be chomped? Distract him? Close my eyes? Why didn't Cameron tell me what he was going to do?

Before I can even decide (I have so got to get over my indecisiveness), Mr. Benoit executes a spiffy little pirouette to come nose-to-nose with Cameron. He starts to stumble back and I grab his arms to steady him.

"Wha—" Mr. Benoit starts to say when Cameron leans forward. Oh, crap. He's actually going to bite him! I hold onto Mr. Benoit, not even sure what my plan is, when Cameron stops mere centimeters from Mr. Benoit's face and says in this really deep tone, "You took Mina Smith's picture."

"I took Mina Smith's picture," repeats Mr. Benoit.

What the—?

"You took Cameron Carter's picture," continues Cameron, his eyes like laser beams boring into the dude's eyes. I lean over Mr. Benoit's shoulder to get a look. His eyes are totally dilated. Wow, Cameron must have the whatever it is that Grandma Wolfington has! Some kind of crazy mind-control trick.

"I took Cameron Carter's picture." Mr. Benoit sounds kind of drunk, but hey, at least he's not getting his blood drained from his body.

"Mina," Cameron says quietly, his eyes still on the Mr. Benoit, "go snap two pictures of a plant or something, okay?"

"What? Oh, right." I take the camera (thankfully, it isn't too complicated) and take two pictures of the Banned Books poster on the wall. Cameron continues to give instructions about what he'll see when he processes the pictures (us, not the poster) and what to do (exactly what he normally would), and when to turn them over to the yearbook company (as late as possible). Then he sits Mr. Benoit down and takes the camera from me and hands it to him. Mr. Benoit takes it, but then just sits there.

"Is he going to be okay?"

"The stupor will wear off in about ten minutes. We can go ahead and leave. If someone else comes in, he should be able to carry on a normal conversation. He probably won't remember it, however."

"Great," I say and start for the door. Honestly, it's creeping me out a little bit how the guy is sitting there like some kind of droopy marionette.

Cameron reaches out and stops me. "You might want to get rid of that 'artful' wrap." He winks and I'm suddenly glad that I can't blush anymore since I'm sure my face would be bright red if I could.

"Um, yeah," I say. I try to pull the floral nightmare off of me as Cameron watches, a grin slowly inching its way across his face.

No go. Oh God.

"Perhaps I can be of assistance?"

145

I just nod, totally mortified. He somehow finds the end of the dratted thing and pulls it, unwinding me in one quick motion. Which of course almost makes me fall over, vampire reflexes or no. Cameron catches me in his arms and I hang there for a minute, kind of like a puppet myself.

"Thanks," I say and right myself as gracefully as I can. The boy smells way too good for his own good. Or for my equilibrium. Note to self: stay upwind of Cameron whenever possible. Maybe that whole mind/hypnosis stuff even comes out in how he smells. Pheromones, right? Isn't that what they call it? Whatever it is, it's practically intoxicating.

"I guess I'm getting in the habit of saving you, aren't I?"

"I guess so," I say. Yeah, real good thing I can't blush anymore. Really, really good thing.

I send George an e-mail as soon as I get home. The twentieth one by my count. Not that I was keeping track or anything.

Georgie-Porgie,

Where R U??? I know, I know, I asked tht
in the last umpteen msgs. MISSING YOU. Not
much going on here. *didn't* take my senior
pic today. long story. remind me not to
tell u all about it. :)

Sriously, why hven't u written me bck? R u
mad? u hven't met up w/ tarzan or somehin
hve u? haha

write soon. how's the jungle and all tht.

Min

Serena's also been MIA for two days, which worries me,
especially after that whole dead-bird-parts stuff on the Death
Beetle. Not to mention that I'd been getting the play-by-play every
night either on my cell during my nightly run or via e-mail. Her
parent's divorce drama has been the main topic. (Last big update:
her dad is officially out of the house and living out of some gross
motel . . . maybe even the same one the VRA holed us up in.)

Hey Serena—

Any news? Wanted to check in since I
hadn't heard anything. I'll try and call
tomorrow, if I can get away from the fam
long enough.

LYLAS,

Min

17

We have to drive almost an hour away to get to our first shape-shifting class. Which I guess makes sense, since there's nothing in Cartville. Though Boondale, the same town where the other blood bar is, isn't much bigger, really. At least not by my standards. Mom spends the whole drive telling me how awesome the class will be and how excited she is to be sharing it with me. Blah de blah de blah.

I seriously doubt I'm going to actually come out of it with a bunch of new best friends and mad vampire skills, but whatever. Dad already claimed the TV tonight for some History Channel marathon on the Dead Sea Scrolls so I have nothing better to do.

Mom only gets lost once (a minor miracle) and we get there right on time. By there, I mean Ivetta's house. (Can you say rinky-dink operation?) We carry in a bunch of yarn, since our cover story is we're attending a knitting group. Hopefully our cover story does not also involve actually knitting something. With my coordination I'd probably poke out my eye. Or someone else's.

Ivetta greets us at the door. "Hey, y'all! Good to see you again! Did y'all get a chance to fill in your Class Objectives form?"

Mom and I look at each other. I know I didn't and I guess she didn't either. Though I'm not at all surprised there's a form to be filled out. There's *always* a form to be filled out. Ivetta takes our confused silence as a no.

"No problem at all! I've got copies right here. It's real easy, just a few lines about what you'd like to get out of the class and what your expectations are, that kind of thing. After the last session, we'll have a Class Evaluation for you to fill out to make sure we're doing everything okay!" She whips out a couple of pages and hands them to Mom, along with some pens. "I'd just love to know how we compare to the vampire continuing education classes out in California, so don't y'all hold anything back!"

Mom smiles. "Actually, this is the first continuing ed class for both of us."

"Really!" I'm not sure if Ivetta looks more scandalized or intrigued. Maybe a combination of both. "Well, I'm sure y'all will enjoy it. You can drop off the yarn here in the living room and come

149

on back to the family room whenever you're done with your forms. It's just down the hall. We're waiting on one more, so no rush!"

Mom and I sit down gingerly on a faded plaid sofa covered in, strangely enough, plastic. Like form-fitting plastic made for the sofa, not like Saran Wrap or anything like that.

We both look at each other and giggle just a little, but don't say anything since Ivetta (and whoever else was back in the family room) would be sure to hear us.

What does she think we're gonna do on their sofa? I've been potty trained for a long time.

I can't resist poking Mom and miming sliding off the sofa, and she gives me a huge sappy smile.

"Glad you're having fun. It's good to have the real you back," she whispers.

I bounce on the sofa again so she wobbles back and forth and we both giggle again.

Hey, wait. I leap up. What if the plastic is for blood? Yuck. What do they do, invite people over and then slice and dice on the couch? Grossness.

I finish filling out my form standing up. Mom just wiggles her eyebrows at me curiously but doesn't say anything. Just as well. She'd probably think I was nuts, since she tends to be a glass-half-full kind of person.

The form is actually mercifully short. I don't really have any goals since I didn't exactly want to take the class anyway, so I just put down "I'd like to learn more about shape-shifting" and leave it at that. Besides, I've learned that the less you put on any Council-related form, the better.

We head down the hall into a more comfortable room (i.e., no plastic covers on the chairs). It's kind of a typical family room: well-worn brown leather sectional with poofy pillows, a large-screen TV (Dad would be so jealous—he's totally jonesing for a good TV since the VRA just left us some dinky 20 incher) and a dog sprawled out in the middle of the floor (something really big and fluffy with lots of drool). Very cozy.

We can hear Ivetta off in the kitchen, probably whipping up something hospitality-wise. There are four other people in the room already: two older ladies who look almost exactly alike, one *really* old dude, and a thirtyish looking guy with glasses. We sit down by the two ladies, who immediately introduce themselves as Reba and Reva Tassin.

"Sisters, not twins," they chime out at exactly the same time.

"Mari," says Mom, "and this is Mina."

"So cute," Reba and Reva chortle in unison. Wow, maybe someone should explain to them exactly how annoying that is. Not to mention the calling me "cute" part.

"I'm Benjamin," says the old guy. He sounds a lot more spry than he looks. He *looks* as old as Dr. Musty sounds. Which is weird if you think about it too hard.

"And I'm Roland," says Glasses Guy. He smiles, revealing a pair of enormous buck teeth. I guess vampirism doesn't come with an orthodontia plan. "You're not from around here, are you?" Boy, if I had a dollar for every time I've heard that in the last couple of months, I could buy my own plane ticket home.

"No, we're originally from California. We just moved here recently. Our first relocation."

"Ah!" The almost-twins turn to Mom. "So it must be your husband that's working for the mysterious Dr. Jonas! Do tell us *everything*!" I'm starting to wonder if they have some kind of paranormal link or something. They're really beginning to freak me out.

Before Mom can say anything, Ivetta sails into the room with a pitcher of something in one hand and a stack of plastic cups in the other. "Is everyone ready to get started? I hear our straggler coming in now!" I'm guessing she was an aerobics instructor in another life. She's very, very perky.

That's when the straggler comes wandering in and my heart jumps just a little.

Cameron Carter. I should have known from the spicy sweet

smell. I manage to hold in any gasps of surprise, but I must have twitched or something because Mom gives me a look.

Cameron, of course, shows no signs of surprise at seeing me there. "Hi, Ivetta," he says. "Roland, Reva, Reba, Benjamin, Mina. And you must be Mari?" He strides over to shake Mom's hand. She takes it, a little bemused.

"I'm at a disadvantage here," she says. "You are?"

"I'm so sorry. I'm Cameron Carter. I thought Mina might have mentioned me."

"I didn't know you were going to be in this class," I manage to squeak out. "Um, Mom, this is the guy I told you about that showed me where Ernie's was."

"Right," says Mom, giving me a bit of the eye. (Great, that means I'll probably get another talking to about not going places with strangers, no matter how cute they are.) "Nice to meet you, Cameron."

"Lovely, lovely," says Ivetta. "Now we all know each other. How about we get started now? How many of you have tried shape-shifting in the past?"

Everyone but Benjamin and me raise their hands. "I just turned this year," I say lamely. I imagine his excuse is that he's just so old he thought he'd break something. Turning doesn't reverse aging, though it does make you strong and kind of repairs what you've got. I wonder why he turned so late anyway? Wouldn't it kind of suck to be old forever? I guess the alternative would be worse.

"No problem, no problem," says Ivetta. "It can actually be better if you've never tried because then you don't have to unlearn anything." She smiles at me. Well, at least her method of teaching is a little friendlier than old Grandma Wolfington's.

"Let me show you an example of what shape-shifting can be about." She moves to the center of the room and motions Cameron and Roland to sit on the couch. Cameron sits right by me, which I try to ignore.

Ivetta looks like she's concentrating really hard and then, slowly, her features start to change. It's almost like her bones are reshaping, taking the skin and everything along with it. Her eyes tilt up at the corners and her lashes extend (ooooh, I so want to learn to do that). Even her height changes a little, maybe an inch or two. Her hair turns from blonde to deep black, starting at the roots and creeping down to the tips. And her teeth shrink until they are just these perfect little pearls. She smiles at us. Whoa. She could almost be a Lucy Liu clone now. In the space of maybe five minutes, she's transformed herself from Southern housewife to Asian glamour queen.

"Now that I've got your attention," she says, "let's talk about the dos and don'ts and the cans and can'ts of shape-shifting." The voice that comes out of the Lucy Liu lookalike still sounds like a Southern belle, which is totally disorienting.

Reba and Reva are practically drooling in their seats. "Yes, yes! Show us how to do *that*!" they both exclaim.

Okay, I'll give it up to Mom. Shape-shifting *is* cool. Way cool. The guys are also all looking very interested, but that could be the whole Lucy Liu-ness of it.

"What you've just seen is a fairly extensive transformation. As you should already know from your introductory classes, you have to work within certain limitations when shape-shifting. The primary one is mass. Now for instance, if I wanted to add a few inches to my, shall we say, personality"—she motions to her chest and everyone laughs (hey, I'm sure all the women, and probably the guys too, were thinking about that)—"I'd have to transfer the mass from somewhere. In a nutshell, you can't make something out of nothing."

I like Ivetta. At least she's got a sense of humor. If G.W. had been more like this, maybe I'd have actually remembered some of the stuff from class. Maybe.

"The other limit is energy, which you've always got to keep in mind." She hands the cups to Roland and the pitcher to Benjamin. "Sweeties, can y'all pour everyone a cup of that lovely red stuff there?" She keeps talking as they pour glasses and pass them around.

I take the cup and look at it before I drink it. I can't tell if it's human or animal. I look at Mom, but she just smiles at me and takes a sip, so I do too. I guess manners trump everything.

"Everyone drink up," Ivetta says."You're going to need it."

"Is this why everyone doesn't just walk around all the time with more, um, personality?" I ask. Because even though vampires are in general buff, I've definitely seen some who could use some improvement in the looks department. Uncle Mortie, case in point. Not that he needs "personality" . . . but more hair would definitely be good. More hair and less gut.

"Excellent question, Mina! Yes, that's exactly right. It takes a lot of energy to sustain a shape-shifting change and the more extensive the change, the harder it is. If you wanted to just do one little simple thing over a long period of time, like changing your hair color and nothing else, it's possible to do so without completely exhausting yourself. However, and this brings me to my third point, shape-shifting also takes a lot of concentration. The more you practice, the easier it is, but it's not automatic by any means. If you get distracted or lose your concentration, poof! There it goes." She lets her changes slip and everything shimmies back into regular Ivetta again. I kind of miss the Asian goddess.

"And we obviously don't want to lose any changes when we're out and about in public. That would cause a lot of questions

156

and definitely create problems. So I must caution you to always practice within the confines of your home before attempting any shifting out in the world. Also, I highly recommend that you never use a shift around humans you see on a regular basis. It can be very hard to explain how your hair grew ten inches overnight!"

Ha, yeah, I could see that. Maybe I could still swing the eyelashes. That wouldn't be too hard, right? And not like they are super noticeable either. I mean, who goes around measuring eyelashes?

"What about changing into a bat or a wolf? Are we going to be doing any of that?" Roland asks. Huh. Looks like he already tried for beaver and got stuck.

"That's covered in the advanced class. Though, honestly, it's really more of a party trick nowadays than something actually useful. Wolves aren't too common in most populated areas. A dog shift is much more useful, but, as I mentioned earlier, you have to work within the confines of your own mass. For most of us, that would mean one pretty darn big dog. Bull mastiffs are popular choices, but they still attract quite a bit of attention. As for bats, it is possible, but something you'd never do in public." Ivetta laughs. "Talk about headline news! A giant bat swooping around would be on at six o'clock for sure!"

"So what is shape-shifting really good for then?" sniffs Reva.

157

(Reba, thankfully, is in the middle of a big gulp.)

"It can be very useful in many situations. Perhaps you are visiting the place you used to live before you were relocated—you could do so by disguising yourself."

Oh really? Hey, maybe if I get good enough at the shape-shifting to hold a disguise, I could talk Mom and Dad into letting me go back to California for a visit. Even the Josh-erator would have to go for that.

I start paying closer attention. This could actually be useful.

"I recommend that you practice a standard shift so that you always have a disguise at the ready. You never know when you might meet someone coming around the corner that you don't want to see. And people do travel today. It's not like the good old days when there were no airplanes or highways. Why, you might run into someone from around here in Paris someday!"

I kind of doubt that I'd run into any Cartville folks in France, but I guess you never know. Running into Nathan in Europe (I think his dad has a chateau somewhere) or some of the other A-listers from back home is more possible, though still pretty unlikely.

"And for those of you who turned at a younger physical age, like Mina and Cameron, you can use shape-shifting to appear older when necessary. Add a few wrinkles, some laugh lines . . . there are lots of ways to age yourself. Of course"—she nods to

158

Benjamin—"the reverse is also true. We can use shape-shifting to appear younger as well."

He looks a little offended, but I'm intrigued. I'll never have to worry about being carded to get into movies or things like that. And once George gets here, we can go to some swanky New Orleans club, the kind of place that wouldn't let a couple of teenagers in.

If he ever gets here. Still no word from him and I'm at 22 e-mails (okay, maybe 25). Not that I'm counting.

We spend the rest of the first class practicing simple shifts, which is good since Ivetta was right: it isn't easy peasy. We go through the pitcher in no time flat. But by the end of the session, I've learned

a) that for once I'm better than Mom at something (I was totally the star pupil),

b) the hokey meditationy breathing exercises Ivetta showed us actually do help, even though I felt completely silly doing them,

c) it would be totally possible to get good enough at this that I could go back home for a visit and check up on Serena in the not too far off future, and

d) I wasn't even distracted by the spicy sweet smell of Cameron. Not even once. But I totally think Reba was.

Ivetta says she's going to show us some concentration tricks next week so a shift can be sustained longer.

I wish I didn't have to wait a whole week for the next class. As soon as I get good at this shape-shifting stuff, I'm going to visit Serena. I can hardly wait to tell her. Finally, I have some news to cheer her up, if I can ever get her to answer her phone.

MYTH:	Vampires don't breathe.
TRUTH:	Only when we don't need to talk and aren't around people who might notice that "Hey, that girl's not breathing" and want to call 911 or worse, the CIA.

18

The next day, I decide to skip lunch. (They're having taco salad again. Gah! My supersmell can't take it!) Instead I head over to a quiet corner of the library to practice my newfound shape-shifting skills. I worked on it all last night (went through like a whole pitcher of Special K by myself), but I've still got a long way to go if I'm going to talk my way into a California trip.

The library is the only place in the school Henny has yet to dig me out of and is far enough away from the cafeteria that it doesn't reek. I'm concentrating on my eyelashes (got the longer part down pat, but I want thicker too) when I hear someone coming around the corner. I quickly let them shrink down to normal and shut my compact like I was just checking out my makeup or something.

"Practicing?" asks Cameron.

"Oh, it's just you." Phew. No wonder I didn't hear him until he was almost on top of me. He must have been doing the whole vampire stealth mode thing.

He laughs. "Nice to see you too, Mina."

"I didn't mean it that way!" Ack, why am I always saying the stupidest things around him? And here I thought I was over the whole can't-speak-coherently-around-cute-guys thing. He must think I'm such an idiot.

"You just startled me is all. Why aren't you at lunch?"

"Same reason you are, apparently. Lowell's house is so crazy with everyone getting ready for John and Wayne that I haven't had a chance to try out my shape-shifting. I thought this would be a good place to practice. Besides, it takes hours for me to get over the taco salad smell."

"I'd have thought you'd already be an expert at shape-shifting." And everything else, oh suave one.

"I've been concentrating on other skills," he says. Yeah, like that crazy mind-control stuff. I really need to learn how to do that. I'll have to ask Ivetta if she has a class on that. Very, very handy skill, that. I wonder if I could use it to talk Dad into buying me a plane ticket? Or better yet, buying me a car to make that California trip once my shape-shifting is up to par.

"Did you take a class for that mind-control stuff you did on Mr. Benoit?"

"No, actually Lowell taught me. He's quite good at it. I'm not that great at it, actually. That's why I had to get so close to him. Lowell can gain control of someone from across the room. He uses it too much, actually. Does it at school a lot on the students."

"Can you teach me how to do it?" Not that I have anyone in particular I need to control other than Dad. Okay, and Kacie. It would be great to cut her off before she tries to cut me down again. Even better if I could do it in some embarrassing but not suspicious way.

"Actually, I was going to suggest that to you."

"Really?" He was? Why? Does he just like to go around and teach people things? How weird.

"Yeah, you know, if you . . . if you want we could get together around midnight? I know a cool spot we could meet at the elementary school playground. No one will see us there."

"I probably should make sure my parents don't mind." I can't believe I just said that. But I did promise Dad I'd be more careful. Or, I guess, more upfront.

"Oh." For once Cameron looks a little bit flustered. "Well, hey, here's my number. If you can't make it, give me a call. In fact, call anytime." He scribbles it on top of my notebook and then starts backing up. "I just remembered I forgot my English homework.

See you later, okay?" He's gone before I have time to do more than nod.

Well, that was odd. But cool that he'll teach me. Watch out, Dad. There is a car purchase in your future! Maybe a convertible.

Did Cameron really say to call anytime?

When the bell rings, I manage to escape Henny's detection until I leave the library to grab my Calc textbook. I'm sporting my new eyelashes (sorry, Ivetta, I know, I know, I'm a total rule breaker sometimes) and it's not too much of a strain so far. After all, eyelashes are pretty tiny.

Henny doesn't notice them, but Grady (who was standing outside the library like a lost puppy) does a bit of a double take. "You look even nicer than normal today, Mina," he says in his aw-shucks way.

"Thanks, Grady." I've been trying to keep my conversations with him pretty short in the hopes that he'd take the hint that I'm not interested. I'll say one thing for the boy: he's persistent. And all that work helping out on his uncle's farm hasn't hurt him any either.

Grady weasels his arm onto my shoulders (honestly, I'm a little ashamed that I've stopped fighting it; it was just a losing battle) and steers me to my locker.

"You know, Grady, I really can carry my books myself." He's been insisting on carrying them for me every day. I thought at first it was just a Southern thing, but none of the other boys seem to carry books for the other girls, so I guess it's just a Grady thing.

"Oh, I know. But then what would I do with my hands?" He winks at me real slow. I have to laugh. He's just such a guy. Henny grins and mock fans herself. At least she's finally starting to see the humor in him too, rather than just swooning all over the place.

We stop in front of my locker and I spin the combination. I pull up the latch and before I can even swing the door all the way open, wildflowers start pouring out. Daisies, black-eyed Susans, and tons of others that I don't even know. Like bushels of them.

"What the—" I sputter. Did a florist die in my locker?

I picked them all myself." Grady's smiling at me, and a crowd of girls have gathered around oohing and aahing. "I would've used roses, but I didn't want you to get hit with any thorns when they came out."

"Goodness, Grady." That's all I can think of to say. I spit out a petal that had attached itself to my lip.

"So, I've been wondering, Mina. Homecoming is coming up real soon. What do you say?"

I sigh. "Grady, I've told you before—I have a boyfriend." I was hoping we were past this.

"Well, yeah, but he's not here, is he?"

He's not even e-mailing me, but I haven't told Grady that. "No, but—"

"You know what they say: absence makes the heart wander." He gives me his sly grin that I know he thinks is irresistible. And it is . . . to all the other girls in school. I see Henny practically melting out of the corner of my eye.

"I don't think that's how the saying goes." I bend over to pick up some of the flowers. This is totally going to make me late for class. Couldn't he have waited until the end of the day for his little stunt?

"Just think about it," he says, like he hasn't heard a word I've said. Then he actually leans over, takes my hand and kisses it before he walks off.

Oh.

Holy.

Moly.

Did he really just do that?

"I can't believe Grady just asked you to homecoming!" pants Henny. "That was the most romantic thing I've ever seen! What're you going to wear?" She squats down and starts picking up flowers, looking at each one as she picks it up like she's never seen a flower before.

"I'm not going. Like I told Grady, I have a boyfriend." Gah. Why can't George just write me or call me or *something*? As sweet as Grady can be sometimes, he's just not my type. And I don't mean that in a blood-type sense either.

"Maybe you're just going to Homecoming with someone else," interrupts Kacie in her best nasty snotty tone. She steps right on the flower I was about to pick up and twists her heel into it, grinding it to a pulp. Drat. I hadn't heard her coming. I almost let my eyelashes slip, but manage to hang on to them.

"Like I was telling Henny *and* Grady, I've got a boyfriend." Yet another T-shirt I should get.

"Maybe you should tell that to Cameron Carter," she says. "I saw you both come out of the library. It's nice and quiet in there at lunch, isn't it?"

Like she would know. I bet she doesn't even read. "Not that it's any of your business, but I was finishing up some homework," I say. "Cameron was too."

"Ri-i-ght." She sails on by, proclamation over. Oh man, Cameron has *got* to teach me his Jedi mind tricks. This girl has so got it coming.

I play the good daughter and tell Mom that I'm going to meet up with Cameron to practice vampire stuff. She gives me a knowing look (ha, like she knows, but I really *am* going to go work on vampire skills—just not the ones from class) but doesn't bother telling me when to be home. When you don't sleep and are essentially (in an Animal Planet kind of way) the top predator around, curfews don't mean much anymore. And I am a senior now. Though it probably also helps that she got to meet Cameron in the shape-shifting class and see for herself that he's a nice guy.

The playground is actually a great place. I've run through here a bunch of times at night. It's quiet—except for the cicadas (which can be incredibly noisy for bugs)—and off to the side of town, so there aren't many houses around. Never any people either, unlike the high school. I ran through there a couple of times and almost stumbled right into some couples making out.

I sit on the swing while I'm waiting. I hope he doesn't think I'm completely lame for checking in with my parents before coming. I called and left him a message that I was going to be here, but he didn't call back. Maybe he won't show up after all.

It's really peaceful tonight. There's a light breeze blowing my hair around (which, happily, behaved really well tonight without any intervention). I decide to shift into longer eyelashes and darken up my lips a little too. The whole insta-makeup applications of shape-shifting are pretty cool. I wonder if Cameron will notice? Maybe it's too much? I'm about to wipe the lip color when he comes up behind me and gives me a light push then steps around to the front.

"Nice night," he says.

Yay! He did come. My heart starts beating really fast.

"Yeah, and the moon is out too." It is actually really pretty out, for once. When we first moved here, the weather was just torture. People say California is hot, but it's nothing like the hot, sticky weather in Louisiana. Since September hit, it has finally started to cool down a little and now that we're getting into the last part of the month, it's almost bearable. Even vampires have a limit on how much humidity they can take.

"Good thing the moon is out, since we'll need some light," Cameron says. He takes a black backpack off and holds it up at me. "I brought a candle too, but I didn't want to get anything brighter so we wouldn't draw any attention."

I get off the swing and follow him over to a picnic table where he unpacks the candle, some matches, some glasses, and a couple of bottles.

"What's in the bottles?" I sure hope it isn't any booze. I didn't drink before and now the stuff really smells rank to me. Besides, it is pretty pointless to drink once you're a vampire anyway. Someone should break the news to Roy and Lowell.

"A bottle of really nice A positive Lowell had stashed away and some Special K. I thought we could use some refreshment while we work. Mind control takes about as much effort as shape-shifting. Maybe more."

Oh, good. I can't believe he brought the pig's blood just for me. Though I hope he didn't sneak it out. Lowell didn't strike me as the kind of guy you'd want to tick off. I've heard some horror stories about his shop class. Not, like, how hard the class is, but more like you don't want to mess with his stuff.

We sit on top of the table and Cameron pours us a couple of glasses and lights the candle. It actually looks really romantic, under the moon and everything, all the cicadas chirping (or whatever it is you call it that they do) in the background. It really makes me think of George. I wonder if he's thinking of me at all? It sure doesn't seem like it. I've sent over thirty e-mails now, which is kind of pathetic.

"So," I say. "Where do we start? What's the trick?"

"All business, huh? Okay, the first thing to do is clear your mind as much as possible. Kind of like how we did with the shape-shifting, but a little deeper. You know how there's your conscious mind and your subconscious? Your goal is to open your conscious mind up to another person's."

"I'm supposed to open my mind up? Isn't that kind of the opposite of what I'm trying to do?"

170

He smiles, his teeth all shiny and perfect in the candlelight. "You didn't let me finish. It does sound like the opposite, but the trick is that you'll be using your mind to control theirs. Mind control is really a two-way street. So you want to clear your mind of everything but what it is you want the other person to see, think, and feel. Push everything else down."

Hm. Sounds a little new agey to me, but I'll give it a shot.

"Controlling humans is fairly easy, since the advantage is on your side. Controlling a fellow vampire is much more difficult."

Well, that broke my concentration. "So how am I supposed to practice on you?"

"Pick something really simple. That's the best way to start anyway. You need to keep eye contact with me the whole time, the closer the better to start off with. Like I said before, Lowell can do it from across a room, but I work better close up. Why don't you scoot closer?"

I move over until I'm feeling a little uncomfortably close. Cameron's whole spicy smell is nearly overpowering at close range.

Then I remember that I don't technically have to breathe and I stop in midbreath. Now I just have to deal with the lingering smell, but I can get past that. I hope. I stare deep into his eyes and concentrate on clearing my mind of everything. Ivetta's breathing exercises would actually be a big help here, but too bad for that.

Cameron stares back at me and I see the candle flame reflected in his eyes. Wow, it would be easy to just lose myself in the blue.

Okay, having some trouble concentrating here. I close my eyes for a minute to gather myself and then start over. I'm starting to think this would be easier to do on anyone other than Cameron.

"Take a drink," I say slowly, but deliberately, with the last bit of breath I have in my lungs.

His hand wavers for a moment toward his glass and then he just starts laughing like crazy. "Sorry," he gets out between fits. "You just look so deadly serious."

I can't help it. I start laughing too, which means I have to breathe again. I slide back a little to give myself some room.

"I guess I'm not very persuasive, huh?"

"No, you did fine for a first time. I did feel it. You just need practice. Come on, we've got all night anyway."

We practice until about four in the morning. I manage to

a) hardly breathe at all the entire night, which is no easy feat (breathing is really an automatic kind of thing, I don't care how undead you are),

b) finally get Cameron to drink from his glass, and

c) almost but not quite get used to the feeling of staring deep into his eyes from mere inches away.

MYTH:	Vampires have a super high pain threshold.
TRUTH:	Yeah, but there are limits to everything.

19

I'm getting really worried about Serena. It's been almost an entire week since I've heard from her. The last text I got from her just said "ARRGGGHHH" and that was it (which isn't totally unusual, but usually that kind of stuff is followed up by a lengthy explanation of the evil that is Alexis or the latest exploits in Divorce Land). Did Raven do something creepier than leave dead bird stuff on her car?

I'm only able to hold my shape-shifting disguise for like thirty minutes now, but maybe I should just risk it and hop a bus to California to check on her. I have been saving my allowance. It's not like there's anything worth spending it on around here anyway.

I even e-mailed Lorelai to ask if she'd seen Serena since my funeral, but I couldn't be specific about why since I can't tell her Serena knows about us. If Linda (who is the only person who *always* responds to my messages) wasn't a gung ho recruitee of the Vampire Goon Squad, I'd e-mail her and ask her to check on Serena. She did say she hadn't seen Raven since class, but that didn't help much.

I'm wishing I could talk to Mom about it, since I know she'd be concerned too (she loves Serena like another daughter . . . ha, probably like the good daughter she never had), but she can't know about Serena knowing about us. I never even told George after Serena talked me out of it.

Secrets suck.

Cartville sucks.

If I didn't know better, I'd think Kacie was a vampire too, since she's got some kind of sixth sense or blooper radar where she's always around whenever

a) I do anything remotely embarrassing (like the accidental water-fountain shower I gave myself yesterday), or

b) Cameron is talking to me (her knowing looks and oh-so-snotty comments are driving me nuts). Not like I'm even doing anything with Cameron besides practicing the whole Jedi mind-control stuff. (I'm slowly progressing with that . . . though I have to wonder if it'd be easier if I weren't so worried about *him* being able to see into *my* mind.) As I keep reminding Grady, I have a boyfriend.

174

Or do I? At what point do I just give it up? I'm now officially up to over fifty e-mails, a bazillion texts, and probably thirty voice mails. Either he's dead-dead (which isn't very likely, considering) or he just doesn't want to talk to me anymore. I just never would have thought George would be this way. Mom has stopped asking me about him, which I guess is good, since I was having trouble thinking up any way to put a positive spin on it. I hate it when she's right.

I'm sending Serena the umpteenth e-mail of the day when I hear a car coming up the road that sounds exactly like the Death Beetle. *Sigh.* I've even got her on the brain. It putters to a stop in front of our house, which is even weirder, so I get up to go see who it could be (or if I'm just totally losing my mind and nobody is there at all, which is probably about where my brain is these days: total mush).

I peek out the window and it even looks just like the Death Beetle. So I am losing my mind. Then I see Serena coming up the walk and I literally shriek like a banshee.

Mom calls out, "Who's here? What's going on?" but I don't bother answering because I'm already out the door and spinning Serena around in circles.

I'm babbling something along the lines of "Ohmygodwhatare-youdoingherewherehaveyoubeenI'vebeentextingyouallweek" and we're both laughing and crying when Mom comes out the door and lets out a shriek of her own.

Oops. Busted.

She hauls us both in the house and slams the door so hard I think it cracks. She pulls the curtains and then sits us both down on the couch.

"Just what is going on here?" she demands.

Happy is definitely not her middle name right now. Not even remotely.

"It's my fault, Mrs. H," says Serena. "I know I shouldn't have come, I know it. But I just couldn't take it anymore at home. It's just been awful." And then she bursts into tears. I put an arm around her and Mom sits down on her other side and does the same. She looks at me over Serena's head while she pats her on the shoulder.

"How did you know we were here? And, *ahem*, alive, for that matter?" She's totally giving me the eye.

"It's okay." Serena hiccups. "I know all about the vampire thing. But I haven't told anybody. I didn't even tell anyone where I was going or who I was going to visit. Nobody knows I'm here at all."

Yikes. If Mom's eyes were machine guns, I'd have about a billion bullet holes in me right now.

"Her parents are getting a divorce," I tell Mom. "Her dad moved out. He's living in a hotel. Alexis is, like, running the house."

"Mina, how long has Serena known?"

Trust Mom to get right to the point. "Um, just since right before I turned. Not the whole time or anything."

"Do you have any idea at all how much trouble we'll all be in if The Council finds out Serena knows about us? I've got to call your Dad. I don't know what to do. This is bad, Mina, really, really bad."

"But I want to turn too. Won't that help? They can't be mad then, right?"

"What?" Mom and I say in unison. We both look at Serena in total shock.

"I thought about it the whole way here. It took me a week to make the drive." She hugs me. "I'm sorry I didn't call, Mina, but my phone died and I forgot my charger." She turns back to Mom. "The whole time I was driving, I just kept thinking I've got nothing back home. And if I turn, Mina and I could travel the world together forever. Or I could be like one of those vampire scientists she was telling me about. Or go to one of the vampire colleges."

"But what about Nathan?" I know she was saying he was too perfect, but I'm still shocked.

Serena shrugs and looks down. "He'll be fine. You guys are more my family than my family is. You always have been. Now that Dad's gone, you're all I have left."

"Honey," Mom says, "just because your parents are getting a divorce doesn't mean your mom and dad love you any less. That's no reason to make a decision this big."

"I told Mom I wanted to live with Dad and she told me I could live in a cardboard box for all she cared. And now Dad's dating some girl he just met. She's only five years older than me!" Whoa, that's news. I'm not all that surprised about her mom (she's always been on the evil side), but I am kinda surprised about her dad. He's always been pretty nice. I bet that was the final straw.

"Still," says Mom, "it's a really big decision. It's not something you can take back, Serena. I'm sure Mina told you"—here Mom stops to glare at me again—"that she had to think long and hard about it before she decided."

"I did think long and hard about it. I thought about it the whole way here. It's what I want."

Wow, she sounds so sure. I wasn't that sure at all, not until the end right before I turned. And it wasn't like I was leaving behind my family—I was joining them. She always has been more decisive than me, though.

Mom sits back and rubs her head. "I've got to call Bob. You girls just stay here for a minute, okay? Stay inside."

Not like we were going to go anywhere anyway. We have a lot of catching up to do.

WHY MOST ADULTS SUCK

1. Adults think they're all adultlike, but half the time they act worse than little kids. They say and do stupid, hurtful things, but then act like we're the stupid ones.

2. And they don't listen to us. Did Serena's dad listen when she tried to talk to him? No-o-o-o, he started playing kissy-face with some twenty-year-old bleach blonde bimbo whom he met in the bookstore while picking up car magazines. (Turns out he's ditched the station wagon for a convertible too. Total midlife crisis.)

3. They get just as caught up in idiotic fads and have low self-esteem just like they always say we do. Like, take Serena's mom. When Serena's dad moved out, she totally freaked out and went on an all grapefruit diet (and she was already a complete anorexic wannabe anyway). Which then made Alexis freak out and walk to the store all by herself to buy out half the candy aisle and then eat almost all of it in one night and bounce off the walls from all the sugar and their crazy mom made her throw it all up so she wouldn't get fat and ruin her beauty pageant chances. Thank goodness Serena never bought into all that stuff and just did her own thing. There's no hope for Alexis. She's just a lost nutcase like her mom.

4. But most of all, when they fall apart and think only about themselves, they drag the rest of the family down with them. That's why I'm stuck here in the middle of nowhere and why Serena basically just ran away from home. Not that the two compare, but you know what I mean.

20

Mom comes rushing back after a few minutes. I'd been so pre-occupied with Serena that I hadn't even tried to listen in on my parents' conversation, which is probably just as well since there were likely a few choice words in reference to me. Which is exactly why I hate secrets. They always come back to bite you somehow. At least now I didn't really have any to speak of. The Serena one was my big one (and it has totally been burning a hole in me, so I'm honestly kind of glad it's out).

"Okay," says Mom. "We're going to New Orleans. Pack an overnight bag. Serena, we need to move your car into the garage. We'll take ours. We're going to pick up Bob on the way."

"New Orleans? Why?" Are we on the run or something? Seriously?

"That's where the Southeast Regional Vampire Council is headquartered. We talked it over and we think it best that we go

181

to The Council immediately. Now, Serena, I ask you again: are you positive this is something you want to do? Once we get there, there's no turning back. You'll be enrolled in classes and you will have a choice, but I'm sure Mina has explained to you what happens if you decide not to turn at the end."

"Yes," says Serena, nodding her head emphatically. "I'm absolutely sure. I'm done with my family dramarama. I want to turn."

Oh, whoa! It hits me. We really *will* be together forever now. Like forever-forever. I let out a little *squee* and try not to completely crush her in a hug.

Mom doesn't look very happy. "I don't like this at all, but I don't know what else to do. So let's get moving, girls."

We pack up some stuff quick (easy for both of us since Serena's stuff is already bagged in her car and everything I own right now would just about fit into one bag) and hit the road, stopping to pick up Dad from Dr. Musty's. Dad gives Serena a hug, but looks just as serious (and so-o-o-o not happy) as Mom.

Me? I can't stop grinning. I know, I know, it's huge and probably bad timing (I wonder if Dad told Dr. Musty why he had to leave?), but I've got my best friend back. And she's safe.

We're a few miles out of Cartville when I remember I was supposed to meet up with Cameron to practice the ol' evil eye. I call him on my cell.

"Is it okay if we reschedule for Friday after school? I can't do it tonight after all."

"Works for me," he says. "Everything okay? I heard someone in a black car stopped by your house."

Yeesh, Dr. Musty is totally right. Everyone knows everything about everyone in Cartville. "Yeah, we're fine. Everything's fine. Great, actually. I'll talk to you later, okay?"

This whole small town thing is a little eerie. I mean, what, Serena's car was parked outside our house for, like, twenty minutes, right? And like an hour later, it's all over town. Creepy. I still think it's weird that there are so many vampires in the area. How do they keep anything a secret?

Serena actually falls asleep on the way there. I guess she'd driven the whole last stretch in one shot since she was so close and she'd run out of hotel money and didn't want to sleep in her car again. Which I can definitely understand. The Death Beetle isn't exactly spacious.

Her sleeping gives Mom and Dad the opportunity to give me a talking to. Which, okay, I expected. And I do learn a few things, including

a) we're actually still on some kind of probation because of all of our past misdeeds (not telling The Council about me, me turning without filing the proper forms, etc. etc. ad nauseam),

b) Mom and Dad are trying hard to be on better terms with this regional council (the Southeast one) because they're sick and tired of the whole cycle of fines and black marks on their record (hence the quickie trip to New Orleans), and

c) even Uncle Mortie is toeing the line and playing respectable. He's opened a blood bar called The Cask and Casket around the corner from where a bunch of vampires first arrived in the area.

We head over to Uncle Mortie's new digs as soon as we get in town. It's pretty much exactly like what you'd expect from my uncle—down a seedy side street in the French Quarter with an old-fashioned looking sign. The front room of the blood bar is obviously for non-vampire (I hope) tourists, with kitschy, junky knickknacks (most of which are vampire themed).

"Isn't this stuff a little obvious?" I ask Uncle Mortie after the obligatory family hugs.

"Good to see you too, oh favorite niece of mine." He picks up a really goofy-looking black casket-shaped purse with a bone-shaped handle and feather trim. "But of course this stuff is obvious! It's for tourists! New Orleans is known for vampires and voodoo and all kinds of other marketable stuff. The Ursuline convent just down the street and around the corner has a great old legend going about a bunch of casket-carrying mail-order brides. I sell an amazing number of these little purses. You like?" He hands one to me and I hand it right back. I may not be totally cool, but I am definitely cooler than *that*.

"I'll take it," says Serena, still yawning, and he hands it to her with a smile. *Sigh*. Obviously Serena's somewhat questionable taste is still in full force. I was going to ask her about her new look in the car, actually, but didn't get a chance before she fell asleep. I'm guessing it must be 1980s, what with the big hair, leggings, and the (obviously and slightly disgustingly vintage) Frankie Say Relax T-shirt.

Uncle Mortie leads us to the back room, which only vampires (clearly) get to go to. It has a huge old carved wooden bar in it and cushy (but definitely aging) leather bar stools, all of it barely lit by some ancient stained-glass lamps. Very circa 1800s, very cozy, and very Uncle Mortie. Call it shabby vampire chic, I suppose.

"So," says Uncle Mortie, "I called the local Council representative. Beverly Boudreaux, from a very old vampire line here in New Orleans. She's gathering up all the appropriate vampires so everyone can get their sticky little fingers involved. We're supposed to head over at eight o'clock tonight. Be prepared—they're a little different here from what you're used to."

"Different how?" asks Dad.

"Just different. You'll see," says Uncle Mortie.

Great. Here we go again.

Serena and I steal a tourist map from Uncle Mortie and escape to wander the French Quarter while the grown-ups do some strategic planning (or maybe just some restorative bloody sangria drinking, for all I know). Mom gave us some cash too, and told us to find something a little less colorful for Serena to wear, just in case. Just in case of what, I don't know, but I can see her point. Everything Serena brought with her is pretty, well, *loud*.

New Orleans is even cooler than I had imagined it would be. Why couldn't Dr. Musty have been based *here*? Sure, the city's a little nasty smelling, especially around the bar areas, but it's got tons of atmosphere. The people look cool (except the tourists; they just look like tourists), the buildings are really neat in an old, rusty, ornate kind of way, and it's just got an all around funky vibe. There are even street performers. (We see one dude spray painted completely gold and another one dressed as a robot.) I can definitely see how New Orleans could be a really romantic city (even including Uncle Mortie's Cask and Casket bar, with its mood lighting).

There are tons of cool shops with all kinds of stuff, including some nice outfits. I talk Serena into a basic pair of jeans and a NOLA T-shirt from a tourist trap.

She changes into the new outfit and then points to the gold lettering on the shirt. " 'No LΛ'? What, do they hate Los Angeles or something?"

"Ha, you're such a tourist noob! N-O-L-A for New Orleans, Louisiana." I punch her on the shoulder and she falls into me and giggles.

It feels so good to just be hanging with Serena again. I feel like I've been off balance since we moved. Not having Serena around is like not having a piece of myself. But now life is normal again.

Okay, maybe not entirely normal considering the Council meeting hanging over our heads, but Mina-normal at least.

We still have some time until we need to meet up with Mom and Dad. So we check out a couple more French Quarter shops (an incredibly cool hat place with hats that cost way more than I can afford, a kind of disturbingly weird store with a bunch of exotic animal skins, and the ultimate socialite shop: doggie clothes and trinkets for those itty bitty yappy dogs). Then we make our way over to the original Café Du Monde (also in the French Quarter, but in a mostly less seedy section) and order up some coffee

(Heaven! Good coffee! No espresso, but coffee strong enough to be almost as good) and two orders of beignets (double heaven—fried doughnutty goodness). All of this makes me think about George, since this is what we should be doing together.

Serena, of course, always seems to know exactly what I'm thinking.

"Have you heard from George yet?"

"No," I say and then decide to change the subject. Way too depressing. "Now tell me what's up with you and Nathan. The last time we talked about the possibility of you and a little bloodsucking, you flat out turned it down because of Nathan."

"I know. But that was before all the drama with my family. I really like Nathan and I think he really likes me, but he just doesn't get me."

"Get you? Or get your clothes?" I poke her in the ribs. Not that I get the clothes either, but I'm used to it by now. Retro eighties is *still* better than some of her phases, and I'll definitely take it over Goth any day. At least this look has color.

"Both!" She pokes me back and somehow, ten minutes later, we're both covered in powdered sugar from the beignets. Good thing we'd picked an outside table.

"You know," she says while brushing some sugar off my hair, "death looks good on you."

"Undeath, thank you very much." I know what she means, actually. Lots of things in the Mina-looks department have improved:

    a) no more ladybug-size pimples (not that I was ever a total pizza-face like this poor girl I used to go to school with, but when I did get one, they were always huge and right on the tip of my nose so I looked like Rudolph),

    b) my hair behaves a lot better and almost has what you could call "style," though I have no idea why (that certainly wasn't one of the benefits that G.W. mentioned in class),

    c) not like I was flabby before, but now I'm definitely all toned up—no flab at all, not even like tummy pooch or anything, and

    d) my eyes, which were more brownish hazel before, are now like ultrablue, kind of like a Siamese cat. Which is cool, if I do say so myself.

"Yeah," I say, "the outward physical stuff is all pretty good, except for the pale skin thing. But I guess you're used to that already. I just keep a bottle of sunscreen in my backpack all the time now."

"That's not a big deal," Serena says.

It really isn't. It's actually easier here than it was in California, since there's no beach to lie out on. And it's not like vampires are albino pale anyway. We're just like Canadian pale. I shake some more powdered sugar from my hair.

"And it is kind of cool to never get tired. But I do miss sleeping."

"Oh, yeah, I forgot about that. But you get a lot done, right? I can't count how many times I've wished I could just skip a night's sleep to get something done."

"Yeah, and it'll be way cooler once you've turned too! It'll be like a sleepover every night!" That might be the best thing about her turning. For me, at least. I mean, one night is fine, but you kind of run out of things to do when you string a bunch of them together. Hanging with Serena will be *way* more fun than hanging with my parents. I've always heard a lot of vampires live in New York City. I bet that's why it's really called The City That Never Sleeps. Hey, we could even move there someday! Just the two of us. Oh man, I can hardly wait!

"You think once I turn, I'll end up looking like you?" Serena asks.

It's so exciting to think about her turning. Kinda freaky, but exciting. She'll be like my sister. Blood sisters, I guess, though that sounds more gross than good. Let's just say she'll be part of my family.

"Well, definitely the eyes will look like mine. I don't think turning will do anything for your fashion sense though." That almost kicks off another round of sugar-flying, but we restrain ourselves as a couple of tourists sit down next to us.

"I guess we better get back," I say. Though I really kind of hate to leave. This has been so much fun.

We leave a good tip on the table even though it doesn't look like anyone else is (Uncle Mortie taught me that—if you leave a big mess, leave a big tip and they'll always forgive you).

We start heading to The Cask and Casket to meet up with everyone. Uncle Mortie's found his niche, I think, since on the walk back, like, five people ask us where Serena got her purse. Go figure.

MYTH:	Vampires often yearn for their old lives and remain stuck in the past.
TRUTH:	Or maybe they just dress like it.

VAMPIRE VOGUE

21

The Council building is in what must be one of the oldest parts of New Orleans. Most of the buildings look pretty rundown and the streets are really quiet and dark. None of the street lights are working either (apparently on purpose, or maybe because they all used to be gas lights and no one ever bothered to convert them to electric). The windows are all shuttered, and honestly, it's all pretty sketchy, if you ask me. Serena is really, really quiet as we walk down the street, and she's holding on tight to my hand.

And I guess the vampires we have run into probably aren't making her feel any more comfortable. New Orleans seems to have a high concentration of vampires stuck in the past. We've seen at least a handful dressed in everything from a top hat and tails to one of those crazy flouncy dresses with all the ruffles. I guess they can get away with it here since tourists probably just think they're all part of the show that is New Orleans. Some of them don't even seem to bother hiding their fangs. It looks really bizarre. And I don't know how they stand it. The fangs-out look is not all that comfortable. I swear I bite my lip every time I have them out.

We know the building when we get to it, even without Uncle Mortie's say-so. It's a huge old moss-covered stone building with vines snaking up the front columns and gothic style arches. I bet it's even on some of the city tours—it's that impressive. Well, if anyone would dare walk down here.

I keep hold of Serena's hand as we all walk in with Uncle Mortie leading the way. Her eyes are huge, though I guess I can't blame her. The Council back home in California wasn't anywhere near as impressive or creepy as this. They must have really bought into the whole vampire literature propaganda here. And then they charge people for it, like Uncle Mortie does. Kind of crazy.

The first room is like a lobby with big marble columns and even more marble on the floor. There are about ten or fifteen vampires just milling around, all of them giving us the eye as we walk through. Uncle Mortie nods to a few. "Evenin', Mortimer," says one politely and even tips his hat to me and Mom and Serena. We keep following Uncle Mortie down a hallway with peeling wallpaper and these really dour-looking portraits hanging on the wall. They could seriously film a movie in here. It'd have to be a horror flick, but it's definitely camera ready. I'm actually finding it kind of funny, though I'm sure Serena isn't at all. About now she's probably wondering what in the heck she's gotten herself into. I give her hand a gentle squeeze.

We finally get to what must be the official Council chamber. Seven vampires are seated at a long table in front of this absolutely humongous fireplace. You could probably cook an entire cow in the thing, it's so big. Instead of a fire, the hearth is piled up with different candles of all different colors. There are even candles on top of candles, where the old ones had burned down.

It would have been sort of cool if not for the skull right in the middle of it all with a red candle burning inside of it. Somebody should seriously check out HGTV for some helpful tips on what NOT to do. I mean, really.

Uncle Mortie leads us down the aisle. There are chairs lined up on either side and quite a few of them are filled up with vampires craning their necks to get a look at us. I guess he wasn't kidding about everybody coming down to see the show. Serena's looking around like she can't believe what she's seeing, and I don't blame her at all. There are some very wacky vampires in attendance. The worst is probably the guy in the long black cape, but then again, the lady in the all black leather catsuit is up there on the whacked scale too. I bet this is a great Halloween group. They could just come as they are.

We stop in front of the table and Uncle Mortie actually bows. I attempt a quick curtsy and almost tip Serena over. Mom pulls us both straight and shoots me a look. Well, it's not my fault. They can't expect someone born any time in the last fifty years to actually know how to curtsy correctly. I was just trying to do the whole when in Rome thing.

"Welcome, Smith family and guest." The speaker must be that Beverly lady Uncle Mortie mentioned. She's sitting in the center of the table and is (thankfully) pretty normally dressed in a basic black dress. "We have called this emergency meeting of the Southeast Regional Vampire Council per your request to discuss the application of one Serena Spivey to our ranks."

I'm sure everyone in the whole house hears Serena gulp. But she lets go of my hand and steps forward to curtsy (much better than me). That's my girl.

Another fellow on The Council (thankfully again, just an average-looking dude in a suit . . . I'm sure my dad is now wishing he'd brought a change of clothes and dressed up a little) nods at the rest of us and waves us toward the chairs. We all sit, though I feel weird leaving Serena up there alone. Is this what normally happens when someone declares they want to turn? Or is this just some weird Southern vampire thing?

"So, Miss Spivey, we understand you wish to become one of us. Can you tell us how you learned of our . . . way of life?" Well, I don't think she actually wants to become one of *you* is what I want to say, but I keep my mouth shut since the next bit Serena says may or may not get me into big trouble. Like a craptastic amount of trouble with a capital *T.* Or I guess that would be a *C.* We really should have come up with a cover story instead of just eating doughnuts.

Serena looks straight at The Council member and says, "When my best friend Mina supposedly died, I just couldn't accept it. Especially when there were a bunch of these pale-skinned people at her funeral who didn't look all that sad. Then I saw someone online who sounded and acted just like Mina, even though they were using a different name. So I did a traceroute and figured out where that person was and came here to investigate. Mina and her family were always like family to me."

That's an utter load of hooey and hogwash (and I bet Serena doesn't really know how to trace anything on the Internet either), but The Council seems to be buying it. Heck, even Dad looks kind of teary. I gotta say, Serena's my girl. Her pulse doesn't even give away that she's totally lying through her teeth. Well, about part of it anyway. I do believe her that we're like family, 'cause we are.

The Council confers with one another. One or more of them must have some kind of blocking skill or something, since I can't tell what they're saying even though we're only a few yards away. Finally, Beverly stands up and bows her head to Serena. "We admire your persistence and dedication to your friends. Such perseverance speaks well of your abilities. We have decided to allow your application." Then they all stand up and come around the table to shake her hand.

The other vampires seated around us all stand up too, and all of a sudden it's like we're in the middle of some little social gathering. A tuxedoed waiter guy comes out of nowhere with a tray full of wineglasses (or I guess that's bloodglasses) and another lady appears with a tray of little tea sandwiches.

I let out a (mostly) quiet squeal and give Serena a huge hug.

MYTH:	Vampires eat only raw meat or drink blood.
TRUTH:	Why would we do that when there's chocolate in the world?

22

We finally get ready to duck out of the little Council after party sometime around midnight, mostly in deference to Serena, who is totally about to drop. We met some really nice (and some really weird) vampires and have at least ten invitations to "stop by anytime we're in town" and two recipes for a vampire-style red velvet cake. (Serena was looking a little green at that one and I totally sympathize, but I'm actually looking forward to Mom trying the recipes out. If she makes blood pudding one more time, I just might scream.)

Beverly Boudreaux grabs us before we leave to give us a stack of forms (no surprise there) but tells us to just turn them in when we get a chance so they can file them at the national level. I guess the relaxed Southern style thing extends to The Council here, which is very cool. Unexpected, but cool. If G.W. had a grave, she'd be rolling over in it. Though I guess technically she probably does have a grave. Maybe a couple. She just isn't in any of them.

We walk Uncle Mortie back to his place and then make the drive home. Serena, of course, starts snoring pretty much as soon as we take off. I'm kind of sad to be going back to Cartville. Really, why couldn't Dr. Musty be based in the city? He could be studying some of the vampire legends Uncle Mortie was telling us about instead of whatever he's nosing into about the Carters in Cartville. Other than Cameron, they all seem pretty uninteresting to me.

We don't talk much on the way back, though Mom and Dad make me swear up and down a bazillion times that I didn't tell anyone else. Which I didn't. Who else would I have to tell anyway? Everyone else I'm close to is already a vampire. Well, except Nathan, I guess, but that's definitely not a conversation I ever considered having with him.

I send a couple of useless texts to George, mostly out of habit, and practice shape-shifting the rest of the way home. I've been working on my standard disguise:

a) long wavy red hair (not like the out of the bottle red that's so obviously faketastic, but real honest to goodness red hair),

b) slightly slanted eyes (because I always thought it would be cool to be like half Asian and half Irish),

c) slightly bigger breasts and hips (you know, just to fill out my shirt a little more), and

d) a couple of inches shorter (to go with the whole half-Asian thing and also because I need it for the other, um, *personality* changes).

I have to say, I'm getting pretty good at this whole shape-shifting thing. Mom can only do, like, one little change at a time, but I can hold all of my standard disguise things in place for a good fifteen or twenty minutes without even trying. Finally, something I'm good at.

I carry Serena to my bedroom once we get back to Cartville. She has always been smaller than me, but it still feels weird to be carrying her like she weighs nothing at all. She doesn't even wake up. When I come back out, Mom is on the phone with Ivetta. Seems she's not only the continuing education coordinator, she's also the new member propagandist. (Like G.W., only nicer and not so crazy. I think she actually *would* bake you cookies.) Mom gets Serena signed up for the next class, which starts this coming week. Feels kind of like kismet, Serena showing up at exactly the right time.

"You want to make a cake with me?" Mom asks after she hangs up with Ivetta. "I've got all the ingredients and I feel too wired to read a book."

"Sure. Are you going to try the one from the lady wearing the purple boa and the giant hat with the stuffed owl on it, or the one from the guy with the poofy hair and red velvet smoking jacket?" I'd personally go with the guy's version, since the vampire lady seemed a little off her rocker to me. She kept insisting that everyone call her Scarlett, even though her name was apparently Millicent. I guess if my name were Millicent, I might do the same. But I wouldn't call every guy around Rhett. And she's crazy if she thinks Scarlett O'Hara would *ever* have worn a hat like that.

"The one from the guy. Anson Chevalier, wasn't it? He seemed more like a baker to me."

"Good choice."

Mom gets out all of the ingredients (standard cake stuff plus cocoa, red food coloring and some blood) and we set to mixing and whatnot. Dad hangs out at the counter to watch us cook and stick his finger in the batter and frosting whenever he can. He's almost as bad as Uncle Mortie.

"Shouldn't we make an extra one without the blood for Serena?" he asks after wiping some frosting off of his face. "She won't like blood."

"Not for long," I say. That makes us all pause for a minute.

Mom goes to get out more of everything for another cake just for Serena. "Are you sure this is what Serena wants to do? What she should do?" She's lost all her happy look from cake baking.

"Why shouldn't she?" I start measuring out more flour and dump it in the bowl. "Serena gets away from a terrible situation at home and I get my best friend back. Forever. What exactly is the problem here?"

"Her parents must be worried sick, not having heard from her in a week and not knowing where she went." Dad also looks totally dismayed, even with more frosting on his nose.

"Her dad maybe. Her mom? I doubt it."

Funny. Now that I think about it, I turned because I wanted to stay a part of my family. Serena's going to turn to get away from hers. Kinda sad.

"Do you think we should call her father?" asks Mom.

"What?" I almost knock over the bowl filled with flour. "Mom, didja eat too much frosting or something? A phone call from the dead?"

"Mina's right," says Dad, which is something I ought to write down in my journal considering how often (as in never) I hear that. "We can't very well call Harry out of the blue since we're supposed to be dead. I'm sure *that* would be a fine and a half."

Mom and I finish mixing, then put the cakes in the oven, making sure to mark the human-friendly one so we don't accidentally make

Serena barf. Then we all sit and watch the oven while they bake and think about the whole Serena situation. At least that's what I'm thinking about. Dad might still be thinking about frosting, seeing as how he keeps sneaking a finger full.

By the time Serena wakes up and stumbles to the kitchen, we've all had a slice or two of cake. (Or three—I admit it, I really love the whole not gaining weight thing. It might actually be the best part of being a vampire.) There's still another hour before school starts when it occurs to Mom that yes, today is in fact a school day.

"Serena!" she practically yells, making both of us jump, but especially Serena, who's still in that I'm-not-quite-awake-yet fog. I kind of miss that.

"Yesh?" I'm sure that was supposed to be a "yes," but it only made it halfway there.

"We need to register you at school! I need to call Josh and see if I can get some papers from the VRA for you."

Oh great, the Josh-erator. "It could wait a day, Mom, don't you think?"

"No, no," she says, still all in a panic and frantically flipping through her purse looking for her cell phone. "If we're going to be responsible for Serena, then we need to *be* responsible. That means school. Now both of you, go get dressed."

Mom can be really whacked sometimes when she gets something in her head. Serena's already missed a week of school traveling here and she was probably studying all different stuff in California than here anyway. One more day really wouldn't matter. But then again, it'll make my day that much better. It'll be just like old times again! Except for all the Southern accents and the weird things they say here and the fact that all the kids (except Kacie) seem to think I'm some kind of trendsetter. Did I tell Serena about that? I can't remember. I've been trying to just lend an ear on the whole divorce drama, rather than telling her all about my problems. You know, be the good friend. Though technically, I guess being popular isn't an actual problem. But I'm finding it really annoying.

I put on my standard jeans and T-shirt (ha, I think I might be single-handedly responsible for an increase in denim sales in the area) and watch Serena dump everything out of her bag and start picking through the pile.

"Eighties, huh?" I say.

"I couldn't decide between the seventies or the eighties. I was watching some movies again—"

"Let me guess . . . *Pretty in Pink*? *The Breakfast Club*?"

"Yeah. I was on a John Hughes memorial kick." She smiles at me. "I knew you'd understand." Ha, not exactly, but I do understand how her mind works. We'd watched all those Brat Pack movies with Mom and her friend on a Girl's Night a year or two ago. Feels like forever ago now.

Serena finally picks out some black leggings (probably a recycle from her Goth days), a bright green Teenage Mutant Ninja Turtles T-shirt and a polka-dotted pink and blue tutulike skirt. That plus a bright yellow banana clip completes the look for the day. Seriously. I have no idea where she finds this stuff. The kids at school are not going to have any idea at all what to think about Serena. I can't wait.

MYTH: Vampires can control their temper as easily as their fangs.

TRUTH: I'm working on it.
Really.

23

As soon as Eugenie is done signing Serena in (and mercifully not making any comments on Serena's whacked-out hair), Henny hones in on Serena like a homing pigeon. (Or do they just carry messages? Whatever.)

"Hi, Mina," says Henny, not even taking her eyes off Serena for a second. "Who's your friend? Is she from California? Is she enrolling too?" Serena (atta girl!) stares right back at her.

Officially, Serena is Mom's (oops, Mari's) second cousin once removed come to stay with us while her father is overseas on a diplomatic mission (the Josh-erator totally pulled that one out of his butt). Serena's already committed her cover story to memory. I wish I were that fast.

"I'm Serena, Mari's cousin and Mina's friend. And yes, I just registered for classes. I have the same schedule as Mina." (Thank you, Josh-erator!) "I'm going to be staying here while my dad is in Timbuktu. And I can talk pretty well myself, if you have any other questions."

I try to keep from laughing. The Josh-erator hadn't specified a country, but I sure hope Timbuktu is an actual place in case anyone looks it up. Henny has no shame, though, and doesn't look at all put out. She grabs Serena's arm and starts walking to class.

"So, *are* you from California too? Where did you find that shirt? Have you known Mina long? How long are you going to be here? Is that an actual tutu?"

I follow along behind. I'm actually kind of glad Henny is doing her thing. If Serena does decide to go through with everything (thank goodness she's still almost Goth pale, so the turning won't be as noticeable), I'm sure Mom will make her finish out her senior year here with me. Henny is sure to make her feel, if not exactly welcome, at least like someone is intensely interested in her. Which she is. Because Henny is intensely interested in *everyone*, but especially anyone not from around here. And considering that the buzz about Serena is already building to a fever pitch, it'll be nice to have someone be on the good side of it. Because a lot of the buzz I'm overhearing? Not so good.

It pretty much sounds like this, over and over again:

Did you *see* what she's wearing?

Is she with Mina? Are they *related*?

Is she from California too?

Who is that? *What* is that?

Not that I'm particularly surprised. I love Serena. She's so cool she doesn't care if you think she's cool. She's totally herself and loves to dive deep into all kinds of weird self-expression (at least, that's what Mom always called it when Serena would show up dressed as everything from a sixties radical to one of today's pop stars) and doesn't care at all about what people think of her. The only person who's ever made her nervous about how she looks is Nathan, and she got over that pretty quick.

Most people just don't get her because they only look on the outside (the part with the tutu). I've kicked a bunch of people's butts over the years defending her, and from what I'm eavesdropping on, there's gonna be some serious butt kicking going on here at Cartville High. Or at least verbal sparring, which I also have a black belt in . . . sometimes. Maybe it's more of a brown belt. And we haven't even run into Kacie yet. I'm so not looking forward to that.

Halfway through second period English I'm about ready to go medieval on someone. A few someones. And I mean that in a totally Vlad the Impaler kind of way.

The worst are the girls who act as Kacie's backup singers. Outwardly, they've been nice to me (whenever she's not around, anyway, and whenever she is, they mostly just bobblehead it because they're chickens), but I could always tell that they were total Kacie clones. They even dress like her, and if there's one thing this world does *not* need it's a couple more skinny, buttless white girls in too-tight pants. There are three of them in my English class: Stacey (truly the cloniest clone, right down to her name), Lala (not kidding, and yes, I've had *that* joke on my tongue since I met her, but I've held onto it since I'm sure she's heard it before), and Adrianna (the quietest one).

The three of them spend the entire period whispering and passing notes about Serena. Actually, what they really did was spend the entire time concocting crazy lies and passing them on. And I can't very well do anything about it since I shouldn't be able to hear them from where I sit all the way across the room. First they told some girl (standard prep issue) that Serena was here because she flunked out of boarding school. Then I heard them whispering to a basketball jock that her parents were failed rock stars (though how you can be a failed rock *star,* I dunno) and that she had multiple drug problems and had been sent here to detox. Then they told another girl that Serena was pregnant and hiding it under the tutu.

You'd think Mrs. Thompson might notice that no one is paying attention to a word she's said about Shakespeare all period long, but she's no Ms. Tweeter. She just keeps droning on and on about symbolism in the sonnets and groundlings and tomatoes being in the nightshade family. (Apparently people back then were idiots and thought they were poison, so when they threw a tomato at you, they *really* didn't like you . . . okay, so I was the only one paying attention. Yes, I can walk and chew gum at the same time.)

Lordy. I need to see if I can get Henny started on some good propaganda or something. This is just ridiculous. Gossip is like an art form in a small town. Or a disease.

MYTH:	Vampires use mind control to make you do anything they want.
TRUTH:	Well, not exactly anything, otherwise all vampires would be filthy stinking rich, right?

24

Mom is waiting at home for us when we get back from school. It's still kind of weird to have her home all the time. She's been baking again and the smell of cookies (sans blood, since she's yet to find a good recipe that includes it, though she's tried out some really horrible ones) fills the house. Actually, I can smell it all the way down the street, but Serena doesn't get the brunt until we open the front door.

"How was school?" Ah, that's why she baked. Unlike some parents, I think Mom actually remembers how bad high school can suck.

"Um, fine," I say, lying through my teeth.

"Okay," says Serena at the same time. "Though I had no idea I was such an alcoholic pregnant druggie dropout."

"What?" Mom and I say at the same time.

211

"How did you know?" I ask and drop my book bag practically on my foot.

Serena laughs. "Mina, I'm not stupid. Or deaf. I may not be able to hear as well as you can, but I could hear enough. Besides, from the sour-lemon look on your face all day, I knew something was up. On the way to the bathroom after third period, I had, like, three girls ask me which druggie rock stars were my parents."

"What did you say?" asks Mom, fascinated. She's used to middle-school students from her teaching days. I bet the gossip at that level doesn't remotely compare to what goes on in high school.

"Well, I told one that I couldn't say because they were in the middle of a big legal battle over custody of me. Then I told another one it was one of the Stones and another one it was some heavy-metal band they'd probably never heard of since they probably only listen to country."

"Oh man, that'll be all over town by now," I say while Mom laughs. "Did you catch their names? I'll try and take care of it tomorrow."

"Don't worry, Mina, I can take care of myself. What do I care if a few girls I don't even know think I'm some drugged-out rock-star spawn? It's not like there's a bunch of paparazzi around here waiting to swoop down on me. What can they do?"

"Talk." Serena's never lived in a small town before. Not that

I have a lot of experience with it, but I've already seen how fast things spread around here. I bet Dr. Musty knows all the details by now. It's hard to say whether my (not totally wanted) popularity will be enough to protect her by association or not.

"Sticks and stones," says Serena.

"So, other than that, how was the rest of the day?" Mom pulls another tray of cookies out of the oven. *Mmmmm*, peanut butter.

"Okay. They're studying different stuff here, but I don't think I'll have any problems or anything."

"Good. That's what I like to hear." She hands Serena another cookie. Ha, she's such a mom. But I guess Serena isn't used to that.

"So, what have you been up to, Mrs. H—sorry, Mari."

"Well, I've been trying to stay busy. There really aren't any jobs in this town to speak of, so I'm looking into my options and trying to update my skills. Taking some continuing education classes, including that shape-shifting one with Mina that I'm sure she's told you about. It's been a little crazy, but it's been great seeing Bob so happy with his work. He really didn't enjoy being an accountant."

Does anyone? Though, honestly, I didn't have a clue that Dad hated his old job. He has been practically floating around the house since he started working with Dr. Musty.

"But enough about me," says Mom. I see her turn serious. "Serena, Bob and I really think you ought to call at least your dad.

Just let him know that you're safe. If we were your parents, we would want to know. He must be going crazy by now."

Serena doesn't look convinced. Her dad must have really hurt her. Not that it isn't creepy that he's dating some girl barely older than Serena, but he *is* still her dad. "You could at least send him an e-mail," I say.

"I'll think about it," she says. Which means no in Serena-speak.

I take Serena with me to meet Cameron at a park (I should say *the* park, since there's only one) since we don't want to be the scary older kids hanging out at the elementary school during the day. Besides which, it's hard to concentrate when there might be a bunch of kids around anyway.

We get there first and I spread out a blanket for us to sit on while we wait for Cameron.

"So, who is this guy again?" Serena is wearing a big floppy hat (which is definitely not eighties, so I'm not exactly sure what she's going for there), and I can barely see her eyes.

"He's another vampire. He looks like he's our age, but I'm not actually sure how old he is. He's local, but he's traveled. He's not like the other kids around here."

"Uh-huh. Is he cute?"

"Well . . ."

"Ah. So he's *that* cute. And why didn't I hear about him before? A little George competition?"

"There's nothing to tell. He's just helping me out with some mad vampire skills is all. And I'd be happy to tell George all about him if I could get in touch with him. Apparently, he's busy with all the Brazilian beach babes or something."

"No word at all, huh?"

"Nope. Right now I'd be happy with half a word." Honestly, I think I've skimmed right over the worrying part to just being stomping mad at him. Even though I haven't technically known George for *that* long, I really didn't think he'd leave me hanging like this. It's been months with no word at all. Not a peep. Not even half a peep. Not even an eep. I didn't even get a text message saying "nice knowing you." How crappy is that?

"So this hot vampire guy is teaching you some stuff, huh? What kind of stuff?" I swear I think she's wiggling her eyebrows at me under that hat.

"He's teaching me some Jedi mind tricks. Like mind-control stuff. I've been wanting to use it on this girl at school."

"Cool. Which one? Have I met her yet?"

"No, but you'll know her when you see her." I see Cameron pull up and wave to him. "Now," I whisper to Serena, "behave."

"What?" she says, really loudly. "You want me to BEHAVE? Is that what you said?" Gah, she's such a goober! Where's a pillow when you need one? I might have to start carrying one now that she's here. I stand up and pull Serena up with me so she can meet him all properlike. Though, on second thought, maybe we should have stayed sitting. The tutu isn't quite as obvious that way. But if he's the kind of guy who freaks out over a little thing like a tutu on my BFF, I really don't need to be hanging with him anyway. Even if he is the only vampire teenish guy around.

"Hi," says Cameron when he reaches us. "You brought a friend?" He doesn't look totally surprised, but I imagine he's probably already heard a bunch of rumors. Hopefully not the really bad ones. He doesn't seem to notice the tutu at all. Or at least he's too polite to stare at it.

"Cameron, this is my best friend Serena. She's staying with us. She's going to start the intro class with Ivetta this coming week."

"Ah," he says and shakes her hand. Serena goes a little giggly, which means she's noticed his piercing blue eyes and überfineness. Well, it is hard to miss. I really need to introduce her to some other vampires so she realizes that we're not all total hotties. Not that I'm a total hottie or anything. But I'm not bad now. Though she has seen Uncle Mortie. It's easy to forget he's a vampire though. He's just crazy weird Uncle Mortie.

"Nice to meet you," Serena finally manages to say.

"You too," he says. "You must be the owner of the black VW Bug?"

"The Death Beetle! Yep, that's me!" She giggles again. *Hmmm, I'll have to ask her later. Maybe I'm not the only one attracted by the whole manly man smell Cameron has going on. Not that I'm attracted. Just, you know, he smells really good.*

"Great car. Very classic." Serena looks like she might fall into a total fit of giggles (or maybe just swoon).

I decide I'd better save her. "So I was telling Serena you've been helping me learn how to do mind control. But I mostly suck at it."

"You know," he says, looking from me to Serena and back again, "if you're okay with it, Serena, Mina could use you. It would be great practice for her. No offense, but it's much easier to control humans than vampires."

"Sure!" *Ha, I think she'd agree to let me perform scientific experiments on her if Cameron asked. Seriously, if that pheromone stuff is a skill you can learn, I so want to learn it. Though I don't want to smell all manly man. Not really girly girl either, since that conjures up images of puffy pink clouds. Maybe womanly woman? What would that smell like?*

Cameron has me sit across from Serena and stare into her eyes. It takes us three tries before we can do it without laughing.

I'm sure he thinks we're total dorks. Okay, so we are total dorks. It works for us.

The fourth time, I stare deep into Serena's eyes and successfully clear my mind. I find the center (which sounds all new agey, but trust me, it actually isn't if you're a vampire . . . there's something to it) and concentrate. I open up and say, "Serena, pick up your glass and drink."

I see Serena's eyes go kind of unfocused and she actually does it. She picks up her glass and takes a drink. Then she takes another. And another.

"Oops," says Cameron. "You need to give her more direction or she'll just keep drinking."

"Oh!" Good thing I didn't tell her to do something else. This could be kind of dangerous, couldn't it? "Serena, stop drinking. Put your glass down." I look at Cameron. "Um, what now?"

"Well, why don't you test and see how powerful your hold is? That's just water, right? Tell her she drank really sour lemonade. Then after your suggestions wear off, ask her if she remembers what she drank."

I clear my throat and try to keep my mind all centered. It's a little hard. I admit it. I can be a little flighty sometimes. "Serena, you just drank some really sour lemonade." She immediately makes a puckered up sour face and a gagging sound. Which of course makes me crack up and I look away for a few seconds. Cameron pokes me and points to Serena, who's acting like she's starting to wake up.

"Keep concentrating or she'll come out of it. Your hold isn't that strong."

So I do the whole mind-clearing thing again and try not to think about the sour face. I finally get all centered again and kind of hold Serena in place with my eyes.

"Hey, how long do suggestions hold, anyway?" I ask out of the corner of my mouth. The one he gave Mr. Benoit was definitely long term, though I'm not anywhere near as in control as he was.

"Well, the better you are, the longer they can hold. Since you're new to this, I'd probably say no more than a day or two for actual commands. The memory, though, should stick around forever. She'll always think she drank some sour lemonade." He looks at Serena who is still making a puckered up face, and laughs. "You did pretty well this time. I think you're starting to get the hang of it."

"It's a lot easier on Serena than on you." I shrug. "So do you think I'm ready for something more challenging? I mean making water into sour lemonade is cool and all, but I don't see much practical application, if you know what I mean."

Cameron nods. "Just remember: it matters what kind of suggestion you make. If you try to get someone to do something completely opposite to their nature, they'll resist you. You might not be ready for that yet. Trying to get them to do something that they'd either normally do or would do without much encouragement is much easier."

Hmmm. Okay. Serena might hate me for this, but I have to try. It's for her own good.

"Serena, when we get home, you will use our phone and call your dad. Tell him that you are okay and doing well. Do not tell him who you are with or what you are doing here. Talk to him normally, but don't give him any identifying information about where you are." I hope that covers it. Our number is unlisted (as recommended by the VRA), so he shouldn't be able to trace it in any way. I think that'll be safe. I hope.

Serena frowns and shakes her head, but her eyes at least remain unfocused. I look at Cameron and he shrugs. "I don't think it took," I say. I try it again and get the same reaction.

"She's definitely resisting it. I don't think you've got a good enough hold." He leans over and peers into Serena's unblinking eyes. "Part of the problem might be that it's harder when a subject knows you're trying to make them do something. People naturally resist. We can't help it. It's in our nature, human or vampire."

"She's pretty stubborn normally." Like a mule, that girl.

Cameron turns back to me. "Do you really want her to make that phone call?"

"I think so, yeah." Did Serena just flinch? "Hey, she can't hear our conversation, can she? She won't remember this part, will she?" I scoot back a little. If she comes out of it right now and knows what we're talking about, she's totally going to wallop me.

"No, she's still under, just resisting. Here, let me show you a trick I picked up." He nods at me and I move over so he's sitting right in front of Serena. He leans over and, weirdly enough, I can feel when Serena's focus switches to his control. Wow, he's fast.

Then he reaches over and tickles her. She starts squirming and giggling, but then subsides and looks even more unfocused as Cameron continues to look deep in her eyes. And she's definitely out of it because if she weren't, she'd be blushing bright red at being so close to him.

"What was that for?" I whisper.

"Distraction. I just needed some kind of outward stimulus to distract the part of her mind that was resisting to get her further under my control."

He repeats the command to Serena to call her dad, and this time she repeats it back and just sits there. Looks like it took that time.

"Does it have to be a physical distraction?" Dad's not really all that ticklish and I don't know if Kacie is or not, but I don't really have any desire to touch her.

"No, it can be anything really. You just have to divert their focus." He sits back and smiles at me. "That's it," he says. "She'll come out of it completely in probably about five or ten minutes."

"After she makes the phone call, she won't remember why she made it, right?" I hope not. She'd kill me.

"She shouldn't."

Good. I do feel a little guilty about it, but I have to say I agree with Mom and Dad on this one. Family is family. Well, her dad is anyway. I can't imagine how he must be feeling right now. Her mom? *Pfffft*. She can suffer.

"If she doesn't mind, you should keep working on her for practice. But don't overdo it. You don't want her to wind up with big memory gaps or anything like that. If you mess around too much, it can be bad."

"Gotcha."

Hey, I bet this is like what the Vampire Goon Squad does to people. They must just be really, really good at it to wipe out memories. I wonder if this is what Linda is learning how to do now? Scary.

"So . . . " Cameron says. " I probably shouldn't ask, but how did the whole Serena situation happen?"

I look at him close. "You won't tell The Council or anything, right?"

"The Carters aren't exactly on The Council's best side." *Hmmm*, interesting. Understandable though. I mean, join the club.

"Well, Serena has been my best friend for forever. When The Council back home made me go through the whole class stuff and decide whether or not I wanted to turn, it was driving me crazy not to tell her. So, one day, I kind of caved. She's known about the whole thing since just a little before I turned."

"And she's decided she wants to turn now? She came all the way from California to here to do it?"

"Yeah, her home situation got a little dicey . . ." I don't really want to say more than that. It's really Serena's business and not anyone else's.

"I'm assuming she's not actually a drugged out alcoholic." He grins at me.

I groan. "Oh, no, you heard all that too, huh? It's awful."

"Small towns," he says. "When I first got back there were rumors that I was the long-lost illegitimate son of the mayor."

"Really?"

"Yeah, you got off pretty easy. The strangest thing I heard about you was that you used to model but had to quit because you weren't tall enough."

"*Really*?" Whoa. That's actually a flattering rumor. So totally untrue since I think the whole modeling thing is just a really surreal way to live. I mean, how weird would it be to know that there are pictures of you everywhere and guys drooling all over them? Not that I'm all that droolworthy or anything. And never being able to eat. Well, before being a vampire made that a moot point. *Hmm*. I wonder how many models *are* vampires? A lot of them are really pale . . . and a bunch of them live in New York . . . but I guess it would break the whole no-photo rule. Unless they used shapeshifting before their photo shoots. Huh. That could explain a lot.

"So I guess that's not true then?" Cameron asks.

I laugh. He's kidding me, right? "No, definitely not true. But thanks."

"Could have been true," he says. "You never know."

Wow, maybe he really wasn't kidding. I've never been called model quality before. Well, at least not to my face. Once again I'm glad that I can't blush.

"So, how was the whole family reunion with John and Wayne?" I ask. "Everyone roll out the red carpet? Was the fatted calf trotted out?" We'd heard secondhand from Eugenie that while we were in New Orleans, two handsome strangers had swooped into town and were staying at Lowell's. From the way Eugenie said his name, I'm guessing Lowell must have tried his drunk-dude tricks on the human side of the population too. And that the Carter brothers were total hotties. She seriously fanned herself.

Cameron drops the smile. "Why, did Dr. Jonas ask?" Whoa. I think the temperature must have just dropped about five degrees from his change in attitude.

Yeesh, I know Dr. Musty is a little annoying. Okay, a lot annoying. I hear something new nearly every day from Dad about his wonderful (read: incredibly nosy) techniques. But still weird. Cameron should know by now that I'm not the kind of person who would spy for Dr. Musty.

"I was just asking. I'm not exactly buddy-buddy with the doc. If it weren't for him I wouldn't be stuck in Cartville."

Cameron shrugs. "I really need to go, actually. I'm supposed to meet Wayne about something." He gets up to go without any more ado.

"Um, okay. Thanks again for the lesson." I wind up saying "see you later" to his back.

That was a little weird.

Actually more than a little weird.

Now I'm totally wondering what exactly John and Wayne are trying to hide from the good doctor that's got Cameron so tied up in knots.

MYTH:	Vampires can't digest regular food.
TRUTH:	Sure we can. Though you don't want to eat *too* much . . . or it kinda messes you up. ⟩⟩⟨

25

Serena doesn't snap out of it until we're on the way back to my house. All of a sudden, it's like the fog has lifted and her eyes come back in focus.

"Hey . . . ," she says. "Where'd Cameron go? How'd we get here?" She stops walking and looks around. I can see it dawn on her. "Wow, so your mind-control thing really works, huh?" She punches me on the arm. "You better not have made me do anything stupid! You didn't make me, like, stand on my head or anything, did you?"

I laugh. "No, goober, I just had you get up and dance and sing that old Britney song you like so much."

"You didn't!" She stops dead in her tracks. "Not in front of that hot guy! No-o-o-o-o!"

I practically pee my pants laughing, but I finally get out a no that she believes. I would never do that to her. Best friends should never (and I mean *never*) embarrass each other in front of a guy, even if neither one of them is interested in him. Or in front of a girl either, I guess. Other girls can actually be worse, come to think of it.

We're still laughing when we get in the house. Mom has disappeared somewhere. (Probably bringing some cookies over to Eugenie. She really has been trying to be neighborly and besides, Eugenie's better than watching the news.) I watch Serena to see if she'll actually act on the suggestion Cameron planted or not.

She pauses for a second as we go through the door and then stops. "Mina," she says, "can I use your phone for a minute?"

"Sure," I say and get it for her. I hold my breath.

She holds it for a minute and looks at it, then starts dialing. It's actually going to work.

"Hi, Dad?" Serena's face looks a little blank, but other than that she looks okay. "Yes, it's me. I just wanted you to know that I'm okay. Everything's fine." She listens for a while as he talks. She's holding the phone so close to her ear (and it's a crappy phone provided by the VRA) that I can't hear what he's saying other than a word or two that don't mean anything on their own. Hopefully he's not reading her the complete riot act. "No, I'm not coming home right now. I'm staying with a friend." She listens some more. "No, I can't tell you where." That kicks off a long tirade on her dad's side. Serena sighs. "No, I can't. But yes, I'll call you again." Another small pause. "Okay. I love you too." She hangs up and hands me back the phone.

"That wasn't too bad, was it?"

"No, I guess not. Hey, do you mind if I use your computer? I want to check my e-mail."

"Sure, it's a piece of junk. But my junk is your junk."

I get her all logged on and then sit and do my homework while she starts furiously clicking and scrolling, pausing every now and then to read another e-mail. I know she's got like twenty of them from me. Who knows how many she's got in there from everyone else. At least she'll know she's loved.

Henny gives me a call while I'm working on my Calc homework. A phone call from Henny is actually a rarer occurrence than you'd think, mostly because I told her my "brother" has me on phone restriction because he thinks cell phones give you brain tumors. She totally bought it, I think probably because we're from California. They think we're all vegan hippie freaks out there, though really we're not. That's more Oregon.

After a couple of nonsense questions about homework (Henny is many things, but studious is not one of them), she finally gets to the point. "Mina, do you have anymore friends staying with you other than Serena?"

"No, why?"

"Just wondering. I thought I saw a new girl over in Boondale and then again here in Cartville. She looked really . . . interesting. But maybe I was just imagining things. Anyway, thanks for the help. I'll see you guys tomorrow."

Yeah, like every weirdo around here belongs to me. Did they not get anyone who wasn't a member of the herd out here before me and Serena? "Okay. Hey, Henny—"

"Yeah?"

"Just so you know, Serena's not a druggie. Or an alcoholic. Or pregnant. Do you think you could spread *that* around?"

"Oh sure," she says, but you can tell she wishes I'd told her something juicy instead. Well, if she knew the real truth, that'd be juicy enough for her, but I've been in enough trouble with the various councils already. Might as well keep my nose clean for at least a couple months.

"Who was that?" asks Serena, coming up for air from the computer.

"Henny. The girl with all the questions."

"Oh. Yeah, her. She was okay. Nosy Nellie, but okay. Is there anyone cool here other than that Cameron guy that I barely got to talk to before you ensorcelled me?"

"Eh, not so much. He's about it."

"Thank God for the Internet," she says and turns back to the computer.

We have an actual sit-down dinner in honor of Serena being with us. Mom goes all out and makes Serena one of her favorite meals: spaghetti with meatballs and garlic bread. Lots of extra garlic for Dad.

"I guess that whole garlic thing is out the window, huh, Mr. Hamilton?"

"Don't forget, it is Smith now," he says. "But you can call me Bob anyway since I'm supposed to be Mina's brother."

"Oh, that's right. Sorry. And Mari, right? It's hard to remember!"

Tell me about it. I catch myself almost slipping up all the time.

"Not to bring up a sore subject, Serena," Mom says, "but we really did want to talk to you again about you calling your dad. The more I think about it, the worse I feel."

Serena's face goes a little wonky for a minute, and then she blinks and says, "I did call him. Didn't I, Mina?"

I swallow a big bite of meatball. "Yep. While you were at Eugenie's, Mom."

"Oh good," says Mom. "I'm proud of you, Serena. I think it was the right thing to do."

"I guess so," Serena says. "Though won't I have to fake my death and everything when I turn?"

Oh. *Hmm.* Yeah, I didn't think of that. Would he feel better or worse to have heard that she *was* okay only to find out that she wasn't?

"You won't have to die necessarily right away," says Dad. "The Council around here is far more lenient than the one back in California. They probably wouldn't allow you to see him again after you turn, but you could speak to him. At some point in the future, whenever you need to relocate and go through the whole process with the VRA, they'd probably stage everything then."

Serena nods and goes on eating. I give myself a mental "whew." Looks like I got away with my meddling. No harm, no foul.

Which reminds me . . . "Hey, Dad. Bob. Whoever you are. Did you hear that John and Wayne are in town now?" Not sure if Mom gives him the Eugenie scoop or not.

"Not directly," he says. "Though Dr. Jonas had surmised as much." Surmised? Cheese, Dr. Musty is definitely wearing off on Dad. Who else talks like that?

"What exactly are you and Dr. Jonas trying to dig up anyway?"

"A lot of things actually." Uh-oh. I think I've unleashed Dad's historical beast. I can practically feel him rubbing his mental hands together in glee that I actually asked a question about his work. "John and Wayne Carter have a very interesting history. Dr. Jonas traced a lot of their path through Europe before coming here to finish his research. Though they've only been in the States for a relatively short while, they've been around for much longer than that. They may be some of the oldest living vampires today. Dr. Jonas was able to follow them back quite a ways, back before they called themselves the Carters."

"Cameron said they got caught once in New Orleans."

"Yes, there was quite a to-do over that!" Again with the weird language! A "to-do"? Dad needs to get out more. "They had lured a number of people to their home, mostly young women, and trapped them there while they drained their blood slowly from their bodies through shallow cuts in their wrists."

"Bob, that's not exactly good dinner conversation!" Mom points her chin at Serena, like I'm not totally grossed out too.

"Oh, sorry. Anyway, they were discovered when one of their victims escaped. When the police went to their house they found a number of"—he looks at Mom—"well, let's just say they found that the brothers weren't good neighbors. They freed a number

232

of people, including one crazy fellow named Felipe who had been there for quite some time. Felipe went on to become one of this county's more prolific serial killers."

Yikes. So I guess the brothers spread mayhem wherever they go. Nice. NOT. It's crazy to me that Cameron is in with them. But I guess you can't pick who turns you. Or, at least, he couldn't.

"But what's Dr. Jonas trying to dig up on them here?"

"Well, they made this area their headquarters in the States and settled here for quite a while. We think they have all of their Carter family recruits make a pilgrimage here after they are turned. Which, I might add, it seems they have often done surreptitiously and not with Council approval." There he goes with the big words again. "They even still call themselves a clan, though that term is frowned upon in today's vampire society. Clans are no longer recognized as official groups, you know. The Councils are supposed to be the only governing bodies now. Dr. Jonas thinks that they store their clan history and bloodlines here somewhere, rather than filing them officially with The High Council, which rules over all the other councils. He also thinks he might be able to tie them to some notorious vampire groups, both past and present. John and Wayne may be responsible for starting some of the more divisive factions within vampiredom both in this country and abroad."

Vampiredom? That just sounds silly. I can tell Serena is trying not to giggle. Even Mom looks a little amused. "So why do you think John and Wayne had to come to town?"

"Well, if they are responsible for some of the groups, especially ones that are still active today, The Councils will be very, very interested. So I imagine they want to block Dr. Jonas from either finding anything incriminating or releasing it."

"So he's not exactly their buddy-buddy."

"Probably not. Hey, did I tell you about how Dr. Jonas showed me the proper method for restoring old documents? We successfully restored a copy of Wayne's Ellis Island immigration records! One of them, anyway. He's entered the country a few different times under different names."

That kicks off a whole conversation—okay, a whole lecture, since technically a conversation involves more than one person talking—about document retention timelines and archival methods and even something about the different types of ink used in old records. I should know better than to ask Dad about anything involving history. At least Serena's here with me now and I don't have to pretend to listen alone.

26

The next day at school is pretty much a repeat of Serena's first day, except for me trying to run interference with the gossip hounds (which totally doesn't work) and Serena making it worse by making up even more crazy stories about herself and telling them to whoever asked (like the one about how she was found as a baby by her parents in the bush while they were on African safari).

By Tuesday afternoon, I've completely given up. I bet Henny has a headache from trying to keep all the stories straight. I know I do.

"You ready to get vamped up?" I ask Serena when we get home from school.

"You bet," she says, and Mom laughs as we do our happy dance.

Serena's first vampire propaganda class (okay, sorry, her

"information session") is also at Ivetta's, where apparently every local vampire thing is located. Mom and I drop her off on our way to do some grocery shopping.

The cover story this time is a painting class, so Serena went all out and wore a beret (purple, of course), a paint spattered T-shirt dress (white, with blue, pink, and green splotches . . . very Pollocky, Mom says), and flip-flops (with her toenails painted ten different colors). I have no idea how that ties into the eighties other than the whole Prince *Raspberry Beret* thing, but I'm working at not mentioning it. I mean, hey, I'm still glad she's not wearing all black anymore. Kind of the exact opposite, I guess, but it's still better than the same thing every day.

Mom and I pick up Serena after shopping at The Pig (i.e., the Piggly Wiggly). It's kind of strange buying groceries regularly again. Weird how fast you get out of the habit of eating normally. Well, except for the Pop-Tarts. But that's just me.

Serena meets us at the car and climbs in, kind of quiet. "How was it?" I ask. "History stuff, right?"

"Mostly." She pulls out a brochure (same one I got) and waves it. "Ivetta gave us, like, the thousand foot overview and then talked about some of the more famous vampires in history. I never realized some of the stuff I've read in novels is actually true. Not exactly like in the books, but, you know, based on real stuff."

"Not *Dracula* though. That one is totally bogus. It's like anti-vampire propaganda."

"I was kind of surprised at some of the famous people—I mean vampires—she was telling us about. I never would have guessed some of them."

"Then there are the ones who you'd swear were vampires who aren't," Mom says. "But that's usually a good thing."

"Uncle Mortie says a lot of pro sports guys are," I say. Which makes sense, though I bet they have a fun time working around all of the medical testing and whatnot. Not the steroid stuff, since they obviously wouldn't need it, but any other kind of medical stuff. I mean, how do you explain how you never get tired or hurt? But maybe some of the team doctors are in on it too. Hard to say. The more I learn, the more I figure out that vampires today are pretty much everywhere. And organized. Or maybe the goons just step in and do a little mind control whenever something comes up. It could happen.

Good thing being organized isn't a required skill though, 'cause I would have been rejected for sure. Serena too. "Organization" is not her middle name. More like "creative mess." But I mean that in a good way.

"Were you guys happy when you turned?" Serena looks all serious. I bet the whole enormity of the decision must have hit her in class. And it's not like she's got someone forcing her to make the decision now, like I did. I would have much rather not even thought about it until I was like maybe twenty-five or so. I probably should have talked to her about that before we went all gung ho and took her to The Council, but it was kind of panic mode when she got here.

"Well," Mom says, since I've been sitting there all silent and introspective. "I don't know that I'd say that I was happy when I turned, exactly. It was a very crazy time in our lives and Mina was just a baby. The timing could have been a lot better, but I suppose that's how everything in life is. Though it did help out with the 2:00 a.m. bottle feedings." She reaches over and messes my hair up.

"Ditto," I say. "I mean, not the baby thing, but the timing thing. I'd rather have waited and not have had The Council breathing down my neck."

"But how about now? Are you happy?"

"I'm happy," says Mom. "But I think I'd be happy if I weren't a vampire too. It's my family and my life with Bob and Mina that make me happy."

Aw. I have to admit that gives me a bit of the warm fuzzies. And it's true. I was perfectly okay before I turned. Or, as Uncle Mortie would say, as okay as any teenager ever is. Which is more okay than he is, so I don't think he's got a leg to stand on there.

"But didn't it make your life better?" Serena asks.

"Some things," I say. "Some better, some worse. But I think Mom is right. If Uncle Mortie had never been turned and hadn't turned Dad and all that whole mess, I think we'd have pretty much been the same way we are now. Well, except for the living in the middle of nowhere part." I point out the car window to the cow pasture we're driving by. There's even only one cow in it.

"Okay, okay," Mom sighs. "I admit that Cartville is not exactly a happening kind of place."

"And the Understatement of the Year Award goes to . . ." I stick my tongue out at Mom and she rolls her eyes at me.

Serena laughs. Ha, ha. She's been here less than an entire week. It hasn't hit her yet. She'll see.

I'm working on a particularly nasty Calc problem (too bad turning doesn't improve your math skills either) when Serena picks up the conversation again.

"Turning has been good to you, right?"

"Meaning?"

"Well, you've got that whole perfect skin thing going. And the strength and all of that. And the eating without gaining weight . . ."

"Yeah, that does rock." Now I can eat that extra cookie or three and not feel guilty about it.

"So wouldn't you say it's been good to you? That you made a good decision?"

"I guess. I wouldn't take it back or anything. I'd do it again in the same circumstances. But it wasn't like I had much of a choice. I mean, I did technically have a choice, but I think I did the only thing that made sense for me." Well, that was about as clear as mud.

Serena just looks at me and raises one eyebrow. She must have been practicing. Last time I saw her try that, both of them went up.

To be fair, I suppose I should tell her that not everything about being a vampire is all that great. Above and beyond the propaganda they tell you in class. I get up from the desk and sit next to her on the bed. "There are bad things about it too. It's not all sweetness and light or anything."

"Like what?"

"The blood thing, for one." Duh.

"Yeah . . ." Serena makes a face. "It does gross me out. But you like it now, right? I mean, you drink it . . ."

I have to laugh a little at the look on her face. "Honestly, it still creeps me out a little. But I can't be undead without it, so, you know, down the hatch and all that." And a little blood on a rainy afternoon does brighten the day up . . . as long as I don't think about it too much.

"So, what else?"

"Okay, there's the not sleeping thing."

"But isn't that a good thing? That like doubles your time!" She looks totally surprised. Heck, I would've been too. It sounds good in theory.

"Yeah, but it can also be really, really boring. There's no good TV on at night and there's only so many places you can go. Really, if it weren't for the Internet, I think I'd be insane already." Though I am getting kind of YouTubed out. You can only watch so many stupid videos before your brain turns to mush. "But having you around will really help! And someday I wanna live somewhere cool again where we can actually do stuff at night other than watch cows."

"I guess I can see that. I didn't think about it that way."

I do want her to really consider this and make sure she makes the right choice. The right choice for her, that is. If it were just me to think about, I'd want her turned tomorrow. It'd be Serena and Mina forever. Like, literally. I take a deep breath.

"And there's the whole relocating thing. Mom says I should think about it like an opportunity to reinvent myself, but until you came, it really just sucked. I had to leave everything behind. You know Mom even had to ditch her wedding dress? And all my baby photos?"

"Huh." Serena turns back to her homework (she's rocking the Calc compared to me, darn her), so I guess that means conversation over for now.

I hope I said the right thing.

WHY BEING A VAMPIRE KINDA SUCKS

1. Besides the obvious drinking blood thing (still gross, sorry), there's the whole getting blood thing. That is, if you have any qualms about sucking your neighbors (or the neighborhood dog) dry. Which I do. It's probably pretty easy in a big city where there are lots of blood bars and whatnot, but in tiny places, your choices are more limited. And then what happens if you're out and about trekking through some far-off land? Or, you know, Timbuktu? (I looked it up and it does exist. It's in Africa in some country called Mali. Not that I particularly want to go there or anything.) You can't exactly tote around a month's supply of blood with you without looking suspicious.

2. And the no-sleeping thing, which I already mentioned to Serena. I don't know if she bought it, though. It does sound good on the surface, but I kind of miss sleep. And I am bored at night. Like, ready to watch infomercials bored.

3. Another really bad thing, at least for me, is having to hold on to your temper. I'm so itching for a fight with Ms. Tight Pants but I know I can't do it. I could kill her totally by accident. With, like, a finger. The other day Kacie said something really horrid and I accidentally crushed my Calc textbook. Try explaining that to your teacher. I had to pretend I'd lost it since I couldn't exactly show Mrs. McNeal my textbook with five finger holes through it.

MYTH:	Vampires are evil.
TRUTH:	Some of them, sure. But so are a lot of humans. There's no vampire monopoly on evil or anything.

27

Grady won't stop hinting that I go to homecoming with him. It's really coming up soon, so the pressure is on. Not just from him either. Henny and Eugenie ask me about it every time I see them, and with Henny, that means I hear it about ten times a day.

After the whole flower incident, he kicked his game up another notch and got the school's choir to actually sing an invite to me over the PA system. I guess it helped that Eugenie's his mom, but I bet Mr. Fleming, the principal, wasn't too thrilled. Serena thinks it's kind of sweet. Which I guess it is. But really, I'm just not interested. He's cute, but he doesn't make my heart do flip-flops or make me feel all warm and fuzzy inside like George did (before he went AWOL on me).

Even worse is that he always seems to corner me when Kacie is around. At this point, I'm not sure if he's just totally clueless or if he's actually *trying* to make her mad. Though why she gets mad at me instead of him, I don't know. It's not like I'm doing anything other than just existing. I've even tried to offer the olive branch a few times and talk her up to Grady right in front of her (which is hard since it's almost impossible to think of something nice to say about her). But she still acts like I'm some kind of man-stealing bimbo.

At least my home life is finally good again. I'm talking to everyone again and Dad did actually kind of apologize for dragging us to Cartville (in between telling me about Dr. Musty's revolutionary filing system and how he's perfecting his lock-picking skills under Dr. Musty's tutelage). We've settled into a routine at home. It's really like Serena's my sister now. And the VRA has finally, *finally* released some of our stuff. The first boxes were mostly Dad's books (bummer) and Mom's good kitchen stuff (yay), but the Josh-erator did call and say that we could expect our clothes by the end of the week. Good thing. I'm so sick of my not-so-new-anymore red shirt that I've actually been debating about wearing some of Serena's vintage eighties stuff. Almost.

The shape-shifting classes are going awesome too. (For me, anyway. Mom's still working on holding more than one change at a time.) Ivetta even let me bring Serena to a class as one of her official field trips so she could see something of the cool side of vampire life. Well, except for Reva and Reba, who are still annoying as anything. Cameron is getting pretty good though. He can do, like, three different actors, but honestly, he looks better as himself.

Mom is officially sponsoring Serena and they're out on another little vampire field trip visiting Dad and Dr. Musty so she can get a close up look at just how interesting (boring) vampire jobs can be as opposed to regular jobs. That leaves me at home alone on a Friday night. Sad, that's what that is.

I figure I might as well e-mail George again. So I open up my laptop and pull up Google mail. Serena must have logged in earlier today because she's still logged in. And her inbox is completely full up with a bazillion messages from Nathan. A good handful from her dad too, but a ton from Nathan. I mean a TON. In the last two weeks. He must be e-mailing her like practically every hour. Judging from the time stamps, he's not even taking a lot of time off for sleep.

I don't even need to read the e-mails to get what they're about. You can tell just from the subject lines. It starts off pretty easy . . .

Nate» Dinner tonight?

Nate» Got reserv @ ur fav!

Nate» Hey S, pick up the phone!

Nate» Where R U???

Those must have been from the day Serena took off. Then by a few days later, it's a lot more frantic. And sad. But also romantic, I guess.

> **Nate»** WHERE ARE YOU?
>
> **Nate»** worried, call me!!!!
>
> **Nate»** PLS CALL
>
> **Nate»** pls be ok, pls call
>
> **Nate»** S, love u. PLS please CALL today

Finally, he must have talked to her dad again after I got Serena to call him. Maybe I should have tried to put a suggestion in there to call Nathan too.

> **Nate»** I talked to ur Dad CALL ME
>
> **Nate»** y haven't u called me?
>
> **Nate»** don't care whr u r, just CALL
>
> **Nate»** Serena I love you why won't u call??????

Oh, man. He's got it bad. He actually said the *L* word. More than once. Mom has always told me that teenage boys are pretty much allergic to that word, no matter what all those sappy teenage dramedy movies say. George and I hadn't used the *L* word before he left, and now it seems pretty obvious that there wasn't any *L* there on his side, otherwise he'd have at least texted me by now. I hope Nathan doesn't feel as crappy as I've been feeling about George not e-mailing me back. Though I never threw in the *L* word. I guess I'm kind of glad I didn't. I mean, okay, if I'm honest, I really did think I was heading that way with George. But how pathetic is it to say it when the other person won't even answer you back?

I can't *believe* Serena hasn't e-mailed Nathan back yet. But then, what's she going to say? "Oh, sorry, I decided I want to live forever and be a bloodsucking freak. Don't really have time for a relationship with some dinky human. Ta-ta!" Maybe it's better if she doesn't respond to him. But still. It's *Nathan*.

I had a crush on Nathan for *years*. And after getting to know him better beyond the whole ohmigod-he's-*so*-hot thing, he's even better than the packaging, though I did figure out we don't exactly have the same sense of humor. If I were Serena, I don't know if I could totally turn my back on him.

She must be thinking about him though. You can tell she's read every single last one of the e-mails that he sent. She's only read a couple of the ones that her dad sent her. Her mom didn't even send one, the old cow. She probably doesn't even know what Serena's e-mail address is.

I wonder if the whole mind-control thing works for asking people questions and getting the truth out of them? Not that I would do that to Serena, though I do want to know what's really going on with Nathan. Being too perfect is so not a reason to cast off a boy. And hey, he *is* perfect. But she knew that going in.

I think about sending George one more e-mail, but decide against it. What's the use? I'm over seventy-five e-mails now with no response. At this point, I just feel like a pathetic loser. Maybe I should take Mom's advice (though how did she *know* George was gonna ditch me like that?) and keep my options open. But Grady's not the one I want to talk to.

I try Cameron on his cell, but it just goes straight to voice mail. I wonder if he's at Ernie's? He says he hangs there a lot since it's

    a) the only place around you can be with a bunch of other vampires,

    b) you can (obviously) get away from all the Cartville drama there (well, the non-vampire drama . . . it's not like humans have a lock on the dramarama thing), and

    c) it's kind of cool in a really earthy hidden bunker kind of way.

Maybe I'll get lucky and he'll be there. I could use a friendly face about now and it doesn't hurt that his is attached to a mighty fine, very manly-man smelling body with a decent sense of humor.

I don't see Cameron's car in the parking lot up top, but figure I might as well get a glass of something while I'm here, so I head down the tunnel anyway. Hopefully Roy and Lowell are off annoying women somewhere else today.

I haven't even completely shut the tunnel door at Ernie's behind me when a voice that I'd recognize anywhere (and had seriously hoped to never ever hear again) hisses "Mina!" with such venom you'd think I was a puppy killer or something.

I turn around and there she is.

Raven.

What is she *doing* here? I can't believe it's her.

My least favorite vampire wannabe. And she's definitely still a wannabe. I can tell from across the room that she hasn't turned. So what's she doing *here*? In a blood bar? Why didn't the vampire police wipe her little brain? Or was there so little there that they couldn't do anything?

"Raven." I try not to sound remotely concerned. I could've kicked her butt before I was a vampire. There'd be completely no contest now. I'm just glad I don't have Serena with me. I'd been thinking about taking her by Ernie's as part of her education.

She marches right up to me and sticks her finger in my face. Okay, did she not get before how annoying that is? There's no Grandma Wolfington here to break it up either. I suppose I'd better just be careful not to, you know, break it off. That would be rude. Since I've got the whole super-everything advantage now (not that I need it) and she's still a super zero.

"I should have known you were in town!" She's practically got spittle flying from her black lipsticked lips, she's so worked up. She had so-o-o-o better not get any of that on me. That's just gross. "I was wondering why that stupid girl came here, but it all makes sense now!"

She must be talking about Serena! I was right. Raven *has* been up to something. I decide to play stupid and see what she'll spill. "What are you talking about?" I demand.

That's when I see her put two and two together and actually come up with four, maybe for the first time ever. Her eyes light up. "You're supposed to be dead! Like, VRA dead! I saw her at your funeral. But she's here, so that means that she knows. You told a human!"

"So?" I ask. "What do you think you are?" Though arguably, she's only human in the technical sense. As far as humanity goes, she's pretty lacking. "And didn't The Council turn your skinny butt down and wipe your little mind?"

She draws herself up as tall as she can, which still puts her at about the level of my nose. "They wanted to and it's all your fault. But the Talons saved me. They broke me out and protected me. I'm going to be one of them and you can't stop me."

So the little Goth girl did actually know some Black Talons. Amazing. It wasn't all hot air after all. I'm not the only one shocked either. I hear a couple of gasps from around the bar and I see Ernie grab his cell phone to call someone. I guess they're like the Evildoers-Who-Must-Not-Be-Named. Not that Raven is any kind of Harry Potter. She's not even Draco Malfoy.

"How's that work exactly? Since you're looking awfully vampire wannabe to me still." That, of course, makes her go even more ballistic and I can see that she's turning beet red underneath all that white makeup of hers, which makes her look even more deranged than normal.

What's black and white and red all over? Angry Goth girl.

"You obviously don't know *anything*," Raven says. "The Black Talons don't just take *anybody*, like The Councils will." She sniffs pointedly at me and I'm about to point out that, hello, they didn't take *her*, when she keeps going. "I was going to drop out of class anyway once the Talons tapped me. *You* were going to be my initiation."

"You need to get over here *right now*," Ernie tells whoever it is he called.

"I was going to be your initiation?" I try to keep my voice calm, like I'm talking a suicidal person off a ledge. "What does that mean, exactly?"

She starts jumping up and down like she can't contain herself anymore. It's like some kind of scary, weird marionette.

"It means you ruined my life! *Everything*! I don't know what you did to Aubrey, but he decided not to turn and they wiped his memory before I could get to him. He doesn't even remember me now! Doesn't. Even. Remember. ME!"

I can't help it. I back up just a tiny bit. She's having a total insane fit. Is she really this worked up over some hot guy? I mean, I know she gave me a bunch of grief over him while we were all in class together, but please. Ernie hangs up the phone, but then stands there like he's not sure what to do either. Nobody in the rest of the place even moves. I don't think anyone wants to touch her. I know I don't.

Raven keeps on talking. "Don't you get it? The Talons only let you in after you've proven yourself by *killing* a human. Unfortunately, by the time they tapped me, it was too late to do anything to you, since you'd already turned. But then I remembered how you were always talking about that stupid best friend of yours. So I found her." She smiles an evil cat-ate-the-canary smile.

254

Say what? She wanted to kill me? And since she couldn't do it, she followed Serena halfway across the country to try and *kill* her?

I don't think so! This is one Goth girl who's going down!

I reach out to grab her but someone steps in between us and my hand just meets a solid, muscular, very male chest instead. Cameron. When did he get here?

"Thanks, Ernie," says Cameron.

What?

"I figured I'd better call," says Ernie. "You got here fast."

Cameron just nods. Why did Ernie call Cameron?

"Out of the way, pretty boy," hisses Raven, batting Cameron's hand out of her face. "I'm in the middle of something here."

"No, you're not," he says firmly to Raven. He nods at Ernie, who jumps over the bar, grabs her by the collar, and hustles her away to the back room, still shrieking. I go to follow, but Cameron holds me back.

"Mina, I think you should leave."

He thinks *I* should leave? Excuse me?

"Raven wants to kill Serena! She wanted to kill me!"

He doesn't know me very well yet, that's for sure, if he thinks I'm going to back down over this. I've been wanting to kick her into next week since I met her and I've got more than enough reason now. I don't care if I do break her finger off or how big an advantage I've got now. Girl is going *down*.

"I understand that. But now is not the time or the place." He pointedly looks around the room where everyone in the bar is watching our little melodrama like they are glued to some reality TV show.

He pulls me over to the front door and opens it. "I'll talk to you later," he says, pushing me through and then shutting it behind me. I hear the unmistakable sound of a lock.

Un-frickin'-believable.

He did *not* just do that. Who does he think he is? I don't know why I even came here to try and talk to him. George would never have done that to me. He'd have at least held Raven down while I got the rest of the story. Or something. Not just slammed a door in my face like I can't take care of myself or my friends.

Raven might be safe for now, but she's got a world of hurt coming. And hello, has she never seen a horror movie or read a book? It's just stupid to tell someone your evil plot. But I guess she's just like the supervillains in all the comic books—can't resist the monologue. Well, I'll be more than happy to foil her evil plans.

No matter what Cameron has to say about it.

MYTH:	Vampires can run super fast.
TRUTH:	Yeah, but you can't do it in front of anyone, so no olympics for me.

28

I run home, just barely catching myself from running too fast in front of Eugenie. I slow it down and give her a wave that I hope looks more friendly than frantic and go in the house.

Then I stop.

No one is due home for a couple of hours. Craptastic. What do I do now? I've got to warn them and make sure Mom and Dad protect Serena on the way home if Raven gets out of Ernie's.

I leave a voice mail on Mom's cell phone to call me as soon as she gets the message. Then I call Dad's and do the same. I'd call Serena except (a) we still haven't bought her a new phone charger (geez, wonder how many messages from Nathan she has?) and (b) she's with Mom anyway.

Though I guess Raven's probably still with Cameron right

now. Did he know her already? He didn't look totally surprised to see her. And why did Ernie call *him*?

I pick up my phone again and then put it down. Then pick it up. I call Cameron and get his voice mail. I skip the message. I'm sure he knows I'm going to want to talk to him. And I don't even know what I want to say to him. Nothing good. I just don't get it. I really thought he was my friend. Maybe even more than a friend.

So I guess I have to wait until Mom and Serena get home. To do what exactly I don't know. But something. GAH. I *hate* this. I'm a doer, not a twiddle-my-thumbs-er.

Maybe I should call Uncle Mortie? Would it do any good to notify The Council? The Southeast Regional Vampire Council doesn't seem that bad, compared to the one in the Northwest. And Raven was already on the wrong side of The Council back home. But they obviously flubbed up big time if they let her get away.

I still can't believe she wants to kill Serena! Or wanted to kill me, for that matter. Aren't vampires supposed to be the blood-thirsty ones? *I* don't want to kill anyone. Well, except maybe Raven. But she's totally got it coming. I can't believe she's this upset because Aubrey can't remember who she is. I mean, sure, he's hotter than hot, but he's just a guy. And not all that great, really. *Definitely* not worth killing over. I don't think he was all that into her even when he knew who she was. She just wanted him to be. And killing over a guy? That's just dumb.

I'm about to call Uncle Mortie for lack of anything else constructive to do when the doorbell rings. Yeesh, I was so distracted I didn't even hear somebody coming up the walk. It must be Cameron. Well, he better have some good explanations up his sleeve. And I mean mighty good.

I yank open the door only to be immediately swept off my feet and twirled around and around and around.

What the—? Is Cameron *insane*? I feel like killing him, not cuddling with him.

I'm about to push off and maybe take a punch or two when I hear a familiar laugh. Like a 9.8 on the George scale.

"Mina! I hoped you'd be the one to answer the door. It'd be embarrassing if it had been your dad. Not that I don't like him and all."

"George!"

He stops twirling and sets me down, and I stare at him like an idiot. For a second. Then I grab him up and twirl, before I realize I'm mad at him and drop him. He stumbles and regains his footing to give me a cockeyed smile.

I glare at him. "Where have you been?"

"Brazil."

"I know *that*. I mean why haven't you called me or texted me or e-mailed me or anything?" It hits me in the chest all of a sudden and I feel like I'm going to cry. Which is so not me. I sniff once loudly and then step back. He's got some serious explaining to do.

"My parents live in the total boonies."

"The boonies?" *We* live in the boonies and I managed to contact him.

"Yep. I'm talking no electricity. Nothing. They're doing this indigenous people study out in the middle of the Amazon. I've spent the last couple of months wearing a loincloth."

"You are *kidding* me." Is this one of his jokes? Because I am so not in the mood for jokes right now.

He laughs but then gets serious. "Okay, I only wore a loincloth once. For like an hour. It kind of itched and it was really drafty. But I'm serious about the electricity. And no cell towers either. Totally cut off from civilization. I didn't get any of your many, many messages until I went into Eirunepé for some supplies. Then I figured I'd better just come see you in person to tell you that I'm not mad at you and I don't hate you and yes, I had a good reason for not e-mailing or texting or calling you back. Seriously, Mina, do you have carpal tunnel now?"

"No, *goof.*" I don't know whether to laugh or cry. Or both. I may just explode. "Oh my God, I've got so much to tell you!"

"Should I finish reading your messages to find out about it, or do you want to tell me in person?"

Oh. Actually, I'd really rather he didn't ever finish reading my messages. I'll have to see if I can delete them or something. I debate telling him about the Serena situation, but Raven can't possibly do anything evil in the next ten minutes. Serena is safe with Mom and Dad and Dr. Musty.

"Or how about a better welcome for your long lost boyfriend?" He steps forward to embrace me, but I duck out of his arms before I even think about it. Does he really think he can just waltz back into my life like nothing ever happened? George looks a little hurt, but he doesn't say anything.

And I'm glad. Right now I've got bigger issues. Life or death issues.

MYTH:	Vampires store blood in secret vaults.
TRUTH:	Uh, how about the fridge?

LEFT OVERS

29

Dad finally gets my message and calls while I'm filling George in on all the details about Serena and Raven and everything else (well, okay, except for Grady and Cameron).

"What's up, Mina? Everything okay? You sounded a little frantic in your message."

Well, duh. How would you sound if you heard some crazy Goth girl wanted to kill your best friend?

I get Dad to stop talking long enough to explain just how crazy Raven is and how much danger Serena might be in. It takes twice as long as it should since he keeps interrupting me.

"I—oh, my. I have to talk to Dr. Jonas. Hold on a second, Mina."

Shoot, I didn't even get a chance to tell him about George. Maybe I should have led with the good news instead of the homicidal stuff.

"Okay, Mina, we're all coming home. Dr. Jonas is coming too. Just stay right there." Then he hangs up. Immediately the phone rings again.

"Hello?"

"Oh and Mina, can you set out some liquid refreshment for us? Thanks." Then he's gone again.

"Yeesh, Dad is still seriously hero worshiping Dr. Musty's dusty coattails."

"What? What did he say?" asks George.

"Dr. Jonas is coming over, so I'm supposed to get out the good stuff for him. Can you believe Dad's more worried about keeping the doctor fed than over Raven wanting to kill Serena?" I go over to the fridge, open it up, and push the button for the false back to open up.

Dad ordered us a fancy false inside compartment thingy for the fridge from the Varney Supply Company and charged it to the VRA. (Basically, you want some kind of vampire-friendly paraphernalia, Varney's is the go-to place.) Especially handy since there aren't that many places to run out and pick up a pint (not to mention that Eugenie's so comfortable with Mom now that she'll just help herself at the fridge). I pull out a bottle and turn around to find George standing in the middle of the kitchen with his mouth hanging open. Oh no, not him too!

"Your dad is working for Dr. Jonas? *The* Dr. Jonas? He's coming here? Here? Right now?"

Sigh. "Yeah. I don't know why, but he's coming." You know, you'd think Dr. Musty was a swimsuit model from the way all the guys I know react around him. Maybe I should skip perfume and just dab dust behind my ears.

I watch while George scurries around fixing his hair and wiping off invisible specks of dust from his clothes. Luckily, wherever Dr. Musty was annoying people today must not have been too far since everybody arrives within about five minutes. Any longer and I might have had to throw a glass of water at George.

"That Goth girl actually wants to kill me?" Serena says as soon as she walks in the door. She looks remarkably cheerful about it. Then she notices George, who is stuck in neutral staring with awe at Dr. Musty. "George!" She attacks him in a Serena-style bear hug (flailing arms, pogo-sticking legs, squeals of delight). "When did you get here?"

"George?" say both my parents at the same time. Jinx.

"That was my other news, but you hung up on me too fast. George got here today. He's been in the Amazon going all tribal."

"Oh, are you with the group studying the Korubo?" asks Dr. Musty.

George nods and gently disentangles himself from Serena after giving her a more subdued hug back. He probably didn't want to look silly in front of Dr. Musty. "Yes, my parents are studying them and some other tribes." He looks cat-that-ate-the-canary pleased that Dr. Musty has heard of it. Figures he would have, nosy old guy.

"Do you have any other news you haven't told us about?" asks Dad. Like what else would I be hiding? Not that I was hiding any of this news. I mean, it all happened *today*. It's not like I've been keeping anything from them.

"Nope, that's it. Dr. M—Jonas. Would you like something to drink?" Might as well get some brownie points.

"Love some, dear," he says in his whispery, paper-thin voice. Dad smiles approvingly, then gets serious.

"So you're sure that this girl intends to harm Serena? And you think she's actually connected with the Black Talons?"

"Okay, do you remember when that Goth girl in my class went all commando on me?" Oh, shoot, wait . . . did I tell my parents or did I just tell Uncle Mortie? Maybe I have been keeping stuff from them.

"No," says Mom. Drat.

So I start over and give them the whole spiel about how Raven hated me because she thought I was getting in the way between her and Aubrey and how she threatened to set the Black Talons on me. I guess I'm not surprised that Uncle Mortie didn't clue them in. He's good like that. Though this time it would have been useful if he'd been more like a normal adult and all up in my business.

"Such a strange coincidence that this girl winds up here, of all places," says Dr. Musty. Um, *hello*, she wound up here because Serena wound up here because I wound up here because Dad wound up here wanting to work for you. But I don't say that, since Dad is nodding his head sagely like he just couldn't agree more. At least Mom looks a little confused.

"Why is that a strange coincidence?" asks Serena.

"Because I have been working on proving that this area is perhaps the primary stronghold and birthplace of the Black Talons. The High Council enlisted my help to do so, as they haven't been able to gather enough evidence on their own to act."

Okay, didn't see *that* coming. "What are you talking about?" He can't mean the Carters, can he? Cameron so doesn't seem like a crazy, bloodthirsty, all-humans-are-evil kind of vampire. And Lowell was kinda creepy (okay, a lot creepy), but he didn't seem all I-like-to-kill-people crazy. I don't think. But Raven *was* at Ernie's. And Ernie *did* call Cameron . . .

Oh, craptastic. I've been fraternizing with the enemy.

"John and Wayne Carter spread discord and mayhem everywhere they have ever traveled. They created a group in the English countryside called the Bloodhounds in Elizabethan England, whose sole goal was to spread terror among the illiterate masses. Before that, they were responsible for a vampire uprising in the 1600s that claimed the lives of over ten thousand humans and over a thousand vampires across Europe. Their record in France is atrocious. And when they came to the States, it is my belief they started the Black Talons." Yeesh. It sounds even worse in Dr. Musty's dry, old whisper. But he keeps going.

"The High Council has wanted to put a stop to them for years, but their hands are tied up with all of that red tape they generate unless they have documentable proof." I can't argue about the red tape. I've seen that myself. I can only imagine that The High Council, head of all the regional Councils, is completely bogged down in it.

"But you think the Carter family *is* the Black Talons? All of them?"

"There are definitely Black Talons who aren't Carters, but I think I can say with some certainty that most, if not all of the Carters, are indeed Black Talons. Now, you say you came upon this girl at Ernie's? And Cameron was called to pacify her after her rant?" I don't know that "pacify" is the word I'd use. More like make her shut up and go away.

"Pretty much. Ernie must have called him. Is Ernie a Carter too?"

"Wait," says Mom. "Bob, did you know that this Cameron guy that Mina has been hanging out with might be a Black Talon?"

George does a double take at that. *Ugh*. Just what I need right now. I just found out I still *have* a boyfriend.

"Um," Dad says, but I interrupt before he can incriminate himself so I can unincriminate myself.

"Mom! I haven't been *hanging out* with Cameron! He's just been helping me practice some vampire skills! And he's always been a perfect gentleman." I look sideways at George to make sure he got that part. Not that Cameron hasn't been a gentleman. I mean, he's never done anything but stare deep into my eyes. It's not like it's his fault that he smells good.

"It is a historian's duty to never assume without evidence," says Dr. Musty. "As far as I know, Cameron Carter is not a Black Talon." Whew. Thanks, Dr. Musty. "Of course, this new evidence does tip the scales a bit." Drat. I thought he was on my side there for a minute.

"Hey," says Serena. "Time out! Okay, now, I've only just started my classes. Who are these whatchacallit Talons?"

268

We all start talking at the same time, but Dr. Musty wins since (a) he probably knows more than all the rest of us combined and (b) Dad makes shushing noises at the rest of us once the doc starts talking.

"The Black Talons can be considered a faction within the vampire dominion. They are a relatively small group and they believe that humans are, for lack of a better term, mere playthings. No offense, my dear, but to a Black Talon you are an expendable commodity, useful only for entertainment and food."

"Ouch," says Serena. I have to agree. That's pretty harsh.

"Indeed. And, as your erstwhile Goth friend indicated, you must kill a human in order to be accepted. We have been working at connecting the Carters, especially John and Wayne, with this nefarious group for some time. I've been met with quite a bit of opposition. Some years ago, after the system of Councils was first formed, John and Wayne pledged that they were no longer troublemakers and would respect the law of The Councils. As of right now, officially the Carters are relatively well-respected members of the vampire community with full voting rights. That would change, should we prove that they are, in fact, integrally involved with the Black Talons."

"So that's what you've been working on? Trying to prove that they're all human haters?" No wonder John and Wayne rode into town. I bet they came as soon as they got wind that Dr. Musty was asking about them. I wouldn't want to be on the bad side of The Councils. Been there, actually. And I only bent some of the little rules. I can only imagine what they do to you if you break the biggies.

"Yes. We've been interviewing some of the more dissatisfied Carter Clan members. We also recently located a record storage location out near Ernie's. Our next step is to secure the records before they can be moved. However"—Dr. Musty gives me and Serena an up and down once-over—"your situation might prove useful to us."

I don't know if I like the sound of that. Who knew Dr. Musty was like James Bond in disguise.

THINGS THAT SUCK ABOUT DR. MUSTY'S BIG PLAN

1. Dr. Musty thinks we can use Serena as bait to draw Raven out into making some point-the-finger accusations about who is and who isn't a Black Talon. Which, you know, might sound good if my best friend weren't on the line.

2. I have to keep acting like nothing has changed, especially with Cameron, which sucks because
   a) I'm a miserable actress,
   b) I'm really kind of pissed at Cameron for that whole shutting the door in my face thing,
   c) George is here, and
   d) Cameron still smells way too good for me to be hanging around with him while my boyfriend is here, not to mention trying to "make nice with him," as Dr. Musty put it. Though maybe it's safer than when George wasn't here and I thought he was off gallivanting with Brazilian beach babes or had given up on me. I mean, let's be honest. Just don't tell him that.

3. And the sticky part? Just in case Cameron is interested in me as something more than a homework study buddy (which I totally assured everyone was a no-go, but Dad just muttered something about how "all boys are the same"),

271

I have to pretend that George isn't my boyfriend. Instead, he's supposed to be Dr. Musty's new intern. Which George is entirely too excited about, if you ask me. Shouldn't he be more excited about just spending time with me again?

4. But the suckiest thing about it all? Dr. Musty's bright idea means I'm actually going to have to try and get Raven to talk to me. On purpose. While wearing an oh-so-comfortable (ha!) recording device that Dr. Musty "just happened" to have lying around. I wonder what other spy gadgets he's got hanging around.

5. Which also means that I totally have to watch what I say since I'm being recorded and my parents might hear it. That actually might be the suckiest thing yet, on a scale of 1 to 10 suckiness.

30

So Operation Foil the Goth officially kicks off the next day. My job is to stick like glue to Serena (while wearing that stupid listening device, which itches like the dickens, not to mention I have to wear this really baggy shirt to cover up the wire taped to my belly). Thank goodness we have all the same classes (thank you again, Josh-erator). George is off with Dad and Dr. Musty doing who knows what at the hidden record vault. Mom is busy manning the wire in case there's an emergency.

"Are you sure you're okay with this?" I ask Serena on the walk to school. After all, it is her life that's on the line.

"Sure. I guess. I know you'd never let anything bad happen to me."

"Of course not!"

"At least Raven will stick out like a grandfather at a Hannah

273

Montana concert around here." True enough. Cartville isn't exactly crawling with Goth girls. "It's just kind of surreal that someone actually wants to kill me."

"Seriously."

"I had no idea the whole vampire thing was so dramarama."

"It's not normally. Not really. I mean, you've known Mom and Dad for years. They're pretty much your average, normal, boring parents." Who suck blood.

"Hmmmmm," says Serena. We don't have time to say any more since Henny accosts us as soon as we get on campus. As per usual.

"Mina! Serena! Wait up!" Like we could get away from her if we tried. It's a good thing she's not a vampire. Then she'd be truly inescapable. We stop and let her catch up. "You guys are going to help with the annual homecoming fundraiser, right?"

"Um . . .," I say at the same time that Serena says, "Sure!" I need to talk to that girl. Don't we have enough on our plate already?

"Great! Here, all you have to do is sell bingo tickets. Anyone can buy one. They don't have to be a student or anything. Make sure they know that this year we're going to be drawing numbers instead of people getting to pick their own square. Last year nobody bought the corner squares and it was a pain." She shoves a stack of entry forms at me.

"What's it for, exactly?"

"The money? It goes to paying for prom decorations at the end of the year."

"No, the number. Isn't bingo like that thing that old people play? The whole b-i-n-g-o thing?"

She laughs. "No, this is cow patty bingo. It's part of the home-coming festivities, right after the game, since we can't do it before 'cause of the obvious reason."

Not obvious to me. I still haven't figured out what these people are talking about half the time. "Cow patty bingo?"

"Oh, I guess they didn't have that in California, huh?"

Not so much. We didn't have anything remotely related to a cow as far as I know. At least in the part of California that I lived in. They aren't exactly common beachgoers.

"Well," Henny explains, "the football field is marked off into squares after the game. Each square has a number and people who bought an entry get assigned a number. Then they turn loose Eugenie's cow and everybody waits for her to go. Whichever square she poops in is the winner. That's the cow patty part. They get half the prize money and the rest goes to the prom committee."

Serena starts cracking up. I just stare at Henny. I've never known her to be a joker before. She doesn't really have the subtlety for it. "Are you kidding me?"

She looks confused. "About what?"

"People sit around and wait for a cow to poop?"

"Oh yeah! It's the biggest homecoming event, actually. Some people don't even show up until after the game is over, just so they can cheer Baby on. That's Eugenie's cow. It used to be Mr. Fleming's cow Bossie, but they ate her a few years ago." Serena starts snorting, but Henny continues on like nothing is out of the ordinary. Which I guess it isn't—for her.

"It doesn't usually take that long for the whole thing to be over. Eugenie is going to make sure Baby eats a lot that day. Lots of silage—that's her favorite. Then there's the bonfire and the dance."

O-o-kay. I've officially heard it all now. I have an almost uncontrollable urge to call Uncle Mortie. I think he'd truly appreciate the weirdness that is Cartville. And maybe he'd come save me. But probably he'd just come to watch the cow and lay a bet.

I actually manage to sell all the cow patty tickets by lunch (ha, unwanted popularity is good for something), with the last one going to Lonnie Pratt. I've been keeping an eye out for Cameron all day with no luck until I see him heading into the cafeteria. Might as well get it over with. I nod at Serena (we're still like glue) and she nods back. We go into the cafeteria and get in line behind Cameron.

"Hey, Cameron," I say, all casual-like. Then stop. Once again, didn't quite think through what I wanted to say first. How best to bring up the whole "hey did you happen to do anything with that crazy Raven chick, or is she still around just waiting to jump out and kill my best friend? And, oh, while you're in the mood to spill some secrets, can you tell me if you're one of those nasty Black Talons?" thing. All I really want to do is yell at him for how he handled the whole Raven situation. And me.

He just gives us the standard Southern hello head bob, a little uncomfortable. I open my mouth again and then Serena jumps in. "So, I hear some crazy chick wants to kill me. You know anything about that?"

Well, I guess there's always the direct route.

"Um," he says in probably only the second time I've ever seen him remotely at a loss for words. "Maybe we should talk about this somewhere else?" He grabs the first thing in the lineup (french fries and an apple) and goes to pay. Serena picks up a yogurt and a sandwich and I get a salad and a couple of cookies. (I still like to mess with their heads.) We find Cameron in one of the far tables in no-man's land (i.e., mostly band members and the Future Farmers of America club, all wearing their little jackets).

"Maybe we should talk after school?" He looks a little nervous.

"Why? Nobody's paying any attention to us." Which isn't strictly true, since half the cafeteria watched us walk over to sit by Cameron, but it's not like anyone else here has superhearing, so I don't see what the problem is. Lowell almost never eats in the cafeteria. I hear he hardly ever even leaves the Shop classroom, the freak.

Serena steals one of his fries. Still up to her old tricks. "Besides," she says, "I could be dead by then, right?" *Groan.* I guess she's not gonna let him off the hook at all. Though, you know, I do see her point.

He sighs. "I'm sure you'll be just fine. I talked to your friend—"

"She is *so* not my friend," I say. As if.

"Okay, I talked to *that girl* who showed up and made a scene at Ernie's."

"And?" Serena and I both ask at the same time.

"And hopefully she's calmed down now."

"Hopefully?" Serena steals another one of his fries.

He sighs again. "Yes, I'm sure she's calmed down now." Ha, I seriously doubt that. He doesn't know Raven very well. She was obviously worked up enough to follow Serena halfway across the country. I really don't think one little talk is going to do anything. Except possibly tick her off even more.

"So," I say, again trying for the casual voice. "Why did Ernie call you anyway?"

"He didn't call me specifically. He called Lowell's and I happened to get the phone." He doesn't look all that happy about it either.

"Okay, so why did Ernie call Lowell?" I have to admit I feel a little better that he didn't call Cameron directly. And it does explain how he got there so fast. Lowell's is really close to Ernie's.

"Mina, I—" he stops talking as Grady heads straight at us. Oh, cheese. Just what I need. Grady might think he's all Romeo to my Juliet, but I'm no Juliet. Heck, he's no Romeo. And who'd want to be either one of them anyway? How about some characters that *stay alive* for love for a change? Or undead, at least. Not that I'd do any one of those things for Grady. If only he would understand that.

"Hi y'all!" Grady plunks himself down beside me and does his annoying over-the-shoulder arm thing. He steals one of Cameron's dwindling supply of fries with the other hand. "Mina, I hear there's some guy staying with y'all now. Don't tell me that he's that boyfriend you keep claiming you have?"

I grit my teeth as Serena kicks me under the table. "No," I say, "he's an intern with Dr. Jonas, that guy my Dad works for. We're just giving him a place to stay." Grady grins even bigger than

279

normal. Cameron looks quizzical. Serena bites her tongue. I feel like biting mine.

"Good! So, what time should I pick you up for the homecoming dance? Did you want to go early to watch the game and bet on Baby, or just go for the dance? I'm okay either way. Lonnie's running the off-the-books pool this year on Baby so I can get my bet in anytime."

Oh holy cheese. This is the last thing I need. I can feel Kacie's eyes burning into me from across the cafeteria. Why can't the boy just go out with Ms. Hot Pants? Then all would be right with the world. Not that he deserves that kind of evil, but still.

"I'm afraid that will be rather inconvenient," says Cameron. "Since Mina's going with me to the dance."

We all do a double take at that and Grady gets this wounded puppy dog look on his face. "Really? When did that happen? Why didn't you say something, Mina?" Okay, yeah, right, like he gave me any kind of opportunity to do that.

"I told you I had a boyfriend," I say.

Wait. Crap! Why did I say that? Cameron's going to think I'm talking about him. And I promised Dr. Musty I wouldn't bring up George.

"And it's always a lady's prerogative to keep her love life private, don't you think?" says Cameron sweetly, but with a little bit of an edge to it and a kind of steely glint in his icy eyes. Grady takes the hint and gets up.

"Sure," he says. "Well, I—"

"Will just be going now," Cameron intones.

Grady just nods and leaves.

Du-u-u-u-de. I wish I knew for sure whether or not Cameron is on my side, 'cause that kind of power should only be used for good.

"Uh, thanks, I guess?" I say. I feel kind of bad for Grady, but I am kind of glad to not have to put up with him hounding me anymore.

"Like I said before," says Cameron, standing up and taking the plate of fries (what's left of it) and putting it down in front of Serena, "I guess I've just gotten into the habit of saving you, haven't I?" Then he takes his tray and leaves.

"Well," says Serena. "I guess you've got a date, huh?"

Serena and I are walking back home after school when I hear a car rev its engine and come barreling toward us.

I knew Raven wasn't all pacified!

I tackle Serena and we both wind up in a bush—a very prickly bush—as the car skids to a stop right next to us.

The driver rolls down the window and a very non-Goth, very pointy-chinned face pokes out.

Great. Ms. Hot Pants has moved up her game a notch. Just what we need, another homicidal wench in town.

"You've got a lot of nerve turning Grady down that way in front of the whole school. *No one* treats him like that. You'd just better watch out, that's all I have to say." Then Kacie guns it and speeds off, kicking up some gravel.

Serena looks at me and pushes a branch out of her face. "You're just all about the drama now, aren't you?"

"Me?" I say and stand up and then haul her out of the bush after me. We both look like we've seen better days. "I'm so *not* about the drama. It just keeps finding me."

I hope we can make it home before someone else decides they want to kill one of us.

MYTH:	Vampires hold onto souvenirs of their past life.
TRUTH:	Well, people do too. Not like it's weird or anything. So long as they aren't holding onto, you know, like, body parts or something.

31

George insists that we both escort Serena to her next vampire session because

(a) she needs protection,

(b) this is our only chance to hang out together without any adults around (we're doing the stakeout thing and sitting in the car), and

(c) did you notice (b)?

I'm a bit worried that George is planning something hot and heavy. But I'm not really in the mood. We just need to talk. Alone. I have to find a way to break it to him that I've apparently got a date who isn't him.

I twist around in the passenger seat of the Death Beetle so that I can face him. "How's work?" Might as well start off with something neutral. And, as Lorelai drilled into me, you should always show interest in the stuff your boyfriend is interested in. It's part of her twenty-step plan to true love.

"Oh, Dr. Jonas is all that I thought he'd be and more." Great, Dad and George should start a fan club or something. I just don't get it. He's just a nosy old vampire guy. With a secret mission. "We started excavating the records today. It looks like they were stashed back in the 1800s from the newspapers that some things were wrapped in. But some of it looks much older. It might be one of the Carter's original stashes when they first came over."

"Mm-hmmm." I can't help it. I'm zoning a little here.

"This stash is in a large reinforced metal locker buried under a cryptomeria tree. We never would have found it without some hints from the angry Carters Dr. Jonas has been talking to."

Cryptomeria? Where have I heard that before? Oh, yeah! "Just like Ernie's!"

"What?"

"The local blood bar. It's underground too and the tunnel to it is marked by a cryptomeria tree." I leave off the part that it was Cameron who told me about it. I'm not quite ready to tackle that topic yet.

"Hmmmm, that's interesting. I'm surprised Dr. Jonas didn't mention that. Hey, do you remember my sponsor? The museum guy?"

"Yeah . . ." I think. I don't know that we were actually introduced, since we wound up ducking out early at George's turning because of his absentee parents showing up and acting all we-didn't-do-anything-wrong.

"Well, this is exactly the kind of stuff he taught me about. A lot of the Old World vampires created stashes of things they'd picked up that they couldn't keep where people could find them. And the Carters are definitely old school. They even used some old-fashioned booby traps on the stash."

"Booby traps? Like what?" Dad sure hadn't mentioned that. I bet Mom would freak if she knew.

"Well, most of them were obviously intended for humans, not vampires, since they were just minor annoyances. Stuff like spike boards buried in the pit, spring-loaded stuff, some trip-wired alarms . . . but Dr. Jonas is a master. He's seen everything. It was really amazing to watch him deactivate everything. I learned so much."

"You said most of them were for people? What about the rest?" A spike board sounds bad enough to me. Dad better not be going all gung ho and getting himself in trouble. I know how excited and distracted he can get when he's going all historical.

"Oh, a few were dangerous. A decapitation trap, a UV beam . . . stuff like that. But Dr. Jonas took care of all of it."

285

Huh. A *decapitation* trap? George sounds way too blasé about this. I mean, Dr. Musty *is* ancient. What if he forgets something? I don't want to lose my dad over the Carters. Or a boyfriend, for that matter.

Which reminds me . . . "George, I need to tell you something."

"What? You missed me desperately and can't stop thinking about me in my loincloth?" He leans over to kiss me.

"No. I mean, yes! Wait, I mean . . ." Now that he mentions it, I do kind of wonder what he looked like in a loincloth. We kiss for a second and then I pull away. "That's not what I was talking about. I'm being serious. I need to tell you something about Cameron."

"The Carter guy you've been hanging around with?"

"Uh, no. I mean, yes." Gah. I'm making no sense at all today! "That's the guy, but I haven't been hanging around with him. I mean, not like all the time or anything. Just every now and then. Before Serena got here." When will I learn to practice what I'm going to say before I say it?

George laughs, but it sounds a little forced to me. And there's not even the flicker of a smile. "Well, you didn't do anything with him while I was away other than hang out, right?"

"Of course not!" Just the staring into the eyes thing and trying not to breathe. But I had to since it was part of the whole Jedi mind trick training. The staring, that is. Not the not breathing part. And there were candles involved, but . . .

Okay, I'm just not going to mention any of the practice sessions to George. That might be best.

George grips the wheel of the Beetle. "We're fine. I'm not jealous." Huh. His eyes have gone all stormy looking. He may say he's not jealous, but his eyes say differently.

"Okay," I say. I guess I've got to just go ahead and say the bad news. "Um, good. 'Cause, you know, we kind of have a date. Me and Cameron. But it wasn't on purpose or anything."

George looks at me like I'm speaking gibberish. "What do you mean, exactly?"

I sigh. My life *is* a soap opera. Maybe Serena is right. Maybe I am all about the drama now. Not that I want to be. "Okay, see, Grady was basically demanding I go to the dance with him. The homecoming dance."

Now George looks completely confused. "Who's Grady? I thought you were talking about Cameron."

"Grady is this local jock boy who has a crush on me. Well, he acts like he does, but I think it's more like he just can't believe I'd turn him down." I decide to leave out the whole singing choir thing and the shower of wildflowers. Don't want to panic George even more. It's bad enough I'm telling him about a date with one other guy. "So he's been bugging me about this dance forever and I keep telling him I have a boyfriend but he doesn't believe me.

287

And then he asked me about you being here, but I couldn't tell him that *you* are my boyfriend, I had to tell him you were Dr. Jonas's intern like we said, so Cameron saved me by telling Grady he was taking me to the dance and to back off."

"Hmmmm," says George. I can't tell if that's a good *hmmmmm* or a bad one, but his eyes are almost purple. That doesn't look good for me.

"You can ask Serena," I say meekly. "She was there."

"Mina, are you still mad at me for not writing you while I was in Brazil?"

"I wasn't mad . . ." Not at first, anyway.

"I finished reading through all of your e-mails last night. You sure sounded mad to me."

Oh. I was hoping he wouldn't read all of those. Especially the last ones I sent.

"Well, you did just drop off the face of the Earth. I was ready to give up on you." I pretty much had given up, actually. But I don't say that. I look out my window. "My whole life turned to major suckage and you were just totally gone. Did you even think about me or how I was doing?"

"It's not like I was out there *dating*," he says. "Or hanging out with evil vampire clans. I was with my parents."

Huh. Tell me he isn't jealous. "*I* didn't know what you were doing. You were gone for months. With no word at all. Not one."

I turn back to look at him. Right in the eye. "I mean, do you have any idea at all what I've been through since we moved? I was so worried about Serena and I had no one to talk to. Dad's, like, off the deep end and the people here either completely hate me or love me, but none of them know me. And you said you'd do your best to keep in touch."

"I *did*." He leans over and takes my hand. "I told you, there was no Internet there, no cell phones, no nothing."

"How long did it take you to get to Eirunepé?"

"What?" He pulls back his hand and his eyes go a little green in the center.

"Isn't that the name of the town you said you went to for supplies? When you finally read my messages? How long did it take you to get there?"

"That's beside the point."

"Is it?" I looked up Eirunepé. It's not that big, but it looks like it wouldn't be that far, mapwise, from where the indigenous whatcha-callit tribes his parents are studying are.

"What are you trying to say?"

"Why can't you just say you're sorry? Admit that you could have called me if you really wanted to. You just didn't try."

George just stares at me. Nice.

I turn away from him and look out the front windshield so I don't have to see that blank look on his face and then my day gets even better. Not.

My least favorite Goth girl is striding toward us with a grim look on her face. (Well, even grimmer than normal. Not like it's hard to look grim when you're all Gothed up.)

"Crap," I say.

"What's *that* supposed to mean?" asks George, but then he looks up and sees her too.

Raven leans her head in the open window on George's side of the car. Maybe it wasn't such a good idea to have driven Serena's Death Beetle after all. It does kind of stick out in Pickup Truck Land.

"Well, if it isn't Curious George," she sneers.

I sneer right back. "Is that supposed to be an insult? 'Cause everyone I know loves that little monkey."

"I suppose you're the intern, then, huh?" She glares at George. "Figures. All my favorite people in one place. And aren't you two just all adorkable sitting out here in the car waiting on wittle-ittle Serena to get out of class."

Hey, I only told Grady and Cameron about the intern thing. And only Cameron knows about Serena taking the orientation classes. That can only mean one thing: Cameron must be talking to Raven.

"So, Raven, what brings you here?" I try to sound nice and sincere, but it falls a little flat.

"What do you think?" She's all sneering again. She better watch it or her face is going to stick that way. Not that it would make a difference.

"You know," says George, "I've been wondering something since I heard what you were out here for: what's taking you so long?"

Say what? Is he on her side or something here?

"What do you mean by that, little boy?"

"I mean why didn't you kill Serena on her way out here? She was alone in her car for a week. Or what about before that? Before she even left California. It's been a few months since you got kicked to the curb by The Council and the Talons helped you avoid getting your brain wiped. So you're running out of time, aren't you?"

Now I'm confused too. "What do you mean, she's running out of time?"

"The Black Talons aren't interested in wannabes. They want results. They've usually got a deadline for new recruits. If you don't kill your target within a certain time frame, then they'll kill you instead, won't they Raven? How much more time do you have on the clock before you're Talon bait?"

291

Raven gets a funny look on her face that at first I can't identify, and then I figure out what it is. Fear. I can see her try to play it off like she's just barking angry instead, but there's definitely something else back there. Heck, I can smell it on her. Raw, naked, nasty, sweaty fear.

"Don't worry about me. I can take care of myself, George. I suggest you start worrying about little Miss Serena instead." She starts waving her finger in his face.

"Not to mention," I add, "when Serena turns, she's not exactly going to be a legitimate target for you anymore, is she?" That's two deadlines she's got to worry about, not just one. Of course, I suppose she could just kill someone else. Like some random person on the street, right? Or do you have to kill the target you tell them about? Like calling a shot in pool?

Raven is literally shaking now, about equal parts fear and anger. This girl could seriously use some therapy. Someone needs to 9-1-1 Dr. Phil.

She finally just spits out, "You. Will. See. Me. Later," turns around, and stalks off the way she came.

Not sure if that was a promise or a threat. Probably both.

"Well," I say. "I guess Little Miss Blackheart is under some serious pressure."

"Yeah, I was talking with Dr. Jonas about it. She's probably only got a week or two at best before it's too late and then"—he makes a slicing sound and draws his finger across his neck. "I do wonder why she didn't do it before. Do you think she's got some doubt or remorse?"

"I've always thought she was all talk and eyeliner." Though now she's got her own life on the line. Who knows what she'll do?

The idea of a desperate wannabe vampire Goth girl is not something I'm happy about. Not even remotely.

"We need to wrap this up quick and get whatever proof Dr. Jonas needs," I say. "If Raven suddenly develops some guts, I don't want anything to happen to Serena."

I will *not* let anything happen to her. No way, no how.

MYTH:	Vampires aren't ticklish.
TRUTH:	Ha, they just don't want to admit it. Bad for the image, you know.

32

George and Serena and I are still discussing—okay, arguing—about the best way to get Raven or Cameron to give up John and Wayne and the whole Carter-Talon thing when we get home. Serena (of course) favors the direct approach, basically just ask Cameron or pound it out of Raven (which, okay, does have some merit). George thinks we can trick it out of Raven or even get her to turn on the Talons if we promise her some kind of amnesty in return (he's way too nice).

Me, I'm really not sure. On the one hand, I don't think Raven really has the guts to go through with killing anyone. Sure, she's a total idiot and she tries to talk a good game, but I think she's a coward at heart. And I really don't think there's any appealing to her better side since I don't think she actually has one.

And as for Cameron? Not that I've known him that long, but

I just can't connect him and the Talons in my head. Like, it just doesn't compute. Is it possible that John and Wayne are the bad guys and Cameron is just caught up in it somehow? Does he necessarily have to be all evil? Or, you know, evil at all? He's always been nice to me.

"You just think he's pretty," Serena says.

I snort. "I wasn't the one batting my eyelashes at him."

George gives us both the eye. "Just how pretty is this guy anyway?"

Uh-oh. We didn't finish our conversation in the car after Raven interrupted us, but I don't want George getting any more jealous than he already is. I can't deal with that, not now, not with everything else going on. "Not *that* pretty," I say. "Nothing compared to you, pretty boy." And I tickle him in his one ticklish spot (right ribs, halfway up, slightly to the back).

He falls to the floor laughing and Serena piles on top of him too, though she doesn't know where his spot is, so he winds up tickling her instead. Since she's ticklish, like, everywhere, soon we're all just gasping for breath. Gets them every time. Tickling is my secret weapon and an excellent distraction technique. And right now I think we can all use a laugh.

Then Dad bursts through the front door like a really large, really angry pack of wild dogs is after him. Or, I guess, more like

295

a pack of pitchfork-wielding, torch-carrying vampire hunters. Mom's high-alert alarm must have gone off (she'd kindly been leaving us to our own devices and hanging out in the kitchen) and she comes running in with a knife like she's going to go all Ginsu on somebody.

"What's going on, Bob?" she says. "What's wrong?"

George and Serena and I struggle to get untangled and stand up. The look on his face is really dreadful. Did somebody actually die-die?

"Dr. Jonas is gone," he says. "Gone."

George gasps. Mom says, "What do you mean, he's gone? Gone how?" Which is exactly what I was going to ask. Dr. Musty is ancient. He's been around for literally eons. What could possibly get the better of him?

"I went by the dig to see if I could help him out since I knew he was going to be out there tonight. When I got there, everything was a shambles. The vault contents were missing, our tools were scattered everywhere, and Dr. Jonas was gone. All I found was this note." He holds up a piece of paper with "Trespassers" scrawled on it in a heavy hand. Really freaky looking handwriting. And is that a splash of blood in the corner? "I checked his house and his office and he's nowhere. I think the Carters took him. Or worse."

Mom stops waving the knife around, which is a good thing. We all kind of stand there for a minute and then Dad says, "I'm going to go after him." Like he's Indiana Jones or Nicolas Cage in those "National" whatever movies.

"Dad," I say, "you're an *accountant.*"

"Not anymore I'm not. I'm a historian now and it's my duty to do what I can to further our mission and find out the truth."

Even Mom is looking at him like he's completely lost it, which he totally has. I don't care if he *is* a historian. Like that's going to make anyone quake in their boots. He's still an accountant at heart. I haven't even seen John or Wayne yet, but I'd bet anything they'd take one look at Dad and laugh until they peed their pants.

"I'm going with you," says George.

"What? Are you both totally off your nut?" I look from one to the other and they both just look determined. Not to mention insane. "Mom!" I say, turning to my one (hopefully) sane relative. "Do something!"

Mom puts the knife down and grabs up her purse and starts digging around inside. "Bob, don't go rushing off like a crazy person just yet. Why don't we call Mortie? I never thought I'd say these words, but maybe he can help."

I have no idea how Uncle Mortie could help. I mean, what's he going to do? Throw lame jokes at the Carters?

ALL THE STUFF THAT SUCKS
(i.e., EVERYTHING)

1. I now live in Nowheretown. In the South. Where people watch cows poop. For entertainment.

2. Some deranged Goth girl wants to kill my best friend so she can join some homicidal maniac vampire group or die herself.

3. A group that may also contain the only person (Cameron) I can really count as a new friend in this tiny town. (Well, vampire friend, anyway. I guess Henny could be counted as a friend. And Grady, kind of.)

4. Said friend being the one who's supposed to be taking me on a not-date for homecoming.

5. While my boyfriend is here, living in the same house. (Which, admittedly, should be a mostly good thing in the middle of a majorly sucky situation, except that he's jealous and not happy with me for having said date but, you know, hey, I'm not exactly happy with him for having dropped off the face of the Earth for months either.)

6. And then Dr. Musty disappears, more than likely because he ticked off John and Wayne Carter, who are more than likely the head homicidal maniacs around.

7. Which makes my dad and my boyfriend both decide to go all commando and go on some kind of misguided rescue mission where they'll probably get killed. Like dead-dead, not just undead.

8. And my mom thinks my crazy uncle Mortie will somehow add to the fun.

MYTH: Vampires can be killed by decapitation.

TRUTH: Uh, duh.

33

Uncle Mortie tells Mom to tie Dad to the couch until he gets here and not to let anyone do anything crazy. Which is craziness in itself. Uncle Mortie's usually the one doing something off the wall, not my dad. I mean, *really*. It's *Dad*. Somewhere, there are demons ice-skating in hell right now.

While waiting on Uncle Mortie, Dad and George spend the time huddled together discussing different approaches with Mom listening in and adding her two cents. Everything they are coming up with sounds completely insane to me:

(a) a full-frontal attack on the main Carter house (Lowell's) where John and Wayne are probably keeping Dr. Musty (provided he's still alive—undead . . . whatever);

(b) a sneak attack in the dead of night (like that makes a difference, I mean, hello, we're all vampires here); or

(c) trying to round up the various Carter family members they've been talking to who weren't all that happy with John and Wayne, and forming some kind of little mini-vampire militia.

In other words, total bloodbath all the way around. I just hope Uncle Mortie actually does talk some sense into Dad. And George. I don't want to lose both my dad and my boyfriend in one night and especially not over some ancient nosy vampire geezer. Let's be honest. He really *was* trespassing. I'm just glad Dad wasn't there when they came. Not that I'm happy Dr. Musty was. I'm just saying.

I pour myself a glass of Special K and go looking for some sanity. I find Serena pecking away on my laptop with one hand and twirling and retwirling a hunk of her hair with another. Uh-oh. That's not good. I haven't seen her this stressed since the PSATs.

"So, guess you didn't know what you were getting into when you came, huh?"

She looks up, startled. I forget sometimes that she's still human and can't hear me come up behind her. "Yeah. Like I said, you're all dramarama now."

I guess I can't argue. We've got like a vampire soap opera going on here. That crazy Harriet Melman author lady Uncle Mortie is pals with should write a book about us, but we're probably still too tame for her.

I perch on my desk next to the laptop and take a sip of my Special K. "Are you okay?"

"Yeah, I'm fine."

"Are you sure about that?" I reach over and untwist her hair. She drops her hand. Guilty.

"No." She puts her hand up to her hair again and then grabs my hand instead. "Honestly, Min, this is all kind of freaking me out. Some girl I don't even really know wants to kill me, that weird vampire guy your dad works for might have a stake through his heart or something, I'm supposed to be making a list of reasons to turn for class, and every time I see you drinking blood it makes me gag."

"Oh," I stare down at the glass. "Sorry. I can drink this in the kitchen. I didn't even think about it." I guess the whole blood thing is starting to seem normal to me after all. I stick the glass behind a picture. (It's the one of the four of us at prom. I'm sure the Josh-erator would have something to say about me having that pic out front and center, but he's not here, is he?)

"It's okay," she says. "You go ahead. I guess I need to get used to it." She grabs the glass using as few fingers as possible and hands it back to me. She looks positively green.

I take the glass but set it back behind the picture again.

"I'll drink it later. Don't worry about it, okay?" I need to take her mind off the red stuff before she gets sick. "So, what were you up to? You looked awfully intense when I came in."

She looks a little guilty. "I was just e-mailing Nathan."

I almost say "it's about time," but then I remember I probably wasn't supposed to have seen any of the bazillion messages she had from him. So I just say, "Good." Then my big mouth decides to take over anyway. "Do you love him? 'Cause it sure seems like he loves you."

She either doesn't notice my slip up or figures I'm just intuitive. As if. "I don't know. I think so. Maybe." Then she gets a couple of tears in her eyes, which is serious business. "Yeah, I think I do."

I give her a big hug and don't say anything else. Honestly, I'm not even sure what I should say anyway. Where's Hallmark when you need them? Whoever they are.

"Do you think Nathan would turn?" she says into my shoulder.

"Um," I say. I totally can't see Golden Boy doing the blood-sucking vampire thing. I could be wrong, but it's really hard to picture. That's like Uncle Mortie being a swimsuit model. Of course, I never thought Dad would go all Indiana Jones on me either, so hey.

I rest my chin on top her head and sigh. If Serena turns just because she thinks I want her to, I'd hate myself for the rest of my (undead) life. And that'd be a very, very long time.

"Just remember," I say, "you have to do what's right for you. Don't turn for anyone else. Not even me. Or Nathan. You have to make the right choice for you. I mean, not that I don't want you to be a bloodsucking freak with me for eternity"—ooops, maybe I should have left the blood part out—"but if it's not right for you, I'd understand. I just want you to be happy." There. Now I've gone all after-school special. It really hurts me to say it, but it's true.

"I think I understand now why you had to think about it so hard. I didn't get it before."

"It's not a little decision. We're talking about the rest of your life. Or death." Whatever. Maybe I should see if Mom can talk to her. She's better at this stuff than I am. And hey, she is her sponsor.

My cell phone rings. It can pretty much only be one person that I can think of, since everyone else who even knows my number is currently in the house with me or probably asleep.

"Cameron?"

"Mina," he whispers, "is your dad there?"

"Yes." Wait. Should I have told him that? "Why are you whispering?"

"I can't explain now, but tell him not to go to work tomorrow."

"Cameron—"

There's some kind of muffled noise on the other end of the phone. "I have to go." Then he hangs up.

"What did he say?" asks Serena, and I hear Mom ask the same thing from the other room. No privacy at all, I tell you. I'm surprised Mom didn't butt in with some advice for Serena.

"He said Dad should stay home tomorrow." I guess that confirms that the Carters do have Dr. Jonas. Or they did something to him. Once again, glad Dad wasn't there at the wrong time. Or the wrong place. I can't believe Cameron's wrapped up in all this madness.

"Girls, come back in the living room," says Mom. "Mortie's almost here." Wow, Mom's hearing must be even better than mine. I can hear Uncle Mortie's big old boat of a car. (Can you believe he bought another huge Cadillac? At least this one isn't yellow and it *is* a convertible. That's a step in the right direction.) It's barreling down the street (the phrase "bat out of hell" comes to mind), but I didn't hear it before she said anything. I wonder if you can train your ears to get better?

We join the rest of the party in the living room and wait for Uncle Mortie to come in. Dad looks tense. George's eyes are so dark blue they are almost purple again, which is not a good sign. Serena just looks pale and worried. I probably look the same, except probably even paler.

Uncle Mortie's car screeches to a halt outside the house and literally, like two seconds later he bursts in through the door.

305

Wearing a purple velvet smoking jacket. The New Orleans vibe must be taking over (at least there's no boa).

"Okay," he says, "I'm here. Let the butt kicking commence!"

And so much for him being the voice of reason.

George, Dad, and Mom all start talking at once.

"Wait!" I yell. "Are you guys absolutely crazy? There are, like, a bazillion Carters. If they've got Dr. Jonas, he's probably at Lowell's where everyone has been hanging out. Not to mention John and Wayne. There's no way the three of you could go in there, fangs blaring, and not get totally creamed."

"Hey—" says Uncle Mortie.

"Oh, come on, you guys! They, like, kill people for breakfast! Literally! I'm sure they'd have no problem sticking a stake in you or testing out some of their decapitation booby traps. And Dad, you don't even like to kill spiders!"

"They squish," says Dad kinda lamely. Case in point.

"So what's your suggestion?" asks Mom.

"Can we at least wait until I talk to Cameron and try and find out what's going on?"

"Who's Cameron?" asks Uncle Mortie.

"Some pretty-boy vampire Mina's supposedly not dating," says George, looking right at me. "Who's secretly a Black Talon along with the rest of them."

"We don't know that!" I shout. "Not for sure . . ."

"O-o-kay, and we should trust him why?" asks Uncle Mortie.

I glare at George. "He *did* call to warn us. Unless the Carters saw Dad go by the site earlier, they don't even know that we know about Dr. Jonas, right? If Cameron hadn't called, Dad could have just shown up for work tomorrow and been ambushed with no clue." That's got to be a check mark on the plus side, right?

Mom nods. "That's true." At least I've got their attention.

"And he was whispering and trying to be quiet, so he was hiding the fact that he was calling me to give the warning. Doesn't that sound like he's on our side? At least partially?"

"He seemed really nice when I met him," adds Serena, which doesn't exactly help my case, since she looks starstruck just thinking about him.

"Just let me talk to Cameron and make sure that Dr. Jonas is still alive or undead or whatever and you're not going all commando for no reason. I'll see him in the morning at school. First thing. It's already after 2:00 a.m. A few more hours won't hurt, right?"

Everyone finally agrees and Serena sacks out, looking like death warmed over. I doubt if she'll even make it to school tomorrow. I think the decapitation talk really finished her off.

The rest of us spend the remaining hours until school listening to Uncle Mortie concoct one insane scheme after another. I just keep staring at the clock and worrying. Why couldn't Dad have just stayed an accountant? It's not like tax time is *that* bad. And it only comes once a year. And nobody ever wants to kill you.

Crazy historians.

MYTH:	Vampires are schemers by nature.
TRUTH:	Uncle Mortie especially, but usually it has to do with trying to get a date.

34

Did I mention that today happens to be Friday? Homecoming day? When I get to school, there's a cow wandering around out front in a makeshift pen (Baby, presumably), and everyone walking by is feeding her (him? it?) something. I hope it's actual cow food and not anything from the cafeteria. The decorating fairies (Henny and company, I'm sure) have attacked and the whole school is decked out in blue and gold streamers and balloons. They take homecoming very seriously here.

Homeroom is basically a lost cause. Serena managed to wake up for school, but she nearly falls asleep again as everyone around us talks about nothing except the homecoming game (which "of course" we'll win), Baby (who has apparently favored the southern goal post area in past years), and the Homecoming Court (Grady is a given, naturally).

Mrs. Hebert passes out the ballots to us for voting on king and queen. I hadn't paid much attention to the whole thing at all this year (I've had bigger things to think about, *hello*), so I just write in Grady (might as well) and put Henny down for the heck of it. There's no way I'm voting for Kacie, even if she is the odds-on favorite.

First period has been replaced with a pep rally. They might as well have canceled the whole day instead of just half of it since everyone is in some kind of football coma. I finally see my chance to grab Cameron and talk to him as we all file in to the gym. He's easy enough to spot—just look where all the other girls are staring and it's either him or Grady. And since Grady is with the rest of the class officers in the center of the gym, that makes it even easier.

Serena stumbles after me and we go sit by Cameron, who is (luckily for me) in the very top row of the very far left corner of the gym. Even the girls who would love to drool all over him are into the pep rally enough to be closer to the court, so that leaves just us.

"So you want to give me some clue as to what's up?" I ask.

"Your Dad didn't go to work, right?" Cameron looks a little anxious.

"Nope," I say. "And he'd really like to know why. And why Dr. Jonas wasn't there when he called to say he wasn't coming." I'm glad I was practicing my whole new agey deep breathing stuff. I'm pretty sure he won't be able to tell I'm lying. Of course, it's harder to tell with vampires anyway. With humans you can mostly tell by the pulse. And the sweat. Luckily Serena's too tired to be giving much of anything away.

"I really shouldn't say anything. I shouldn't have called you to begin with."

"But you did," I point out. "I know Dad and Dr. Jonas were researching the Carters and digging up some old stuff. I'm guessing they dug up something they weren't supposed to?"

He looks around all nervous. I don't see Lowell with the rest of the teachers, but even if he was down there I don't think he could hear us over the roar of "Go, Cougars!" and the stomping and clapping. Cameron finally leans forward to whisper in my ear. "They took Dr. Jonas to try and talk some sense into him."

"Took him? Talk some sense into him? Like what kind of sense? What kind of talking?"

Cameron looks really unhappy. I feel a little guilty, but I shift closer to make sure that stupid itchy wire I'm wearing again actually picks up what he's saying so it'll be all official if he does give some incriminating evidence. Serena leans forward too, but winds up yawning. I swear, even life or death situations aren't enough to keep her awake when she hasn't had enough sleep.

311

"Lowell is 'talking' to him."

Oh. Lowell. That does explain why he's not at the pep rally. I bet I know what that means too. Lowell's not exactly a stunning conversationalist. He's more the mentalist. He's probably using some Jedi mind tricks on Dr. Musty. I hope the old geezer's brain can hold out. Otherwise, the gig is up. Suddenly, the wire feels really heavy *and* itchy. And obvious. I resist the urge to scratch it or check to make sure it's not poking out somewhere.

"What kind of 'talking' are we talking about here?" Can I get him to actually come out and say it? He just looks at me. Hard. "Right," I say. "So you're worried he might want to 'talk' to my dad too?"

"Yes. I thought if he didn't go to work today maybe things would blow over. And it's homecoming, so everyone will be at the game tonight."

"They're all going to the game?" Even the vampires are into football around here, I guess.

"Yes, even John and Wayne. Well, everyone but Lowell. And Ernie. He never closes the bar. Look, if you can just get your dad to stay out of sight for the next day or two, I think everything will be fine."

Huh. Fine for everybody but Dr. Musty. Doesn't he see the problem with that? But I just say, "I'll do my best." Serena picks that moment to let out a ladylike little snore and tilts forward even farther. I grab her before she goes rolling down the bleachers.

"Maybe I better get her home," I say. "She didn't get much sleep last night. Too, uh, excited about homecoming."

He looks a little curious, but just nods. "I'll pick you up before the game? Oh, I forgot to ask what color your dress is. I'm out of practice, I guess."

Crapola. Our not-date date. "Um, green." I guess I can wear my Ella Moss dress.

I hope George won't be mad about the neckline.

I give the school nurse the same excuse about Serena and she totally buys it. I guess everyone really is into football and homecoming here. Kinda weird. I don't think I even attended a single game at my old school. Not a big deal anyway, since everyone gets a half day today in honor of the big game, so we're not going to be missing much. Or maybe I should say Big Game, since you can practically hear the capital letters anytime someone brings it up.

We get home and I put Serena to bed since we'll need her awake later tonight. She goes without a grumble and conks out immediately. I do miss that.

"So," says Uncle Mortie. "We listened, but what's the deal with all the 'talking' going on? Who's this Lowell character?"

Oh yeah. I guess all that probably didn't make sense to them. I never did tell Mom and Dad about my side lessons with Cameron. I'm sure Mom thought I've just been practicing my shape-shifting. Which I have been. Just not with Cameron.

"Lowell is another Carter. He's the Shop teacher at school and he's like the Carters' resident brain shrink, kinda like one of the Vampire Goon Squad. So I'm thinking they're either trying to wipe Dr. Jonas's mind or trying to pick his brain to find out exactly what he knows and then trying to wipe it."

Dad jumps up. "No! We can't allow that! Think of all the vital information that could be lost! We have to figure out where they're holding him and get him out of there!"

Okay, Dad, dial it back. Wild historian on the loose.

"He must be at Ernie's Blood Bar," I say. "I thought you guys were listening? Lowell, like, practically lives in the back room there."

"Then let's go!" At least he didn't yell "To the Batmobile!"

"Dad, it's probably packed in there right now. It's homecoming and nobody's working. It's like a Cartville holiday. They're all getting ready to tailgate. And they're on the lookout for you. If you go rushing in there, they're just going to turn your brain to mush."

"Didn't that boy say that they were all going to be at the game tonight?" asks Mom.

"Yes. Everybody but Lowell and Ernie." I'm still having trouble fitting my head around the idea of a bunch of vampires sitting around watching a high-school football game. Especially if they really are a bunch of blackhearted Black Talons. But there's no accounting for taste.

"Seems like that would be a good time to go on the attack," says George. "Since Mina has to go to homecoming anyway on her hot date"—I frown at him—"she can wear a wire and try to get more evidence on tape. And keep an eye on the rest of the clan to make sure that they stay put at the game. Then we can go to Ernie's. The four of us should be able to do some damage, especially if they aren't expecting us." Well, four against two is definitely better than four against a whole bar full. But I still don't like it.

"I've got an even better idea," says Uncle Mortie. I resist the urge to groan. "Ditto on Mina's mission. It just makes sense. But rather than us all just rushing in there like a suicide squad, how about I go in first and get in position? They've never seen me, so they'll have no idea what I'm there for."

"Won't they wonder why you're there and not out at the homecoming game with everyone else?" I ask. "Or why a total stranger just shows up out of nowhere? This isn't exactly Grand Central Station."

"I'll be a traveling salesman!"

Well, that's not a stretch anyway. He used to be one. And it's believable. Like I've said before, Uncle Mortie *looks* like a traveling salesman. But do they even have *vampire* traveling salesmen? "Selling what, exactly?"

"You said it was a blood bar, right? I'll tell them I'm from Varney Supply Company. It just so happens I've got a brand new Blood-Tender 4000 in the trunk of my car. I picked it up for The Cask and Casket. I can pretend to demo it for him. Then once I've got him distracted I can say a code word or something and the rest of you can come busting in."

Hey, I think that might actually work. Even if it is Uncle Mortie's idea.

MYTH:	You can't take a vampire by surprise.
TRUTH:	I've been surprised plenty of times. Maybe it's just me.

35

Serena wakes up around three and we spend about two hours getting ready. It's a little weird getting dressed for a date while your boyfriend is sitting there giving you advice about what to wear (he seems okay with the green Ella Moss dress) and how your makeup looks (less eye shadow, he says, since I don't want to give anyone the wrong idea). I guess he's being a good sport about it though. Kind of. The comment about the eye shadow was a little much.

Of course, George hasn't actually *seen* Cameron yet.

Serena is wearing an old prom dress that she stole from her mom. Why she even brought it with her, I don't know, but it's perfect—for her eighties look, anyway. It's kind of a Molly Ringwald-style pale pink thing with flounces. (NOT, thankfully, like the dress Molly actually wore to the prom in *Pretty in Pink*, since that was just god-awful ugly. You know, that reminds me.

317

I really need to find some new movies for Serena to obsess over.) It's actually kind of cute and the coloring suits her. If Nathan were here, I bet he'd be going ape. I think Serena's thinking the same thing, since I catch her gazing at her keychain. (It's a picture from prom of the four of us.)

Everybody else has been getting ready too, but in the opposite way. I'm not entirely sure what their plan is, other than to rush in on Uncle Mortie's signal. (He's going to yell out "Bottom's up!") The rest of the plan apparently involves a baseball bat, a pitchfork, some steak knives, and some bungee cords. Our house didn't provide much of an arsenal for the intrepid ambush crew. I don't care what Dad thinks, he's no Indiana Jones. Even if he had a leather whip, he wouldn't know what to do with it.

Cameron knocks on the door right at five and George goes to open it before I can get there. He holds the door for a minute, just staring at Cameron. Actually, you could probably say he's giving him the evil eye.

I was afraid of that.

"Hello," George finally says.

"Hi," says Cameron. "You must be Dr. Jonas's intern? I'm Cameron. I'm here to pick up Mina for homecoming." He holds out his hand. After a long pause, George shakes it. Serena gives me a look.

Yeah. We'd better get out of here. The sooner the better.

"Hey, Cameron," I say, coming up behind George and giving him a light pat on the back that I hope he interprets as an apology and not a get-out-of-the-way-of-my-date. "I see you've met George. Serena's coming along with us. Hope you don't mind! She's my unofficial chaperone." I try to laugh, but it comes out kind of giggly and high pitched, so I stop.

"Sure, that's fine," he says. Then he does a double take that I wish he'd kept to a single. "Wow, Mina, you look amazing. Green really suits you." George clears his throat and I just look helplessly at Serena. Do I say thank you? Ignore it? What's the least likely to peeve George scenario here? Why does Cameron have to be so seriously smoking hot?

"What about me?" Serena says, and sashays over and then does a twirl and insinuates herself right in between Cameron and George. "How do *I* look?" God bless the girl.

Cameron steps up to the occasion with a big smile. "Just lovely. A vision in pink," he says. Then he holds out his arms, elbows cocked, one for each of us. Serena slips her arm through his right away. I hover for a moment and then do the same on the other side.

"Bye, Mom, Dad, everybody," I call out. "Good"—yikes, I guess I better not say luck — "um, night! Have a good night! I've got my cell if you need me." George steps back out of the way and crosses his arms over his chest.

Well. All in all, that was just really, really uncomfortable.

It takes all of two minutes to get from my house to the school in Cameron's car, but I'm still glad we didn't walk it. High heels are killer, no matter how high your pain threshold is. Baby is still out front and people are still walking by and petting her and feeding her things. The whole campus is absolutely packed. I think everyone in town (other than Lowell and Ernie and my family) must be here. Actually, probably everyone from the entire parish (which sounds kind of like a religious thing, but it is what Louisianans call counties).

It feels kind of bizarre to be all dressed up for a football game, but most kids are. I'm guessing the ones who aren't either go home to change or just skip the dance entirely to watch Baby.

Cameron leads us toward a section of bleachers on the far right. I scan the people around there and it's vampireless. "We're not sitting with your family?" I ask. Not that I particularly want to, exactly, but I am supposed to be keeping an eye on them.

He looks at me kind of weird. "No, they're up there." He points at the top of the middle section of the bleachers. "Did you *want* to sit with them?"

They look pretty intimidating. There must be about thirty of them up there, maybe more. Probably three or four parishes worth of Carters. You can tell where the vampires end and the people begin too, since there's like a demilitarized no-man's zone around them. I think even if people don't know that you're a vampire, they still know that something is up, especially if you get a bunch of them together in a group. Especially when they're all stony faced, pale, and talking quietly among themselves instead of laughing and shouting and throwing popcorn like the people around them.

"No," I say. "We're fine here." I can actually see them pretty well from down here. Plus they creep me out less from farther away.

"Great. I'm going to get us some sweet tea. Do either of you want anything else?"

Serena opts for some popcorn and a hotdog (she's an eater when she's nervous), but I just shake my head no. As soon as he leaves, I start scanning the Carter crowd to see what I can learn.

John and Wayne would be obvious even if they weren't located smack dab in the middle of the clan. Even sitting down I can tell that they're way beyond normal tall and they almost look like twins, not just brothers. They both have wavy brown hair with these really shockingly electric blue eyes. One has a small goatee, which gives him a really devilish look that I suspect is on purpose. And they've got presence. I now finally understand what my drama

321

teacher back in ninth grade was trying to teach me. Whatever presence is, the Carter brothers have it. Like animal magnetism. I bet that's where Cameron gets that whole manly-man smell from, which reminds me that I need to try and not breathe tonight. Like, at all. Seriously, I need to get over that.

Surprise (not): all the Carters immediately surrounding the two brothers are female, though most of the clan (male and female) aren't stunning beauties or anything. John and Wayne are definitely the stars of the show. A couple of the guys in the second tier of Carters look more or less like Uncle Mortie (paunchy, kinda balding, and very questionable fashion sense—I don't care if we are in the South, can they please ditch the overalls?). One guy actually has muttonchops, and I get the feeling they're probably original. He just looks old. I mean, when did muttonchops go out of style? The Dark Ages? Unless you're in a band, I guess.

"Uh-oh," says Serena.

"What?" Does she see something I don't see? I count the Carters up and all of them are still there from my last count. Thirty-three total.

"I think it's that girl who hates you."

"Raven? What? Where?" I turn around but it isn't Angry Goth Girl headed at us. It's Angry Skinny White Chick. In the tightest purple sheath dress I've ever seen in my entire life. If Kacie even ate a grape, I think you could watch it travel all the way down to her stomach. It's almost hypnotic, watching her bony hips twitch toward us as she pushes her way through the crowd.

"So you did decide to come to homecoming after all. I'm so glad. It took a lot of nerve to show up after our little incident," she says sweetly, hands on those dangerous hips. Our little incident? Huh. I suppose you could call almost running me and Serena over an incident.

"*I've* got a lot of nerve?" I say. "At least people can't tell whether or not I've had my appendix out." That makes Serena snort, which probably doesn't help my case with Kacie. But seriously, I've got bigger fish to fry than some spoiled anorexic wannabe Homecoming Queen.

Kacie, perhaps wisely, just chooses to ignore the comment. She smiles a big crocodile smile at me. I can see all of her teeth. "Grady's here with *me*," she practically coos.

"I'm happy for you," I say. "You make a lovely couple." That's a lie, but hey. Half the couple is lovely anyway. I wonder if she had to club Grady over the head or what?

"Thank *you*. I suppose you're here with Cameron? Where *is* he and his hot self anyway?" She bats her eyelashes at me a few times like we're just big buddies discussing our hot dates. Geez, she's gotta be kidding me. If all it took to get her off my back was to get Grady to date her, I'd have been working on him even harder. Serena's blinking at me like an owl. I feel kind of the same way.

"Um, he's getting us some drinks." I wave over toward the concessions. "I'm sure he'll be back in a minute if you want to talk to him yourself."

"That's not necessary. Oh look," she says, barely glancing over her shoulder. "I think they're counting the homecoming ballots now. I'm just gonna go check on that and see how things are going." She turns to leave and then looks back over her shoulder. "Y'all have a lovely time tonight, okay? I'm sure you will. I *know* I will." She laughs her shrill little laugh. Gah. That just gave me goose bumps.

"Um, thanks," I say. "You too." I have no idea what else to say.

She stumbles a few steps in her too-high stripper heels but keeps walking.

I think the world just shifted somewhere or maybe those ice-skating demons are building igloos now. I resist the urge to pinch myself.

"That was weird. Isn't she the one who almost ran us over?" Serena raises her eyebrows at me and I just shrug. I guess all you gotta do is give a Southern girl what she wants and she's all sweetness and light.

I look to see whether Cameron is on his way back from the concession booth yet. He's still in line, but what I do see makes my stomach clench. There's Raven, just, like, fifteen feet away from us, watching Kacie walk away with great interest. I can't believe I let the skinny snot distract me like that. What if Raven had just kept coming instead of stopping to listen?

I step forward in front of Serena, but Raven just waves at me, turns around, and leaves. Man, I need, like, three sets of eyes. One set to watch out for Raven, one for anymore weirdness from Kacie, and one set for the Carter Clan. Or maybe I just need a swivel.

"Great people you've met here," Serena says.

"Other than Kacie, they aren't actually that bad. Most of them, anyway. If you take away the anorexic chicks who usually want to kill me but now apparently just want me to be happy, and the bloodthirsty maniac vampires who want to do away with my dad, the rest of the town isn't that bad. Really. And you brought the homicidal Goth girl with you, don't forget."

"I don't think you can blame that one on me," says Serena. "After all, she only wants to kill me because of you."

I guess she has a point there. *Sigh.* It is all my fault.

Wait, you know what? I blame it all on the Northwest Regional Vampire Council. If it weren't for them, I'd never have even met Raven and we definitely wouldn't be sitting here in Podunk

Cartville trying to keep from getting killed. Well, not me, but Serena. But still. Definitely The Council's fault. Along with just about every sucktastic thing in my life.

Cameron hands Serena her popcorn and hot dog and passes drinks around when he gets back. The game finally really gets going and we sit and watch. Well, Cameron watches (I guess some things all guys are into) and Serena eats and I mostly hope that Cameron doesn't notice that I'm spending more time rotating back and forth trying to keep an eye on all my enemies. Luckily, the Carters all seem as into the game as the rest of the crowd and haven't moved (other than one older guy dressed head to toe in the school colors, and who has been jumping up and down and screaming whenever the ref rules against the home team). I've lost sight of both Kacie and Raven since they both disappeared back behind the bleachers somewhere. Right about now X-ray vision would come in really handy.

I send George a quick text saying all is well, but don't get a response back. I hope that's a good thing. I'm trying to remember all our James Bond codes, like

a) "cc!" if the Carters start leaving en masse,

b) "gga" for "Goth girl attack" if Raven goes after us,

c) "911" if we need help (which I'm determined not to send since they need all the help they can get as it is)

d) "gme ovr" for, obviously, when the homecoming game is finished, and

e) "hme" for when we're home safe.

Too bad we don't have better spy stuff. Though I guess the wire kind of counts as a spy gadget, just not a very cool one. It's actually driving me crazy since they had to tape it down my side and stick the bulky part in the side of my underwear because of how the neckline of my dress goes. And I thought it was annoying before! I don't have much choice though, since I didn't have any other dresses that would work. I wasn't about to wear Serena's mom's old prom dress, even if it is more full coverage. You have to draw the line somewhere.

"It's halftime," says Cameron, making me jump and almost drop my phone. "I'm sure there'll be a mad rush for the concessions and bathrooms, so if you need anything or have to go, now might be a good time."

"Thanks, I'm good," Serena and I both say at the same time, then laugh. Some things never change. We don't even bother saying "jinx" anymore.

"Actually, Serena, I was wondering if you might do me a favor? I'd really like a word with Mina alone. Could I talk you into getting us all some more popcorn?" He pulls some money out of his pocket.

"Um," Serena says, looking at me. Crapola. What do we say that doesn't sound suspicious? I really don't want to be split up from her at all tonight if I can help it. Though he knows about Raven. Maybe I can just go with a somewhat truth?

"Cameron," I say, "I—"

"Mina!" shouts Henny, practically flying down the aisle at me in an unfortunately bell-shaped bright yellow dress. "Didn't you hear your name on the loudspeaker? Girl, get down on the field!"

"Uh, what?" I guess I've been getting better at focusing my hearing since I have absolutely no clue whatsoever what she's talking about. I didn't hear my name until she shouted at me. Henny's voice could wake the dead though, especially when she puts some volume behind it.

She grabs my arm and starts pulling me to the field. "For Homecoming Court! You're one of the finalists! Get down there!" All the people in our section of the bleachers start chanting, "Mina, Mina, Mina!"

Oh.

Holy.

Crap.

MYTH:	Vampires are the rulers of the undead.
TRUTH:	And Cartville High, apparently.

36

Henny pulls me all the way down to the field where everyone else they called (including Kacie and Grady and even Lonnie Pratt in his football uniform) is already assembled. I look up to find Serena and Cameron in the crowd. Serena just shrugs her shoulders at me and gives me a thumbs-up.

I didn't even know I was on the ballot. All I remember from when I voted this morning were just fill-in-the-blank spots.

I definitely did NOT write my name in.

I go stand with the rest of the girls, as far away from Kacie as I can get. There are actually ten each of us (girls and guys) and I don't ever remember a Homecoming Court being that big, so with any luck I'll just be some kind of honorary whatever-they-call-it and be on my way after giving a couple of Queen Mum-style waves at the crowd.

Mr. Fleming, the principal, makes a few jokes and some yadda yadda about how pretty we all look. Then he starts calling out names for the Court.

"Shanna Harvey and Roscoe Blevins!" A tall girl in a red halter dress and three-inch heels totters forward, along with a short guy in an actual top hat and tails. Maybe he's compensating or something.

"Lala Louise Blanton and Grady Broussard!" Try saying that three times fast. Lala gives Kacie a high five as she walks by, and Grady winks in our general direction. I'm not sure if he meant it for me or for Kacie.

"Kacie Kinsley and Lucas Runnels!" Well, at least she was picked. If the smile on her face gets even bigger, she'll have to reach around to the backside of her head to brush her teeth.

"Mina Smith and Lonnie Pratt!" Crap. I don't even look at Kacie as I step forward. At least I can put big, hulking Lonnie in between me and Kacie. I doubt if her newfound goodwill extends to standing next to her.

"And now, for the moment we've all been waiting for . . ." Mr. Fleming makes a big show of waving the envelope around in the air. I wish he'd just get on with it so I can go back to my seat. We all know Grady's going to be king and Kacie's going to be queen. That's just the way of the world.

"The Homecoming King is . . . Grady Broussard!" Yep, that's pretty much what I expected. I'm doing my dutiful clapping when I see Cameron get up and walk off, leaving Serena sitting there by herself. What gives? I give an underhand wave to try and get her attention, but she just shrugs and gives me another thumbs-up. A thumbs-down would have been more appropriate.

"And while I have everyone's attention," continues Mr. Fleming, "I just want to say thank you to everyone for coming out tonight and supporting the home team!" Everyone in the stands erupts into cheers. Everyone but a certain black-dressed girl who has reappeared in the crowd. Raven really does stick out here, like a little black hole.

I go to reach for my cell phone to text Serena (she borrowed Dad's phone) and realize I'd left it up in the stands when Henny dragged me away. Crapola. I am one sucky spy.

Mr. Fleming finishes his happy dance. "But I won't make you wait any longer. This year's Homecoming Queen is . . ."

I start to leave undercover of Kacie's big announcement. I doubt if anyone will notice me making my getaway while she's crowned. Finally, something useful comes out of Ms. Hot Pants.

". . . Mina Smith!" Mr. Fleming grabs my hand to shake it as I start to walk by. "Looks like she knew it was coming too! Congratulations, Mina!"

331

I can see Serena clapping like a madwoman and jumping up and down while Raven climbs the stands toward her. Cameron is nowhere in sight. I'm trying to dodge around Mr. Fleming when he whips out a cape from somewhere and flings it around my neck.

"Hold still," he says. "We've still got to put the tiara on you." I stop struggling. This will probably go faster if I don't fight it. But it's driving me nuts.

Serena is still clapping and doing her ear-piercing wolf whistle thing (I've never learned how to do that) and is just totally oblivious to Raven, who has now made it halfway across the section.

"There," says Mr. Fleming. "Don't you look pretty now. Goodness you're strong!"

"Sorry," I say. I didn't mean to throw him off like that. Then Grady comes up and does his standard arm thing and I try to push him off. Gently.

"Whoa," he says. "Smile for the camera, my queen!"

Mr. Benoit starts snapping pictures. Gah! This is a disaster all the way around! I keep ducking my head or looking to the side. The Council is going to kill me.

"Now let's get some pictures of just the girls!" Grady steps back and Shanna, Lala, and Kacie step up. Kacie grabs my elbow and tries to pinch me with her fingernails, but only succeeds in breaking one of them instead. Her fingernail, that is. Not her finger.

Though if she'd pinched any harder, she might have broken that too. Didn't hurt me at all, but I'm sure she's feeling some pain now.

"Ouch, you—"

"Kacie!" says Lala. "Don't forget!" Forget what? Not to swear in front of Mr. Benoit?

Kacie literally growls but then plants a big smile on her face right before the flash goes off. "I saw your name on a bunch of the ballots," she says to me out of the side of her mouth, "so I knew you were going to be down here."

"Sorry," I say for lack of anything better. With all the flashes going off, I can't see Serena anymore. My eyes are killing me and I'm seeing stars. If Serena can just stay where people can see her, maybe Raven won't try anything. Or maybe Cameron will come back, unless he was in on it. Please, please don't tell me he has been in on it the whole time.

"I didn't think you'd actually *win*, but there's no accounting for taste." I could point out that she's part of the Homecoming Court too, but I don't. I'm not surprised that all of the sugar and sparkles are gone from her tone.

"A perfect opportunity, according to that girl."

"What girl? What opportunity?" I whip my head around to look at Kacie. She's got an evil grin on. Mr. Benoit keeps snapping away. "What are you talking about?"

"I even had Stacey make up a story to get Cameron out of the way. Something about his car and Baby, I believe. She's pretty inventive, don't you think? And boys do love their cars."

"Kacie," I say, and stick my face right in hers so she knows I mean business. "Spit it out. What are you talking about?"

But it's like she's oblivious to me or maybe she can't stop smiling whenever there's a camera turned her way. "What was it she said, Lala? That she'd take care of everything? I just had to make sure you were distracted for long enough for her to do what she needed to do? Wasn't that it?" She taps her wrist, even though she's not wearing a watch. "And oh look! I think it's just about been long enough!"

I push Kacie out of the way and she falls down on the field, taking the rest of the girls with her. I start scanning the stands as I run. I don't see Raven anywhere now but Serena isn't where I left her either.

"But the pictures!" Mr. Benoit yells after me, and Kacie is laughing like a rabid hyena, even though she's flat on her back on the fifty-yard line. I almost twist my ankle on the turf grass—stupid heels!—so I kick off my shoes and keep going. The cape flies off and lands on a water boy.

My one big mission—keep Serena safe—and I've failed. And I mean Epic Fail.

They can't have gotten too far. Raven's no vampire, not yet (and hopefully never, if I have anything to do with it). And Serena can be a real scrapper, so that should have slowed them down even more. I would bet that Raven's got at least one black eye by now.

Everyone around me is screaming (mostly about me knocking over Kacie) or laughing (ditto) or chanting (for the game to start up again) but I try to focus as much as I can to see if I can hear either Serena or Raven anywhere.

I head under the bleachers first as the most likely place for Raven to have taken Serena. It's darker under there and more or less secluded, but I don't see them or hear anything either. Where could they have gone? I start making my way back towards the school. Raven can't know the area really well and she needs some kind of cover, so it seems like the most logical next choice. Not that I think logic is her strong suit, but I've gotta do something.

I'm halfway to the main school building when I hear Cameron calling my name. He's running toward me from the parking lot.

"Mina, where are you going? What happened to your shoes? What's going on?"

I grab his hand and keep running. "Raven has Serena. She talked Kacie into distracting me long enough to get her out of

335

the stands. I don't know where they are. They aren't under the bleachers. I need help. Can you help me?" He doesn't know me very well or he'd know just how desperate I am. I don't like asking for help from anybody.

He pulls me to a stop right outside the building. "Hold on," he says. "Whoa. That girl is completely insane. I told her you were off-limits."

Off-limits? I shrug off his hand. "Well, she obviously didn't listen. Look, we don't have time to talk, we've got to find them." I yank open the door but he holds me back.

"Mina, you're the one she really has it in for. She's liable to fly off the handle as soon as she sees you. You can't just go running in there like that. It's the worst thing you could do."

He's got a point. "I can't not do anything!"

"Just let me go in and see if I can find them first. She knows I'm a Carter. Maybe she'll listen this time. I'll tell her that her application will be denied or something."

Oh man. Is my wire working? "Her application"? Did he really just confirm that he's a Black Talon? I can't believe it.

"Mina, I—" He runs his hand through his hair, leaving it sticking up in weird places like a mad scientist's. Or maybe a crazy homicidal maniac. Then he pulls the door out of my hand. "I wanted to talk to you earlier. Look, I'll find them. Just wait here, okay?" And then he's gone through the door. It swings shut behind him with a creak and a bang.

Crap, crap, crap, crap! What if he's going to help Raven? If he really is a Talon, I can't trust him. Not with Serena's life. What do I do?

Then I see one of the Carter Clan girly girls making her way to the bathrooms.

Cameron's right about one thing: I can't go after Raven looking like me. But what if I *wasn't* me? I take a good look at the Carter girl (long straight brown hair, way too pouty lips, slim nose, and hips to die for) then slip inside the door. Cameron is nowhere to be seen. I use a trophy case to help myself concentrate on the shift. It takes a moment to calm myself enough to do it but I manage to shift into a reasonable copy of the Carter girl. Yes, finally, some homework that paid off!

I start down the hall when I catch another glimpse of myself in the full glass door of Administration. Crap again. Raven saw me in my dress earlier. It may not occur to her right away, but she's not totally stupid. Even with a new face, I can't go around in the same old clothes. I also can't go naked.

Luckily the gym and the locker rooms are on this side of the building. I run to the girls' locker room and hope one of the cheerleaders left something behind other than a homecoming dress to change into. I can practically feel the clock ticking. But for the first time tonight, I'm in (relative) luck. The cheerleaders are total slobs and there are clothes all over the benches in the locker room. I find a pair of jeans and a T-shirt that fit reasonably well and leave my dress behind.

I've been listening, but I still haven't heard anything from Raven or Serena. The noise from outside is still making it hard, but I think I heard Cameron's footsteps off toward the left when I came in, so I head to the right. The building is basically a big rectangle once you get past all the gym and office stuff, so if I keep going, I should be able to surprise them all.

I haven't been in this area of the building much since all of my classes are on the other side. This is the no-man's land of Home Economics and Shop and the other electives. I think it's where the Future Farmers meet. I hear some muffled clunking noises up ahead and creep forward, my senses all on high alert.

I get to the door where the noises are coming from. Shop class. Ack! Where all the power tools are!

I'm still disguised as the Carter girl. Hopefully it will be good enough to fool Raven. I take a deep breath, stand up tall, and sashay through the door like I own the place since that seems to be how all the Carters act.

MYTH:	Shape-shifting is like second nature to a vampire.
TRUTH:	If second nature means having to really concentrate and not get distracted, then yeah, sure, why not

SHAPE-SHIFTING 101

37

"Rav—" I start to say in a stern Southern accent. Then I stop. Goth girl and Serena are nowhere to be seen. I've walked in on an entirely different scene of mayhem.

Dr. Musty is crouched in front of a metal pole in the middle of the room, facing the door. He looks seriously pissed in a geriatric kind of way. The whole room is a shambles, with power tools and assorted stuff strewn everywhere (screws, nails, boards, and other things I have no idea what they are since you wouldn't catch me dead in Shop class).

Lowell is between me and the doctor. He's got a wooden stake in one hand and a sledgehammer in the other and he looks like he means business.

"Lowell," I say, trying to make my voice sound different and Southern. I wish I'd heard that girl speak. I hope I can fool him.

"Wayne sent me. He wants you to—"

But Dr. Musty interrupts me. "Lowell, kindly silence our visitor. Permanently."

I freeze. What's going on? Lowell turns around and starts toward me. His eyes are blank and unfocused. Is he *drooling?* He runs into a table and tries to keep walking toward me, bumping the table slowly across the floor.

"Lowell, stop. Go around the table. *Then* silence our visitor."

Dr. Musty must have him under mind control! "Wait, Dr. M— Jonas! It's me!"

As soon as I say the doctor's name, Lowell's face goes a little wonky and his eyes seem to refocus a bit. He glances at me and then makes an abrupt turn to Dr. Musty. I swear he's actually growling.

Dr. Musty puts an upturned table between himself and Lowell and starts talking a mile a minute to Lowell about slowing down, dropping the hammer, you name it. Lowell takes a couple of swings at him and stumbles forward a few more steps, but then stops and turns around to come back toward me.

He maneuvers around the table and comes right at me, raising both the sledgehammer and stake high above his head. He's definitely drooling. There's a trail of spit running from the corner of his mouth down the front of his plaid shirt. It ain't pretty.

"Dr. J—" Maybe I better not say his name again. "It's me! Mina! Make him stop!" I dodge Lowell's lumbering stab and run into another metal table, doubling myself over and knocking the breath right out of me. Why won't he listen to me? Then I catch a glimpse of myself in the surface. Gah! I still look like the Carter girl. I push myself off the table.

"Look, it's me! Mina Smith! Bob's daughter! We've been trying to find you!" I shake off the shift as I keep dodging Lowell and pieces of heavy machinery to make my way to Dr. Musty.

"Mina?" Dr. Musty blinks at me as I get close to him. He looks a little fuzz brained himself.

"Would you call off Lowell, please?" Why is this creepy old vampire guy always trying to manhandle me?

"Lowell, stop!" Dr. Musty shouts.

I turn, hoping to see Lowell stopped dead in his tracks and instead find a stake coming right at me. I duck and run. Lowell follows me.

"Lowell," says Dr. Musty sternly. "*Halt.*"

Lowell growls again, deep and guttural, and grinds to a stop. But then he turns his bloodshot eyes back on Dr. Musty. "You-u-u-u—" The rest is so garbled I can't understand it, but there's no mistaking the downward swing of the hammer. Dr. Musty and I both jump back. I'm not sure who he was aiming for that time.

"Why won't he stop?" I yell.

"I'm not sure." Dr. Musty is panting. That's a bad sign. How long has this battle been going on? "He's got quite a strong mind, you know." It doesn't look like it right now, not with all the drool and everything. But Lowell *is* still going and obviously resisting. Maybe the good old doc isn't as über as dad and George think he is. Dr. Musty stares deep into Lowell's eyes. "Lowell, listen to me! Stop!"

Lowell abruptly halts just inches away from me. Then he turns and lifts up the hand with the stake in it. I start backpedaling, but I'm off balance.

"No," I say. "No!"

I'm still falling backward when Lowell drops the stake with a clatter and holds his index finger up to his mouth.

"Sssshhhhhhhhhhhhhhhhhh!" he hisses at me.

I hit the floor.

"Ah," says Dr. Musty. "I think he's trying to obey the first command I gave him and silence you."

I scoot backward until I'm out of the hammer's range. "I don't think—" I start to say but Lowell goes ballistic. His face twists in a snarl and his hands go up in the air like claws. With his scruffy beard, he looks like a bear on the loose.

I shut up. Stupid Neanderthal vampire. *Of course* he only pays attention to *one* of Dr. Musty's suggestions.

"I guess I don't have firm control of him yet," whispers Dr. Musty.

You think? Gah! I don't have time for this. Who knows what Raven is doing to Serena right now!

Dr. Musty bends down to help me up and Lowell shakes himself like a dog. Drool goes flying in all directions.

"Look at me," Lowell intones. His voice is scratchy, but forceful. I feel Dr. Musty go stiff behind me. He lets go of my arms and I go back down on my butt, right on top of a board. I look over my shoulder. Dr. Musty's eyes are looking hazy. *Crapola.* I've got to do something before Lowell takes over. If he gains control of Dr. Musty, we're both toast.

I consider grabbing the board, but even in his current half-drooling condition I think Lowell could whip my butt in any physical fight. He's easily three times my size. That just leaves mind control. Oh man, why haven't I been practicing that instead of making my eyelashes longer? I am so dead. But I've got no choice. I have to try.

Maybe I can distract him like Cameron said. With his attention on Dr. Musty, it just might work. I scramble to my knees and grab up a handful of assorted nuts and bolts and screws and throw them right in Lowell's face.

He howls and drops the sledgehammer right on his toe. He doubles over, one hand over his right eye and the other clutching his foot. Now is my chance.

I grab his greasy head with both hands and pull him down to look him directly in the left eye. Hopefully this will work with just one of his eyes working. Hopefully it will work at all. I stare deep into his eye without breathing so I won't be distracted by the smell of him. I don't bother saying anything or giving him any commands, I just work on gaining control.

I can feel Lowell resisting, but Dr. Musty snaps out of it and tries to hold him too and finally, finally, Lowell's left eye goes completely unfocused. His whole body goes slack and I ease him down until he's slumped on the floor.

"How did you do that? I didn't know you knew how to mesmerize," says Dr. Musty. For once, the holier-than-thou tone isn't in his voice.

"There's a lot you don't know about me," I say.

"Ah," he says. "Well, thank you for your help. If we can just restrain him—"

"I can't. I've got to go," I say. "Raven—that crazy Goth girl—she's got Serena. I've got to go and find her." I start running for the door. It looks like Dr. Musty can handle the rest anyway, now that Lowell is out of commission. "Oh, but watch out. The rest of the Carters are at the homecoming game. Everyone else is at Ernie's trying to save you."

"I'll get them and come after you," he calls after me. "As soon as I get this little matter taken care of. Be careful!"

MYTH: Vampires don't bleed.

TRUTH: Well, that kinda depends.

38

I start piecing together my Carter girl shape-shift as I'm running. I wish I'd had a nice glass of Special K instead of that sweet tea earlier but I don't imagine they had any of *that* at the concession stand. After that little escapade with Lowell, my energy is rapidly disappearing. But I manage to get it back together by the time I've turned the corner.

I'm partway down the long side of the back of the building when I hear (hallelujah!) Serena's unmistakably annoyed voice say, "Oh, don't be so stupid." It's coming from the Chemistry lab. I have to stop and just breathe a minute in relief. Then I pull myself up tall again and push open the door hard enough for it to bang into the opposite wall. Hopefully Dr. Musty will hear it and figure out where we are.

Raven jumps up and whirls around from where she was

crouched down in front of Serena, who's sitting at a desk in the front row. Actually, tied to a desk. With a bunch of rubber tubing. I guess they were doing some weird kind of experiments in class this past week. Other than being tied down and looking extremely pissed, she looks fine. And there's no sign of Cameron. A wave of relief passes through me, but I try not to let it show on my face.

"Who are you?" Raven demands, brandishing a broken glass tube at me. Good, I guess that means that she hasn't met this particular Carter girl, whoever she is. So I don't have to worry about copying her voice. I decide to just stick with a generic Southern accent.

"Honey, I'm Eugenie Carter. And I've heard all about you, Raven girl. So why don't you put down that glass and settle down a mite?" I hope that wasn't laying it on too thick. And apologies to Eugenie, but it was the only name I could think of on short notice.

Raven doesn't put the tube down, but she does relax a little bit and step back slightly from Serena. "What do you want, Eugenie? I'm a little busy here."

"I thought Cameron had told you this particular little specimen was off-limits?" I walk forward, trying to put a Southern swish to my hips and to get close enough to step between Raven and

Serena. Or, more specifically, the jagged edge of the glass and Serena's neck.

"Specimen?" says Serena. "Please." So not helping the situation. I try to tell her to shut up by glaring at her, but that just makes her go more huffy. "If there're any *specimens* here, it's her."

"What do you care anyway?" Raven's back to her snarling Goth girl self. "She's just a stupid human, right?"

I decide to go for the tough-girl act. "So are you. But maybe you don't listen to your betters, is that it? I'm sure John and Wayne will be just thrilled to hear that."

Instead of getting defensive, that just seems to make Raven even madder, especially when Serena laughs. Agh! I wish she'd be quiet, just this once.

"What's with you people anyway?" Raven says, "I've done everything you've asked me to! I picked a target. I even followed her halfway across the freakin' country. I got the tattoo already! What more do you want from me?" She uses her free hand to pull back her right sleeve to show me a ginormous tattoo. It looks like the foot of some kind of huge bird with blood dripping from the tips of the talons, all wrapped completely around her upper arm. Not exactly tasteful and very, very obvious.

"A little big, don't you think?" I can't resist asking. You'd think even the Black Talons wouldn't want to advertise like that. Does

Raven really need to belong to something that bad? That's just sad on so many levels.

"That's exactly what I'm talking about!" Raven says. "What's *wrong* with all of you? Every one of you Carters I've met just has some tiny little tattoo, like you're ashamed of being a Talon. Except for John and Wayne, and they have to get theirs re-inked every couple of months. They're proud of what it stands for. I am too, you hear me! I'm proud! I'm not letting you or any stupid human get in my way any longer!"

She lunges at Serena with the glass tube and I jump at the same time, praying that for once my aim actually works. The broken end of the tube jams right into my side and I can't help but let out a scream as it embeds itself. I catch a glimpse of Serena's eyes getting bigger and bigger as I tumble forward and take Raven and a couple of desks down on the floor with me.

"Serena? Where are you?" I hear Cameron yell from somewhere not too far away.

"Chem lab," yells Serena back. "Help! Crazy Goth girl on the loose!"

I push myself up on my hands and knees. The glass tube is still stuck in my side. I can feel it, but I'm not quite prepared to look at it yet. I just hope it isn't as bad as it feels because my entire side feels like it's on fire. Raven groans and rolls over to stare at me.

"What's wrong with your face?" she says as Cameron bursts through the door. Then she and Serena and Cameron all yell out "Mina!" at the same time, with different degrees of horror. I guess it does look as bad as it feels. I let the last of the shape-shift float away. At this point, there wasn't much of it left anyway.

"Oh God, oh God," says Serena. "Are you okay? Get me out of this!"

Raven just sits there speechless, staring at me in total horror as Cameron helps me sit up. The look on her face would actually be kind of funny if I didn't feel like I was going to die. Like for real die. I know Grandma Wolfington said vampires don't bleed unless they want to, but I've got news for her. We can bleed even if we *don't* want to too. My hand slips in the pool of blood that's gushed from my side and I almost fall back over.

Cameron is the only one of us remotely calm. "We've got to get that glass out of you. It must be holding something open so you can't heal. You shouldn't be bleeding like this. Just—here, hold onto my hand. I'm going to pull it out. Are you ready?"

I take his left hand and just nod. At this point, it's trust him or faint. Or maybe worse. So much for invincibility. This definitely was NOT in the brochure. He grabs the end of the tube that's sticking out of me and pulls. Another scream comes out of my mouth without any prompting whatsoever, but as soon as the thing is out

I can feel things starting to knit back together. Slowly and painfully, but whatever the glass split open inside me starts to fix itself.

"Better?" Cameron asks. "I'm sorry I didn't get here sooner. I was checking the cafeteria kitchen and the storage closets. There were a lot more little rooms back there than I thought there would be."

I nod again and then point my chin at Serena. "Get her out of that mess, will you? Before Goth Queen over here goes postal again. I don't think I can take another swipe like that."

Cameron gets up, all covered in my blood, and starts unwrapping the tubing from around Serena. "I don't think she's going to be a problem anymore," he says.

I look at Raven. She's just staring dully at the blood on the floor. A rivulet of it starts flowing right toward her and she backs up frantically to the door like a crab. That's when the gibbering starts.

"I guess maybe she should rethink her career choice," I say. "Doesn't look like she can stomach blood after all." I try to stand up and Cameron, who just finished untying Serena (who's looking pretty green herself), catches me just in time.

"You've lost a lot of blood," he says. I'm very tempted to say something along the lines of "Duh," but I hold my tongue. "You need to take some in soon."

"I am *not* taking a bite out of Raven," I say emphatically. "I don't have the stomach for rotten Goth girl." She must still have a bit of a brain left, since that makes her back up even farther away from us and pull her legs up to her chest. She starts rocking back and forth and kind of moaning.

"I can do it," says Serena. "Take mine."

"No," says Cameron. "She needs the blood of another vampire. It will fortify her faster." He picks me up in his arms and cradles me like a baby.

"I've never done this before," I say. Does he actually want me to bite him on the neck? That's just so *personal*. This close to him, the manly-man smell of him really is overwhelming. And it's seriously not how I imagined cuddling up to his neck.

"I'll help you," he says. "Serena, can you prop her up?" He sits down in the teacher's chair and Serena stands behind my back and holds me up. He takes an X-Acto knife from the desk and makes a small slice on the side of his neck. "Hurry," he says, "before it closes up. It will stay open while you drink."

I feel like arguing, but I also feel like I'm about to keel over, so I do what he says and lean forward, putting my mouth against his neck. My fangs extend automatically without me even thinking about it. Oh lordy, being this close to him is making me feel even more cloudy, but I just close my eyes and let the blood flow into my mouth and down my throat. It's like how I imagine drinking mulled wine must be. Intoxicating. But maybe that's just Cameron.

And that's our little tableau as the door flies open and George comes charging in the room.

MYTH:	Vampires are above human foibles like jealousy and revenge.
TRUTH:	Heh. Speak for yourself.

39

"Mina! What's going on? What happened?" George rushes forward, almost tripping over Raven in his haste and then skidding a bit in my blood. I must seriously look like a wreck.

I pull back from Cameron's neck and try to stand up to walk to George. I don't care how shaky I still feel. There's no way I'm sucking on some other guy's neck with my boyfriend in the room. George gets there right as I start to crumple again and he grabs me up in his arms. Now he's covered in my blood too. It's starting to look like we got in some kind of twisted squirt-gun fight in here or something. And I would definitely be the loser. At least I didn't ruin my Ella Moss dress. But some cheerleader is going to be seriously pissed at me because I don't think there's any way you can get this much blood out of a pair of jeans. Not to mention the big bloody, gaping hole in the T-shirt.

354

George holds me tight in his arms and kisses me on my forehead and cheeks, which are probably the only (mostly) non-bloody bits on me.

"I'm so sorry I wasn't here," he says. "I should have been here."

"It's okay. I'm okay. I mean, I'm okay now. Thanks to Cameron. Otherwise I'd probably be just lying in that puddle on the floor. He was giving me blood. That's why I was, you know . . ."

"Attached like a leech to his neck?"

"I wasn't—" I pull back to look at him and he's smiling at me. Just a 5.8 on the George scale, but a smile all the same. It hits me then, maybe even harder than Raven did with that tube, that I've really missed that smile. Cameron may smell like the kind of heaven you want to wrap yourself up in, but George's smile has the power to make everything feel right.

"I'm just teasing you. But I am sorry." He loses the smile to look serious. He ducks his head so our foreheads meet. "About everything." He kisses me again. It feels like home. Blood is good, but this is even better.

Mom and Dad come in then, talking so fast I can barely figure out what they're saying. Mostly it sounds like a lot of oh-my-God-that's-a-lot-of-blood-are-you-okay-what-happened! Then Dr. Musty is there, observing everything with his normal detached-historian air. Uncle Mortie jumps into the room last in a kung fu stance, like he even knows how to make chop suey. And Ivetta is here too, clucking her tongue at the mess. Who called her?

I guess this finally puts to rest the question of whether Cameron's on our side or not, Black Talon or no. Though he's probably wondering what's up with me and George. "Cameron, I—" I start to say and twist around to find him.

"He's gone," says Serena, looking at me with eyes about twice their normal size. "He just went out the back door." Did he leave because of me and George? I didn't even get a chance to tell him thank you.

"What happened?" demands Mom. "Is all this blood yours?" She sounds like she doesn't quite believe it. I look down at the floor. I barely believe it either. Apparently, I'm quite the gusher.

"To make a long story short, Raven went for Serena with a broken glass tube but I got in the way. Cameron pulled it out, untied Serena, and gave me some blood to make up for what I lost. Then he disappeared, I guess." Is that it? "Oh, yeah, and I'm the Homecoming Queen."

Uncle Mortie hands me a flask. "Take a drink, Homecoming Queen. You look a little pale." Ha, ha, very funny Uncle Mortie.

I take it and sniff it suspiciously. "What's in it?"

"Just some good ol' O negative. That's all. Always keep some around for emergencies. Or a snack."

I drink it and it does make me feel better. Not quite as strength-ening as eau du Cameron, but definitely more fortifying than a glass of Special K. George is still cuddling me like he thinks I'll blow away any second.

"How did you guys get here so fast?" In some ways it feels like forever ago that I saved Dr. Musty, but I know it can't have been that long ago. My sense of time isn't that bad. "And what's Ivetta doing here? No offense, Ivetta."

"None taken," she says, altogether too cheerfully. I mean, come on, does nothing phase her? We're sitting in the middle of a blood bath here. I have no idea how we're going to explain this to Mr. Fleming.

Mom and Dad sum it up, with frequent interruptions from Uncle Mortie:

a) Uncle Mortie dazzled Ernie with his salesmanship demoing the BloodTender 4000, got into position, and gave the signal, then

b) everyone else came in, overpowering a very surprised Ernie, and

c) rushed the back room where they found absolutely nothing. Surprise.

After that, they went back to the house and called Ivetta to see if she had any ideas. She, along with everyone else, was at the

357

homecoming game and I hadn't returned George's text (he'd sent me a "hme bt no dr?" text), so they figured they'd walk over and see what was up. They were actually just outside the school looking for us when Dr. Musty ran out and told them to get their butts inside. (I seriously doubt if he actually said the word "butt," but Uncle Mortie was telling that part of the story.) Then they heard Serena shout out we were in the Chem lab (good ears, I'm telling you, it's why I never get away with anything). They'd have gotten here even sooner if they'd had a clue where the Chem lab was.

"Now," says Ivetta, cutting Uncle Mortie off from re-creating the mad dash inside, "I think it's time for me to call for some backup. They should be here soon, since some of them are out there watching the game. Then we can get to work cleaning up this mess. Oh, and congratulations on being Homecoming Queen! That's a real honor!"

Eh, whatever. We wouldn't be in this mess if I'd just stayed in the bleachers with Serena. I say as much but Serena immediately disagrees.

"No, it's my fault," says Serena. "I should never have believed that Stacey girl's crackpot story about Cameron needing help with his car and that stupid cow." Ah, that explains how they lured Serena away too. I guess I should have known she wouldn't have just followed Raven all tra-la-la-la-la to certain doom.

"It's nobody's fault," says Mom. "Sometimes, stuff happens."

"I disagree," says Uncle Mortie. "I think we can blame it all on this one." He points to Raven, who's still cowering in a corner. She's kind of just whimpering now. I always knew she was a chicken at heart. I just wish she'd figured it out before going all slice 'n' dice on me.

"It *is* my fault. She followed me here." A tear leaks out of Serena's right eye. I'd throw a pillow at her if I had one. It's so not her fault that Raven was crazy enough to want to join the Talons.

"We'll take care of her, sweetie," says Ivetta. "Don't worry about that. The Council is sending its best agents over as we speak." She snaps her cell phone shut.

"I could take care of it," says Dr. Musty. I stop myself from snorting. I just don't have the energy for sarcasm right now.

"No, no," says Dad. "You've done enough, Dr. Jonas. Why, you've cracked the Talons!"

"Not without help," says Dr. Jonas. "I don't believe I would have gotten away from Lowell without Mina's help, not to mention the information she helped gather." He gives my shoulder a squeeze. "You've got the makings of a great historian," he says.

Dad beams at me like I just made valedictorian. Oh great, I bet I know what I'm getting for Christmas this year—boring history books.

"Um, thanks," I say. "But what about all this mess?" I wave a hand at the blood. Actually, it's making me a little queasy now, the sheer quantity of it. Especially since it's all mine. In some ways, I don't blame Raven for going cuckoo. But then again, it's all her fault.

Serena's gone past green into puce territory. She closes her eyes and Uncle Mortie puts an arm around her and pulls her to his chest so she can't see it anymore. She looks paler now than she ever did during her Goth days.

"We'll take care of that too," says Ivetta.

Ten minutes later, I see what she means. A bunch of serious looking vampires swoop in out of nowhere. In minutes, they've got me cleaned up and back in my own clothes (one of them even found my shoes). They set the Chem lab back into working order then whisk Raven off somewhere to give her the third degree. I guess they've got experience in blood or something.

Ivetta says she'll take care of the homecoming photos herself, though I think I might have been dodging the camera enough that they probably didn't come out. Hopefully. And after the whole fiasco with Kacie, Mr. Fleming might just disqualify me anyway.

"Just leave casually," says the head goon. "One at a time, out of different doors, and head back to your home. We're surrounding the area to round up the Carters now, so please just act like everything is normal."

I wind up leaving last (with many promises to George that I will be very, very careful and not make anyone mad enough to kill me on the way home) to give myself a little more time to recuperate and to down another flask of emergency O that one of The Council guys had on him. Strangely enough, he even kind of looked like Uncle Mortie. Just skinnier. And cooler, except for the blue and gold home-team colors he's sporting.

I have every intention of going straight home as instructed. But then I see Kacie standing at the very back of a long line for the girls' bathroom, looking all smug and cheerful and something inside me just won't let it go. Maybe it's the part of me that's related to Uncle Mortie. Maybe it's because I've just been through a bloodbath (literally) and all she's had to deal with is standing in line to pee.

"Hey, Kacie," I say and take her by the arm and pull her out of line and back behind some bushes before she can even respond. Chalk up one for the mad vampire skills.

"What—" she starts to say but I lean in close and do the quickest centering of my entire undead life and look deep in her eyes. I don't think anyone noticed me grab her, but you never know. And she's

361

just as pea-brained as I thought, since she goes under my spell pretty much immediately. Ha! I am rocking the mind-control stuff tonight!

"You won Homecoming Queen," I say. She repeats it after me. As Cameron taught me, it's good to start with something they're already inclined to believe.

"You forgot your crown out on the football field. You feel just naked without it. You want to show it off to the whole town." She keeps repeating everything I say. Perfect. "The crown is right in front of the goal posts on the south end of the field. Other girls are jealous of you and might try to stop you, but that crown is yours." She repeats the last part with relish and an evil sneer. "The crown is a little different this year, but still absolutely beautiful. It's brown and kind of round and it goes perfectly with your dress. It will look stunning in your hair. Once you find it, put it on. Don't let anyone steal your special moment."

There. That should do it. One of the clean-up goons had been a little chatty and mentioned that Baby had finally pooped right in front of the south end goal posts, just like last year. Maybe it's petty and maybe it's beneath me, but you know what? It still feels good.

I give her a push in the right direction and then follow her out of the bushes after I see her start to move purposefully toward the football field.

"What are you making her do?" asks Cameron.

I jump about a mile. Either I was concentrating even harder than I thought, or he's got some seriously good sneaking-up-on-you skills. Probably both.

I look around to see if any of the goons have made their way out yet. He probably has no idea they're going to round up all the Carters. I still can't believe that he's a Talon. It's just wrong.

"I told her to go look for her homecoming crown around the vicinity of Baby's cow patty."

He laughs. "I'm glad I've never made you mad." Then he turns and looks at me a little sadly. "Though I'm sad I wasn't able to make you as happy as some." He lifts up his hand and just barely touches my face, then takes it away.

"About George," I say, and then stop, not really sure where to go from there. I really don't like actually lying to people. A little fibbing, maybe, but lying just sucks.

He smiles and shakes his head. "I think I can safely say that he's not just an intern working with your dad, right?"

"Um, yeah," I say. Can I just leave it like that? Is that okay?

"Mina, I've never met anyone quite like you. I wish we'd had a chance"—he clears his throat—"to dance at homecoming." Holy cheese, he did not just say that, did he?

"I'm sorry," I say, and stop again. I hate that. Whenever I feel like I have a lot to say, I usually can't say anything at all. At least, nothing coherent. But the least I can do is warn him. He *did* save my life. I owe him big. "I'm sure I'm not supposed to tell you this, but you really ought to leave. A bunch of goons are about to unleash a world of hurt on John and Wayne and the rest of you guys."

He nods. "I expected that. It was stupid of them to take Dr. Jonas. I told them that, but they didn't listen. They've been getting away with so much for so long that it was bound to go to their heads sooner or later." He reaches out a hand like he's going to touch me again, but stops before he does. "I just want you to know something, Mina. I owe a lot to John and Wayne, but I wasn't one of their normal conquests. Wayne really saved me when he turned me. I was about to die. So they aren't all bad. Just mostly bad." He gives me a sad smile and pulls back his sleeve to show me his arm. No telltale tattoo. "I am a Carter and I always will be, but they don't own me."

I just *knew* he couldn't be a Talon. "You should still probably go, just to be safe."

"It's been nice knowing you," he says. "Maybe someday . . ." Then he leans forward and gives me a gentle kiss on the lips. Then he's gone, just like that. The scent of him lingers in the air for a minute or two afterwards.

40

George is waiting for me outside the door to the house. I can hear Mom and Dad and Dr. Musty inside celebrating. Sounds like Dad even broke out the really good stuff.

"Hey," I say. "No one tried to kill me on the way here."

George doesn't say anything, just gathers me up in his arms. "I meant what I said back there, you know. I really am sorry."

"What for?" I take in a deep breath of Georgeness. Like orange marmalade, a summer rainstorm, and fresh-cut grass. Not overpowering or knock-me-over, but something I wouldn't mind at all smelling every day.

"Everything. And I'm sorry I didn't say it before. I should have gone into Eirunepé earlier, if for no other reason than to let you know exactly where I was and what was going on. I was just so excited to be there with my parents and getting to know them

365

that I lost track of time. And I promise I wasn't ogling half-naked Brazilian bikini babes. I did see some naked Korubo women, but it'd be a big stretch to call them babes." He gives me a 7.8 smile on the George scale and pushes a stray strand of my hair behind my ear. Yeesh, I really wish he hadn't read all my e-mails.

"And I should have thought about what you were going through, leaving your life behind. I think it just didn't occur to me since I've never had anything to leave behind before."

I give him a small smile. "I'm sorry too." Goodness knows I'm not perfect either.

He puts a finger to my lips. "If it's about Cameron, say no more. I know I left you hanging and if something did happen, I really can't blame you. But I'd be lying if I said I wanted to hear about it."

I'd blush if I could. Technically, nothing did happen with Cameron (other than the one kiss that *just* happened, but that took me by surprise), though something definitely *could* have if George hadn't shown up when he did. But that wasn't what I was thinking about. "No, this isn't about him. I wanted to tell you I'm sorry I didn't support you going to visit your parents. Honestly, I still don't really see why you want to get to know them, but that doesn't matter. I should have supported you no matter what. I mean, I *do* support you. I think you should spend as much time with them as you need to."

He looks a little surprised (and maybe relieved it wasn't about Cameron). "Thanks," he says. "That means a lot to me. What I'd really like is for us all to spend some time together. I think you'd like them once you get to know them."

I kind of doubt that, but I keep my feelings to myself. If it's important to George, it's important to me. I just give him a big hug instead.

"Come on," I say. "Let's go in and save Serena from the madness." He smiles at me again and turns to open the door. I think better of it and stop him to pull his head down. There's always time for one more kiss.

The Goon Squad is coming tomorrow for Serena. It took her all of five minutes after George and I came in to the house to tell us she didn't think she was really cut out for the whole vampire thing. Not right now. And that she really missed Nathan and her dad and even, just a tiny bit, her little sister. The ten more messages from Nathan that came just while we were out probably helped make that decision, but I can't say I blame her. It's been one big dramasaster after another since she got here. Not to mention the bloodbath we just went through.

If we were still in California, the goons would have probably been here as soon as she even looked like she was going to chicken out. But the Southeast Regional Vampire Council is, well, more Southern. Things are relaxed. They said it was just fine for us to have one last day together before they erase her recent memories and drop her and the Death Beetle off back in California with an implanted memory of having gone on a road trip to the Grand Canyon to get away from all the divorce drama. Of course, they don't know that she knew about the whole vampire thing from back before the funeral. I'm hoping they don't figure it out.

But I've got one more trick up my sleeve too. Serena and I go out to the park so Mom and Dad can validly claim that they had no idea what I was up to if things happen to blow up on me. I'm still not all that sure my Jedi mind tricks are up to par anyway, but I'm hoping that Cameron was right when he said it's easier to implant something that the person wants too. It seemed to work pretty well on Kacie. Homecoming will be a night she'll remember for years. Well, the parts of it the goon squad let her remember. I begged them to leave the cow patty memory and I'm pretty sure they humored me. They ought to, after what I went through helping them prove the whole Carter-Talon thing.

"Okay," I say to Serena, "are you ready?" We're back sitting on the blanket, just like the first time I practiced on her. But this time it's for real.

"You promise there will be no extra goodies like where I'll bark like a dog when someone honks their horn, right?"

I laugh. Trust Serena to always look on the dark side. "I promise. Though I am tempted to make sure you never go Goth again."

She shivers. "Don't worry. After that whole crazy Goth girl thing, I'm definitely through with that one. Besides, why go back? Always look ahead. That's my motto."

"That's my girl," I say. And give her another hug. Probably the umpteenth one of the last hour. I just can't help myself. I'm hoping this isn't the end, but who knows? What's that old saying? If you love something, set it free? Maybe it isn't so cheesy.

I stare deep into Serena's eyes and she stares into mine. No laughing this time. I breathe deeply in and out and do all that centering stuff. Okay. Go time. I concentrate harder than I've ever concentrated in my life. Harder than when I was trying to stop Lowell from mashing my head in. I really need to make this good.

"Serena, somewhere deep inside of you where the VRA and the Vampire Corps cannot reach"—I sincerely hope, anyway—"you will always know that I am alive. Um, undead. Whatever." Crap, I should have thought about what I was going to say more. "And that I will always be there for you if you need me. *Always.* And you will know that I will always love you. If you ever need me, really

369

need me or if you ever decide that you want to turn, no matter how old you are—twenty, thirty, sixty—it doesn't matter." Cheese, I think her eyes would be glazed over by now even if I weren't doing the whole mind-control thing. I am such a goober. "Just send an e-mail to me at willymina@gmail.com. No matter where you are in the world, I will come find you. Can you repeat that e-mail back to me, please?"

"Willymina@gmail.com," she says in this weird monotone. I guess it is working. I hope.

"Do not tell anyone about that e-mail address. Do not think of it at all, except when you get to the point that you need me. Or want to turn." Am I forgetting anything? Oh, wait, maybe I can sneak something in.

"Periodically, send an update on your life to that e-mail address. Write me whenever something important happens or you just want to share." Oh, I hope that works.

I am actually a little tempted to add something in there about her fashion sense (or lack thereof, sometimes), but Serena wouldn't be Serena without her crazy tutus and whatnot. I sit and just watch her as the sun comes up and the tranciness wears off. She finally gives herself a shake and her eyes come back in focus.

"Did it work?"

"I think so. I hope so."

"Don't worry," she says. "I know it will work. I can feel it. We will see each other again. Maybe not soon, but someday."

"Yeah," I say. I feel it too. We're BFF. And I do mean forever.

WHY MY LIFE ROCKS AND SUCKS
AT THE SAME TIME

(or, like Uncle Mortie says, sometimes it sucks rocks)

1. ROCKS: Now that we've proved the whole Carter-
   Talon-Cartville link for The High Council, Dr. Musty
   is ready to move on somewhere else. The Council
   (for once, they're commending us instead of fining
   us) thinks we should leave with him (and Dad's all over
   that) since we wound up being basically like a bomb
   going off in this town between emptying it of Carters
   and the whole homecoming scene. I don't know where
   we're going to wind up yet, but it's gotta be better
   than here. It couldn't be any smaller. wait. I didn't say
   that. That's just asking for trouble.

2. DOUBLE ROCKS: And George is coming too! He's
   going to keep working with Dr. Musty! Maybe I'm
   starting to like that dusty old vampire after all.

3. SUCKS: Somehow, John and wayne got wind of the
   goings-on and disappeared before the goon squad
   could capture them. But most of the other Carters
   were rounded up. A couple proved they weren't
   Talons and were let go (probably with a hefty fine
   or two). The rest? Ivetta says there's going to be a
   big honking trial (vampire lawyers . . . ugh, talk about

bloodsuckers). I think it'll be a long while or maybe never before they're out in the light of day again. We might even have to testify, which I'm not really looking forward to. I just hope we don't run into the Curter brothers anytime soon. Or, you know, ever. Of course, with Dr. Musty on their trail, it's hard to say.

4. SUCKS (mostly): I tried to talk the goons into wiping Raven's mind so hard that her brain would just be a puddle of goo, but all they did was remove all vampire-related memories and drop her off in the middle of Venice Beach. Wearing a clown outfit. (That was my idea.)

5. TOTALLY ROCKS: So many people witnessed Kacie slapping a cow patty on her head (and fighting off Lala and Stacey, who were trying to stop her) that the goons had to leave that memory intact. Yes! They did, however, wipe any memory of Raven and her plot to stick it to me from her puny little mind. So she'll never know exactly why it happened. Which works for me.

6. ROCKS: Grady decided skinny-butted girls with cow patties on their heads really weren't his thing, told Kacie to take a long shower, and asked Henny to the Homecoming dance! On his own! With no help from the goons at all. There's hope for the boy yet.

7. ROCKS? SUCKS? Cameron wasn't picked up. He just disappeared. Maybe I should feel a little guilty about that, but I don't. So sue me. Just don't tell The Council or George. But really, I'm 99 percent positive he's not a Talon. Though I'm 25 percent considering that I might be thinking that just because he smells so good. No one who smells that good can be evil. Seriously.

8. MAJOR SUCKAGE: I miss Serena. Big time. But I know someday we'll see each other again. Somehow, some way. Even if she doesn't know I'm alive (undead, whatever), I'll still always be there for her. Forever.

With much thanks to...

Little Max, for introducing chaos and giggles into my life and my husband, Tony, for trying to keep me sane. (Yes, I know it's a losing battle.)

My nephew Cameron for letting me borrow his name and my nieces Rachael and Natalie for their expert advice on things I am too old to understand anymore.

Nina, as always, for fighting for this book, but most of all, for making it much better than it would have otherwise been.

Myra for periodically talking me off of ledges and just generally being a cheerleader (the writerly kind).

And most especially to all the fans who have written me e-mails and letters and left comments on my site. You guys always make my day (not to mention helping me out with the tough questions in life, like what George would smell like or what a character's name should be). YOU ROCK.

About the Author

Kimberly Pauley would like to state for the record that
she is <u>not really a vampire.</u> *⸌⁼ or perhaps the VRA is just forcing her to say that?*

As her alter-ego, the Young Adult Books Goddess
of yabookscentral.com, she has been reviewing books
for teens since 1998. She lives in Illinois with Max the
cutest baby in the universe and her husband Tony,
who is also <u>not a vampire.</u> *(Maybe.)*

To read her blog,

find more information about her books,

and enter special contests and promotions, visit

www.kimberlypauley.com